The Haunted Plot

The Haunted Plot

Charlotte's Voices of Mystery Series

C.L. Bauer

The Haunted Plot, Copyright © 2025 by C.L. Bauer.

All rights reserved. Printed in the United States of America. No part of this book may be used or reproduced in any manner whatsoever without written permission except in the case of brief quotations embodied in critical articles or reviews.

This book is a work of fiction. Names, characters, businesses, organizations, places, events and incidents either are the product of the author's imagination or are used fictitiously. Any resemblance to actual persons, living or dead, events, or locales is entirely coincidental.

For information contact:

www.clbauer.com

ISBN: 978-1-957015-09-5

First Edition: March 2025

10 9 8 7 6 5 4 3 2

Charlotte's Voices of Mystery Series

The Haunted Lost Rose
Haunted Decisions of the Heart
The Haunted Plot

Dedication

Sometimes there has to be a corner of your heart that is reserved for those who gave love the only way they knew how. That is where forgiveness lives.

Chapter One

My personal storm was just beginning. When I was a child, thunder and lightning made my skin crawl, but for some bizarre reason, rain was my personal nemesis. When it didn't stop in just a few hours, I began to panic. I walked around in circles, and I talked to myself. "It will stop. It will stop." When it didn't, I would begin to shake and find the nearest corner to hide my eyes and cup my ears. I'd face the wall and pretend I was invisible.

As the youngest of six children, I was almost invisible. When everyone else went to school in the fall, there were at least three years when I was home alone with my mother. I became an only child.

Dad, as a federal judge then, usually didn't arrive home until dinner. There were those nights when I was already in bed. I would surprise him by reaching up and holding onto his neck. He'd reprimand me gently telling me I should be asleep.

But most of the time I was with Mom. There was one afternoon when the rain came. It was silent in the house except for the pelting noise. I balled myself up into a knot on the couch. Mom stared at me. "Charlotte Rose, you and I are going outside."

"No."

"Yes, baby. You need to get over this."

She didn't pull me, but I wasn't a willing participant. I planted my feet firmly on the porch and watched her stand in the yard. She extended her arms out and leaned her face back. She smiled. "Charlotte, you need to sing and dance in the rain. Come out."

I watched her for the longest time until she was drenched. Her hair hung straight and her light dress hung to all of her curves. "I want Dad. You're crazy."

"Your father won't be home until late. Charlotte, if you don't tip your chin up and look rain in the face, you'll never be able to survive the storm. Your brothers and sister will tease you endlessly if they know you're afraid of just water from a cloud."

"They won't," I yelled over the noise. "I won't go out."

"What if you have to go out, sweetie? What if you have to go to school or work?"

"I won't. I'm staying with you the rest of my life."

"Charlotte, I won't always be here. I'll always be at your side, but some day, when I'm older and you are too, you'll walk into that house, and I'll be home with God, just like Aunt Celia."

Aunt Celia had died the previous week, and we all cleaned up, wore our best, and had attended her funeral. It was very sad. Aunt Celia was very young, they said. Her heart had stopped for no reason. Did someone break it?

"Mommy, I don't want you to go see God."

"Honey, we all go to God eventually, but don't worry. Right now, I'm just standing here in the rain being happy. Join me, Charlotte."

Her hand beckoned me, and slowly I took a step and then another until her hand grasped mine. The rain was cool on my face, but instead of flattening my hair, it curled. "Look at my hair."

"It's beautiful. Charlotte, when you get older, you'll face every storm, and you'll survive. Who knows? You may even hold hands with a wonderful man who likes to run in the rain with you."

"Boys, yuk."

"That's the spirit." Mom laughed. We danced, and we sang much longer than we should. Even Mrs. Baxter across the street shouted over to see if we were okay.

It rained into the darkness, and surprisingly, I slept all night long. I didn't even notice my father coming into my room and kissing me goodnight. Mom fixed my fear. She could always do amazing feats like that. If needed, I bet she could've fixed everything that was wrong now. She could fix her critically injured son Sean. She would know who shot at him. She would know who killed our other brother Conor. Mom would tell me what to do about the man I loved, and she would help me discover his secrets before I lost my heart and soul to him.

I had placed my hand in his. We had danced in the rain together.

Chapter Two

"Dad? You're here?" I yelled as I entered the house. I was surprised to see his car sitting in the driveway. It was understandable that he spent as much time as he could at Sean's bedside, but I was worrying about Dad's health.

"I'm in the kitchen. Have you eaten?"

Well, he'd understand as soon as he saw me. I dropped my bag and laptop onto the couch, kicking off my shoes as I continued to walk through our family's home.

He looked up from the casserole on the counter and smiled. "Ah, you've been at Max's." His statement was void of any judgment, but he reviewed my current state. He took his fingers and picked something off of my shoulder. He placed it in his mouth. "Tastes good. He made chili. Are you just wearing it or did you eat?"

Shyly, I grinned. "I was taking a taste from the pot and then this happened. Why do the accidents always end up with me covered in glitter, water, and now beans?"

"I'm really not sure. You two are ... well, a unique couple. Why don't you change and share this meal with me? It's a barbeque casserole with brisket, potatoes–"

"I'll be right back. The aroma alone is making my stomach growl." I nearly sprinted upstairs to pull on yoga pants and a huge sweatshirt.

"Charlotte."

I froze in my childhood bedroom, and now my adult one as well, and listened. When I was younger, I was afraid of so many things. Rain terrified me. Too much snow made me search for the closest blanket to burrow under. And, I was always afraid that when loved ones died, I would forget the sound of their voices.

Luckily, or not, I could still hear them, even ones I wasn't related to or ever knew in their lives. Visiting a funeral home or cemetery could be action packed with voices sending me in many directions among the tombstones. Here, in my childhood home, my deceased brother and mother usually spoke to me in the privacy of my room. But I never knew when the strange voice or apparition would approach me at any time or place. "Yes, Mom?"

"Max has problems."

I nodded. We all had problems, didn't we? Max's seemed so much more extreme by normal human standards. He was in his late thirties and discovered he had another father out there, one who was a powerful senator. He was investigating criminals who had indirectly caused the death of one of his friends, and he and I seemed to be targets. "Yes, I know that by now."

"Charlotte, you have to be strong."

"Mom, I had to be strong just to survive in this family. You made me that way."

"More. So much more."

"Okay. I'll try."

"For Max's love. Save him."

Whoa, that was a new one. "Save him? How can I do that when I don't know what I'm saving him from, Mom?"

"You'll know, dear. You will know."

"Okay. Don't worry. I'll try my best."

"You always have. Your father is calling. Dinner is ready."

"Good. I'm starving." By the time I reached the kitchen, Dad had two servings of his new recipe on the table, along with a side salad and two ears of corn.

After we said thanks, I waited through a few bites before I began my questions. "Dad, how are you really doing?"

My father dropped his fork and stared at me from across the table. "I'm tired, Charlotte. I'm torn every time I leave your brother's side. I'm in shock, challenged, and disgusted. How's that for an honest answer?"

I blinked a couple of times. "Well, that was very good. Have you been rehearsing that one?"

"I suppose." He took a bite from his salad. "I don't know if I'm up for this."

"Dad, we will just take it one day at a time."

He nodded quickly. "Has your mother said anything about

Sean? Does she know ..." His voice trailed off. He seemed afraid to ask the hard question.

"I don't think they are included in the decision making when it comes to life and death. I wouldn't want to know anyway."

"But you knew before other deaths."

I looked down at my food, avoiding my Dad's piercing eyes. "I did, but this is so different."

"Ah, I see. So, how is Max?"

The change in topics nearly gave me whiplash. "He's fine. He's busy. I went over to ask his opinion on a will I am working on."

"You could've asked me."

"Dad, you have a lot on your plate." Since Sean had been shot, Dad worried about him every waking minute.

I finally looked up to see my father smiling at me. "Besides, it gave you an opportunity to see him. You two seem different. Anything you want to tell me?"

He would know if I was telling a fib. He always did, darn him. "Not yet. We're talking quite a bit. Learning about each other." Yes, we talked ... before we made love, during, and after. I was being honest with my father, but I wasn't. "I'm using more intuition than spiritual guidance when it comes to Max and any relationship that may grow." Well, that sounded very adult.

"I see." Dad took a drink of water and placed the glass

down in slow motion. "Charlotte, we've all been throwing the two of you together. Maybe that wasn't the best thing to do."

I laughed out loud. "You think? Gio and you have been the worst matchmakers ever. My sister and both of my sisters-in-law have been pushing me into his arms since he arrived in town. He was Tom's best friend and probably still is. Paddy and Sean seem to be the only ones immune to his charm."

"And you? How do you really feel at this very moment?"

I needed to be honest, at least as much as I could. "I'm not immune to his charm. He's wonderful, and yet–"

My father reached over and grabbed my hand. "You have your doubts? It's a lot to take in when you're falling in love."

I pulled my hand back quickly, stood up and began to clear the table. "I don't know. I was falling in love with him, but now I'm a little confused." I wasn't telling my father I was in lust with Max. Now was not the time.

"My biggest fear is that you'll lose yourself." Dad shook his head. "I want you to achieve your own dreams, not become part of Max's plans. You'd be an integral piece of whatever he wants to accomplish, but you need to be you. Be strong."

I turned away from the sink and looked at my father. "Be strong?"

"Yes."

"Mom told me the same thing just a bit ago."

My father gave me a side glance. "You don't always tell me everything they say, do you?"

I suddenly felt embarrassed. "Dad, it's not because I want to keep secrets from you. Sometimes, it just isn't the right time."

Dad's eyes narrowed. "Are we talking about your conversations with those beyond or about Max again?"

I turned away in silence. I began to fill the dishwasher. Now wasn't the time to share the biggest secret I had ever hidden from my father. The truth was I'd never held anything from the family I loved.

Chapter Three

I'd been frozen on the same word for over an hour. The computer screen wasn't my friend today. I needed to read this document before my clients arrived in the office at three. But all I was thinking about was the secret I was keeping from my father and my entire family.

"Charlotte, is it Sean?"

Phoebe, my assistant, stood in front of my desk. The woman, who used to work for my father and retired when he did, happily returned to work to help me start up my family law practice.

"Sean is holding his own and has a long road ahead of him. No, I don't know what's wrong with me. I just can't concentrate." I wasn't about to tell Phoebe about the messages I received from dead relatives, haunted spirits, ghosts who wanted to be noticed ... they were more vocal than usual in the last few days. My mother kept telling me to be strong, to be careful.

And Max had his own agenda. He pulled me into his arms and wanted me to stay with him, to be held by him, to be loved by him.

Phoebe sat down and sighed loudly. "I know exactly what's wrong with you. You've gone and fallen in love with Max Shaw, haven't you? Ever since the storm and terrible flood Labor Day, you've been smitten. Something has changed between the two of you."

"No, nothing has changed," I said quickly.

"Then you've been in love with him all of your life?"

Finally, my eyes left the screen and looked up shyly. "Not all my life. I was a little girl, and he was Tom's friend."

"And now? You and he–"

"Phoebe, we are working here."

Phoebe laughed. "Are we? You haven't scribbled a note on that paper or hit a key on that computer for a couple of hours. Were you thinking about his eyes? His lips?"

"Shoulders and other areas." As soon as I blurted the words out, my hands flew to my mouth. I just couldn't help myself.

"Ah hah. I knew it. Has anyone else suspected that the two of you have been fooling around?"

I knew my face was reddening. "First, it's not fooling around. He's very serious about it. Second, they've all been so busy with Sean they haven't noticed. I think Gio knows. We were holding hands when we came into the hospital the morning Sean woke. Gio gave me this knowing look, but he was very happy about it. I don't think Max realizes that the old mobster has caught on. And then there's that."

"What, Charlotte?"

"I feel so awful about all of it. Here is my brother fighting to stay alive, and I'm in Max's shower with him–"

Phoebe's eyes flashed. "Tell me more."

I shook my head. What was I doing spilling my guts? "Phoebe, you can't tell anyone. No one, or I swear I'll tell Dad about the time you and Mom used his credit card to go shopping."

"You little snot. He never realized what we did. That was a great day with your mother. I miss her."

I slumped back in my chair. "I miss her so much right now. Max needs time, and you know me, I go head long wanting every question answered, and every action understood." And my ghost of a brother had contended Max would know about him. Know what? If Max did know something about Conor, then it made complete sense that Sean wanted to tell him who the murderer was, but so many scenarios were racing in my head I didn't know what to think. I just had to trust Max for now. But as a federal prosecutor, he couldn't tell me anything even if he knew something.

"You are not a patient person, Charlotte, but you get things done that way."

"And then, we have a murderer out there. Conor is dead, and Sean is hurt perhaps because of the same man. Max is a target and may be involved in all of this."

Phoebe tapped the edge of my desk with her pen. "Are we sure it is a man, and that Max could be next?"

"Pretty sure. Sean told Paddy he had seen him. I just know deep in my heart that Max is at the center of this, and for some reason I think it's because of me and secrets." I didn't want to share with my paralegal that my dead people had warned me of the danger to the man I loved.

"Have you told your father and the family?"

I nodded my head. "No. They don't need to know that Max could be the next one."

Phoebe made a noise between disapproval and angst. "Charlotte, not that. Have you told everyone that you and Max are **together**?"

My eyes shot up from what I was doodling in the margin of the legal document on my desk. "Heavens no. Besides, Max and I are hot and cold when I'd prefer room temperature all of the time. Dad knows we talk, and we visit each other, but–"

Phoebe made a disapproving clucking sound. "You need to tell them. This isn't some soap opera where you keep everyone in the dark. This is real life. It'll probably go better than you think."

"Better than Paddy killing Max before the murderer can? Max will become dessert on Sunday." I thought about our family dinner. Dad was insisting that we all meet this week. He was at the hospital almost night and day, and he wanted us to sit down to a good meal as a family. He said it would make him feel better, but I feared he also wanted to discuss the future, and Sean's recovery.

"Max is a big boy. He can handle himself," Phoebe answered calmly. "You can't continue like this. Look at you. You're worried about everything."

"Because I can't do a damn thing about anything," I yelled. I threw my pen down on the desk. "I can't help Sean get better. I can't take away my father's helplessness. I can't solve Conor's murder. I can't save Max when I don't know who the killer is, and why he, or she, is doing this. And I can't take–"

"What?" Phoebe reached across the desk and took my hand. "What is it really, Charlotte?"

"For the first time in my life, I don't know for sure how this will end with Max."

Phoebe fingered the area where my engagement ring from a prior relationship used to sit. He had been the wrong man, and I had dodged a lifetime of unhappiness. "He hasn't committed to anything, has he?"

"No, and I just can't go with the flow. That's just not me."

"Well, maybe it's time to try. Have some fun. Enjoy each other without the ties of an engagement or marriage. Where's the harm in that?"

I smiled. "My soul could go to hell, and Max could meet his demise after we pass the potatoes if Paddy figures it out."

Phoebe patted my hand assuringly. "Don't you worry about your brother. I remember one summer when he came to your father's office and was worried he'd gotten a girl pregnant. He didn't even know her last name."

"What?"

"Oh, yes. Don't you think for one minute your father isn't a man of the world. He can handle it. Paddy had that worry. Jane was living with nice little Brad before they married, and your mother and father knew it. It was cheaper for the two of them back then, and your parents just ignored the situation. Tom and Meg had a fling and broke up while she went on a trip with another guy from college. Charlotte, you're an adult. Frankly, if I had a chance with Max Shaw and was much younger, I'd be waiting in bed with nothing but a smile on."

"Shower." I don't know how or why details of my private life kept popping out of my mouth. Phoebe smiled and laughed uncontrollably.

"Oh my goodness! There must be something really special about–"

"Kitchen too." Now, I was just showing off.

Phoebe fanned herself. "My, my girl. You have got yourself a good one."

"I know, and I really don't want to lose him."

"Lose who?" Max filled the doorway of my office. I wasn't sure what he had heard as I stood at attention for no reason. How did the man just suddenly appear? Phoebe avoided eye contact with the very nicely dressed, looking every bit the U.S. attorney.

"A client. He called to hire me for some fantastic work involving wills and trusts." I noticed Max's one brow arch. He knew when I lied so why did I keep trying to pass one over on him? I needed to hone my skills.

"Uh huh. Phoebe, how are you?"

"Great, Max. I need to get back to work." She lowered her head and almost pushed him to the side as she passed.

Max sat down in the chair across from me, and I finally returned to my seat. "Phoebe knows, doesn't she?"

"She guessed." There wasn't any point in fibbing.

"How much has she guessed?"

"Absolutely everything."

Max shook his head and smiled impishly. "Everything?"

I threw one of my pens at him. "Stop it."

Max caught it and laughed. "You know, I think your suspicions are rubbing off on me. I could've swore Paddy was following my car this morning."

"Now who is acting paranoid?" There was a pause as we both looked at each other. "Max, Phoebe thinks we should tell the family Sunday."

"Charlotte, what else is going on in that brain of yours? I thought we were good when we left the park the other day, but your thoughts have been in another zip code even when you're over at the house. I told you I would find out information on Conor's murder. You won't even talk about Sean. Gio has kept me in the loop more than you have. Now, you're talking about telling the family?"

"Then there was the chili explosion, remember? Wait, what are you doing here? Are you done for the day? I have one more client coming in later." I was rambling and avoiding the subject.

Max leaned forward. He smelled so good, and those eyes of his were burning a hole in me. "Charlotte. What is it? I already said I'd pay for your dry cleaning. Hell, I'll start running a tab at the place."

"It's not the chili or the dry cleaning. I think, well, I do think we are cursed, and it's because of me for some reason."

Max dropped back in the chair and stretched his legs out until they were well under my desk. "For the love of God, you and your family are not cursed. Do you think it's because you talk to dead people? Is it because I'm the devil incarnate on earth?"

"You're not the devil, maybe one of his perfect minions who is a retired guardian angel," I mumbled slowly.

"Tell me now, and please look at me."

I slowly looked up into those lovely eyes. It was always dangerous to stare directly into those caramel orbs. "There has to be a close connection between Conor and Sean's shooter, even though it's been years apart. Now, you are here–" I paused. "Look, I'll just say it."

"I really wish you would."

"My mother, Rose, and when Sean woke up all said Danger, Max. I used to think you were dangerous because of how you made me feel, but now I understand. You're in danger, and I believe that all of this centers around me."

"Why? Who on earth would take their revenge on you by hurting your brothers? What could you have possibly done, and why am I a target too?"

"I don't know, but that's what they're all telling me. It freaked me out when Sean said the same thing like he'd been on the other side of life and returned with a message only I would understand."

Max sat silently, occasionally blinking as though his mind was working like a computer. "Charlotte, we will deal with what we have to, but as I said before, this is war. I won't allow anyone to hurt you. Now, as for Sunday, Phoebe may have a point. We should tell them about–"

"Us? You can't even say it."

"What do we say? We're grown adults. Do I walk in and say, Judge, your daughter and I are having sex anytime we have a chance, except she's feeling so guilty she won't even look at me now?"

"I told you, the guilt passes."

"It hasn't lately. In just two days you became a fixture in my house. I miss you at night. I miss waking up next to you." Max leaned closer over my desk. "Charlotte, I miss your luscious lips when you kiss my chest. I miss those hips beneath me, and I miss your beautiful breasts that fit perfectly in my hands. I miss you."

I missed him too, not as poetically. If I began to think about his body, I'd need a cold shower. In my last relationship, I thought I was in love, but Max brought me a higher feeling, one that didn't wear off. His touch was branded on my body, and whatever his feelings were, they had been assigned onto my heart. "I miss you too. I'm sorry. It is just overwhelming right now."

"I think I understand. There's so much going on. Gio is trying to keep your father hopeful, but he says it seems bad. Do they have a prognosis?"

"Dad doesn't go into details. I guess we will talk about it on Sunday as a family."

"Maybe I shouldn't be there," Max suggested.

"No, he wants you and Gio at the table. He really appreciates the old mobster's company."

"And my dad has been calling the judge every afternoon. He told me last night he's never heard your father so down. Judge O even admitted that Sean's tragedy brings back all of the memories of when your mom and Conor died."

"I agree. It seems as though the oxygen has just been sucked out of him. When Conor was killed, Mom was there, always buoying Dad's spirits. We have no captain of the ship."

"Well, you do, and she's sitting in front of me, but I've been distracting her."

"Well, there is that, but you've been wonderful. You are probably more than I deserve."

Max's soft face hardened. He stood up and came around to my side of the desk, turning my chair to face him as he loomed over me like a tiger ready to pounce. "Don't you ever say that again." He reached down, pulled me up from the chair, and enveloped me in his strong embrace. His lips found mine. His kiss stole the air from my body. Mom was right. Love the man that leaves you breathless. When he released me, I was still held firmly. "Do you understand, Ms. O'Donohue?"

"Yes, Mr. Shaw."

"I knew it!" The clapping gentleman who just entered my office wore a huge smile. I needed to lock my door.

"Gio." I looked out at Phoebe. Did she ever stop any intruder before they reached my desk?

"I knew it when you two were holding hands at the hospital. So now what? Do we have a party? When's the wedding? I can't wait until the two of you have little ones. I'll spoil–"

"Stop. We're taking our time," Max answered quickly. He kissed me once more and sat down on the edge of my desk while Gio took the chair.

There was no point in working. I looked down at my watch. My client would arrive in an hour. Maybe I'd have the federal prosecutor stay around and dazzle the poor man with his legal knowledge. That should mask the fact that I was unprepared because everyone wanted to discuss my love life!

"Time is fleeting. Don't wait too long. I'd like to dance at your wedding. Does Rose know? Of course she does." A concerned look crossed his face. "Charlotte, how does that work? When you two are fooling around–"

I held my hand up. "Stop, please. I don't know, and I really don't want to think about it."

Max grabbed his head. "You two can't talk like this while I'm around. Does my ghost of a grandmother watch me? Do I need to wear a towel while taking a shower or get dressed somewhere else?"

"No, I don't think it works like that. You don't think of God seeing everything you do, but He does. Oh, Lord, he does see everything I'm doing."

Gio looked between us. "Charlotte, the closer I get to God, I know now He doesn't have time to be watching every indiscretion. I'm sure Rose is busy too, Max. She's probably having dinner with Charlotte's mom or maybe she is taking a care package down to her old coot of a husband."

Max threw his hands up. "You two ... I can't. This is very weird for me." He bent down and kissed me again. "You, I respect you, and you deserve everything good. I will see you soon. Call me when you are finished with work tonight." He pointed to his grandfather. "You, do you need a ride?"

"I do indeed. I took the bus here to visit Charlotte."

"Well, come on. I'm taking you out for a late lunch, and then back to the house to look at the ceiling in one of the upstairs bedrooms."

"I could eat. I'll visit with Charlotte another time. So what's up with the ceiling?"

Max sighed. "The cornices are unique, and I'm not sure we can save them."

Gio stood up slowly and blew me a kiss. "Mr. Fancy Pants has no solution for a mere cornice. He needs me. I bet that is the room finished by this unusual Hungarian by the name of Rudy. Charlotte, he could hear dead people too."

Max grabbed Gio by the arm. "That's enough. You two can talk about your ghosties when I'm not around." He turned back as he escorted Gio to the door. "I'll expect a call from you."

I saluted. "Yes, sir, Mr. Fancy Pants." The man who was usually so serious stuck his tongue out at me. Max had the uncanny ability to lighten my heart. I'd never noticed it before, but he knew how to do it. "Ghosties." And he made me laugh.

Later, my clients stayed longer than I liked, and I headed directly to the hospital. There had been no change, and Sean was sleeping more than the doctor liked. Scans were scheduled for the next morning. I did persuade Dad to follow me home. It was nearly ten before I called Max.

"Where are you?"

"I'm at Dad's. Jane brought over meatloaf so he and I sat at the kitchen table and ate dinner. He was so tired after the meal, he could barely make it up the stairs."

"So you're spending the night there?"

I shut my eyes. "Yes. I have court early tomorrow morning. It's a civil protection order so I need to be up on my game. It was good to see you today."

I could almost hear Max thinking. The silence seemed to last forever, but he cleared his throat in a minute. "Charlotte, let me take you out Saturday night. Let's just go to a neighborhood restaurant, eat, and talk. We don't even have to dress up. What about it? May I take you out?"

"Of course, as long as nothing has changed with Sean."

"I understand completely. Alright, I won't bother you until then. Goodnight, and good luck tomorrow."

Chapter Four

As I shook hands with my client and began to pack up my notes, I glanced to see the back of a nicely dressed attorney speaking with one of the officers of the court. I knew those shoulders very well. He turned and smiled.

"Hello, counselor."

"Hello, the Honorable Mr. Shaw. What is the U.S. attorney doing here?"

"Checking out a certain family attorney. Your summation was very good. We might have a position for you at the federal level."

My laughter was a mix between no way in hell and uneasiness. Did Max always have an angle? Why was he dangling a hook in my direction? "No way. Feds don't play fair. Besides, I've heard what you're like as a boss."

Max waved at the judge's assistant who was leaving the court. "I'm bossy?"

"Very. I've also heard you are demanding."

"I'm demanding in other areas of my private life as well."

As my face reddened, Max laughed. "Someone might hear you."

"Are you free for coffee? Or maybe a walk over to my office with me?"

I took a quick look at my watch. "Just for a bit?"

"I'll take that, Ms. O'Donohue."

It felt so natural to walk side by side with Max, but when we entered the security checkpoint of the federal courthouse, the differences in our lives were evident. Max was treated like a king, and I was, well, treated much like the peasant I was. As we walked through his office, everyone watched me, wondering who I was, and why I was walking in with the boss.

"Ms. O'Donohue, it is so nice to finally meet you." Max's personal assistant Carolyn smiled genuinely at me.

I shook her hand as she stood. Max checked his messages. "It's wonderful to place a face with a voice."

Max grimaced as he held up one of the notes. "Tell me he's not waiting in my office."

"I could tell you that, but I'd be lying."

Max uttered profanity under his breath. "Charlotte, stay out here with Carolyn while I get rid of this guy."

I saluted in comic fashion as I was shown a comfortable chair on the other side of his assistant's domain. "I won't be staying long. I've got to get back to my own office."

"How is your brother?" The woman's concern was real.

"Thank you for asking. He is holding his own. He has several tests this morning." As my new acquaintance answered a call, I reviewed the emails on my own phone. I heard a familiar friendly voice coming from Max's office.

"Brody?"

"Charlie, Charlie O'Donohue? What are you doing here?"

As I embraced my father's former clerk, I saw Max cross his arms in front of his chest. He watched from his doorway. It seemed Max was always watching with those deep caramel eyes.

"I was just visiting the offices. Mr. Shaw is an old friend of Tom's, remember?"

Brody stood back and seemed to review me from head to toe. "Oh, I remember the entire group. I saw your father the other day. It's such a shame what happened to Sean."

I nodded, but gave up no additional information. I kept noticing Max watching me out of the corner of my eye. His fists were clenched. "He's in bad shape. Where did you see the judge?"

"I dropped by the house with a fruit basket. I didn't know how I could help. I caught him taking the dog out."

"That was very kind. I know you were there for him when Conor and Mom passed. He really relied on you."

Brody smiled. "Truth be told, I miss being around him. I was lost when he retired, but I'm doing well now." He pointed back at Max. "I've been trying to secure a position here with our star prosecutor. It's wild that we are all the same age, yet here he is."

Max finally had an opening and stepped forward to sit on the edge of Carolyn's desk. "If we have an opening, we will have you in for an interview. Your credentials are very good, but I have to admit I brought in a few people from my Atlanta staff. The attorney general and the president preferred I hit the ground running, and a new staff would've been a hindrance."

Brody nodded. "I understand. I should be going. Thank you, Max. Charlie, it was so good to see you." He leaned in and kissed me on the cheek. After he left I shrugged. Max's eyes had impossibly darkened, and I was beginning to understand that wasn't a good sign. I didn't dare tell him that Brody had been interested in purchasing my house but had been outbid by a couple with a baby on the way.

"I've known him almost all of my life."

"How well?" Max's tone had an underlining of suspicion.

"Could we talk in your office?"

As soon as Max closed the door, I turned on him, fluttering my eyelashes. "Why, Mr. Shaw, are you jealous?"

"No."

I looked around the room. "Wow, you are super organized. I haven't seen my desk since I moved into the office space." I went to the wall and saw various dignitaries with Max. Again, one of the best photos was of Max and his father at the FBI headquarters in Washington. "Will your dad be coming to Kansas City soon?"

"I'm not sure. I'll have to go to New York for Thanksgiving. That's the one date of the year my mother insists I be present." Max headed for his desk and removed his jacket. "Do you want a coffee or something else?"

"No, I really will need to go in just a few minutes. Max, what is it about Brody that bothers you?" As formidable and confident as Max was, I really couldn't believe he could be jealous of Brody's attention toward me.

"Nothing really, but he assumes his connections to your father can get his foot in the door. His resume is good, but I have no room for him. He's pushy too, and I don't like how he calls you Charlie."

I placed my briefcase and purse on the coffee table near the seating area by the windows. "Brody has always called me Charlie. He treated me like a little sister. He was sweet, and it seems like he still is."

Max shot me a side glance. "Sweet? I wouldn't want a woman to consider me sweet."

"Sweet is nice."

Max feigned real pain. "Nice is worse."

I walked behind his desk and leaned down. "Well, I think you are sweet and nice."

"I thought I was the devil. Weirdly, I prefer that."

"Well, yes, that's the dangerous part about you, but I'm beginning to be comfortable with your hard exterior."

Max grasped my hands and pulled me onto his lap. "I'll give you a hard exterior."

His kiss reminded me that he was indeed dangerous, but deep down I knew he was the most considerate man, except for my father, whom I had ever known. His hands began their way down my back, and I quickly surrendered to more kisses. When he began to unbutton my suit jacket, I pushed back.

"You start this, and I'll never get out of here." I stood up quickly as he released me. "You seem very good at this seduction thing. Have you done this before with a woman in your office?"

"No, I haven't. Truthfully, never in my office. It seems you are again a first for me. I break a lot of my own rules with you."

I smoothed down my skirt and grabbed my things, ignoring his low voice and statement about my influence on him. "I have to go. I will see you Saturday night. You'll pick me up at Dad's?"

A knock interrupted his answer as Carolyn walked in. "I'm so sorry, Max, but the governor is on the line."

Max looked at the flashing button. "I'll be at your Dad's at six. I've got to–"

"I understand. Go to work."

I walked out behind his girl Friday. "Do you need an escort to your car?"

"Oh no. It's a beautiful morning for a walk, but thank you. By the way, please call me Charlotte."

"I will. I'm sure I'll be speaking with you soon."

"If he keeps working this hard, we may be only conversing through you. Have a good day."

Carolyn smiled. "It'll depend on my boss."

"Good luck with that. I'll pray for you." I walked past the desks of men and women who eyed me as though I was a fish just pulled from the water, on the hook, and waiting to die. Was my hair sticking up? "You all have a good day." I received a smile from one female attorney.

As I walked the downtown streets to my car, I noticed Paddy lumbering toward police headquarters. I yelled, and he stopped to wait for me.

"What are you doing down here, honey?"

"I was in court, and then I took a visit to Max's office. The walk was longer, but I had a quick look around." I might as well tell the truth. My oldest brother still eyed me suspiciously.

"Really? So how is the fair haired boy wonder?"

"Good. He's in a precarious position with some old staff and bringing a few from Atlanta to integrate. They don't look like happy campers."

Paddy snickered. "I've heard rumblings that the leftover staff doesn't like how Max moved those people into premier positions. It's his office, and I guess he should have the right to fill the desks with staff he trusts."

"Just like you, brother dear. Have we heard anything about Sean?"

Paddy took a sip from his coffee. "I was just there. His vitals are improving, but not as fast as the doctors want. He has his tests this morning."

"I know. I'm heading back to my office, but I'll leave early to visit this afternoon. Dad is exhausted. I did get him to go home for dinner and to sleep in his own bed again."

Paddy suddenly kissed me on the head. "You're the only one who could do that. I don't know what he'd do without you, or what we'd do. Since you're there, we all just don't worry."

I appreciated his gracious comments, but I also heard other words. Because I was there, **they** didn't worry. No wonder they were frantic to find me when I stayed with Max. They had to step up and take a little bit of time out of their lives. That's how it had been when Conor and Mom had passed. My latent resentment crept more into my thoughts. "Paddy, there may come a time when I won't be there."

"Where will you be?" He laughed as he asked the question.

"Maybe I'll have a husband and a family of my own, and we'll all have to share the responsibility?"

"Right. Don't you need some guy before that happens? Do you have some imaginary blow up or some secret love?"

His smug look made my blood boil. Without any words, I slugged him hard on his arm.

"What the bloody hell?"

"Don't take me for granted anymore!" I began to stomp off, but he caught up with me.

"I know we're all under a lot of stress, but what has gotten into you? Is it your new little career?"

My eyes flared. I pushed past him. "Paddy, no one has ever considered your job a little career. You are such a jerk."

"Stop, Charlie. What is wrong with you?"

I turned on my heel and faced him. "I love you all, but I'm tired of basing my decisions on what all of you think, or what Dad may say. In fact, I do care what Dad thinks, but as for the rest of you, well, go to hell, Paddy."

I continued walking, but this time, my brother hadn't followed. Telling off my eldest sibling made me smile. It felt good to address his constant demeaning comments. By the time I reached my car, I was having that darn guilt setting in, but I fought it. Phoebe was right. We needed to tell everyone at the very least, Max and I were going to kiss each other every now and then. The details of our relationship would stay between just the two of us, until both of us were certain. Because, despite my feelings of love for Max, there remained so many secrets I needed to uncover about the man who gave me butterflies.

Chapter Five

This Sunday dinner the grandchildren were exempt. Just in case there needed to be a serious discussion about Sean, Dad didn't want them worrying or upset by the news and plans. Gio fixed several of his favorite Italian dishes, and I was warming the items before everyone arrived.

It was freakishly quiet without Sean's loud voice booming upon his entry into the house. Jane and I filled the table as everyone else sat in the living room watching the football game.

"Have you ever noticed that once the season begins, you and I do all the work?"

I nodded at Jane. "It does seem that way. I like this idea of a buffet. We have more room on the table for the bread and salads."

"The aroma from this sausage dish is making my mouth water. Gio is an amazing cook."

"He's been doing it a long time, Janie." The doorbell rang, and I threw my towel at my sister. "I'll get it."

There was no rush to get the door. Apparently, it was a tight game. Gio smiled at me as I greeted the two men. "Jane is ready to eat all of that one dish with the sausage."

"Ah, did she melt the mozzarella on top like I said to do?"

"Yes, sir. They're all in the living room watching the game." I hoped he'd take my suggestion so I could greet Max properly.

Max stood on the porch, holding a large box in his hands. He looked very unlike a powerful attorney dressed in his faded jeans, sneakers, and a loose sweater. "I brought the cannolis."

As he handed me the box, he leaned down and kissed me quickly. "How are you?"

"I'm okay."

As he entered, he stretched to see the crowd. "Is Paddy talking to you after your temper tantrum?"

"Is that what he called it?" I looked inside the box to see the most amazing sweet pastries.

"Tom told me. Paddy told him. Do any of you know how to keep a secret?"

I leaned against him. "Lucky for you one of us can."

"Yes, very lucky for me, but I wanted you to stay all night," Max whispered. He kissed my cheek this time. "Last night was very nice for a few hours."

"I thought you didn't like nice," I joked as I kissed him back.

Max winked. "It depends on your definition. I better go in. Are we still doing this today? We didn't really talk about it on our date."

"Yes, no secrets." I answered with a firm tone. "So, if you

want to hold my hand, or put your arm around me, they'll just have to live with our relationship."

Max grimaced. "I hate that word. Can we figure out something else?"

"I'm not going to say we're dating like teenagers. Do you have any suggestions?"

Max pulled me closer to the wall. He leaned down to whisper in my ear. "I was very, very disappointed when you didn't stay the night, and I want them to know you're moving in with me."

"Stop. No. I can't do that just yet. Besides, we're not sure where this is going, and then there's Sean's situation. I'm worried about you too, and that you'll be the target because you're near me."

Max placed his hands on my shoulders. "Stop, breathe. Your family isn't cursed, and I'm not going to be hurt because of you. It's not your fault."

I shifted out of his arms and headed into the dining room. "I'm not so sure about that. I've been thinking about all of this. I shouldn't have told you my suspicions. I just should've walked away from you."

"But, you shouldn't." His voice was low, as sweet as honey, and my face began to redden.

"What shouldn't Charlie do?" Jane came out of the kitchen carrying the salad dressings.

"Um, add staff right now. I think she should wait until next year. What do you think, Jane?" Max smiled smugly at me. The man was so smooth and very quick on his feet.

"I agree, Max. You're the expert on this stuff. She should wait. Why are you in such a hurry all the time, Charlotte? Take your time. Enjoy it and make sure this is what you really want."

I knew what Jane was referencing, but my thoughts were on Max. "Isn't that good advice, Max? I should figure out if this is really what I want. Isn't that interesting?"

"Very. You should always take your time and never hurry. Slower is much better."

Jane had no idea what she had set in motion. Max was seducing me verbally in front of my sister. The rest of my family was in the other room. I couldn't take him up to my room before dinner, could I?

When my sister turned her back, I stuck my tongue out at him, and he only smiled.

"I'll just follow your lead," Max whispered. "Whatever you want to say, I'll be there with you."

My eyes sparkled as though I had been given the best gift ever. "I'll just tell them we're engaged. How's that?"

"And you said I was the devil?"

It was interesting that he hadn't become instantly offended or berated me for the mere thought of marriage. When Jane turned back around, Max was at one end of the table, and I was at the other end. When we all sat down to eat, Max maneuvered to sit at my side.

No one even cared. Casually, we ate the wonderful food, and everyone updated each other on what had been going on in their lives. Usually, they never got around to me, fixating on the cost of Tom's latest sale. The tone became serious as the discussion turned to Sean and his future. So many things were unknown.

"Eventually, he'll have to leave the hospital. He may go to a rehabilitation center first, and then he'll come home. He will come here." Dad's statement was definite. I wasn't sure if he was commanding it to be so or just wishing and hoping.

"We can fix up the room downstairs just like we did for Mom," Paddy suggested.

"I can have a contractor here on Monday to take a look," Tom added.

"Let's not get ahead of ourselves. Sean would need so much more," my father said, thankfully slowing down hammers into the walls.

"Charlotte's schedule will work the best to help you out, Dad." Paddy smiled at me from the other end of the table as he offered the suggestion. Was my brother actually taunting me?

"And Jane," Tom added. He seemed to be the second man in on this creative plan.

"I'm sorry, but I'm a grade school principal, and I have four kids," Jane answered defensively. I'd heard all of this before.

"Charlotte is living here and is used to helping. She was wonderful with Mom." I saw my father frown at Paddy's insistence.

"Charlotte has her law practice." Dad's eyes seared into Paddy. "Besides, she was wonderful with Mom, but Sean is a large man, almost twice Charlotte's size. We need to slow the jets, please."

Paddy shook his head as though he was jabbing me with a very large stick. "Charlotte can work her schedule around, Dad. She's the one with spare time. She's the youngest, and she can stop her career and start up again. It's not like she has a secret relationship or a few kids hidden away." Paddy's direct assault fell on me. He added a wink. He was challenging me.

Max threw his napkin on the plate. He touched my hand. "Charlotte, you can hate me, but I don't care," Max whispered. "You're not going to lose yourself again just because the rest of your family doesn't consider your feelings." When his voice raised, everyone heard. He stood slowly. "Charlotte is tired of working out her schedule. I won't allow that."

Paddy pushed back his chair, but Dad glared at him. "You won't allow it? Who in the hell do you think you are Max Shaw? You are nothing. We allow you to be at this table. You don't have to be here."

I heard Gio's chair pushed back. A line of defense was forming. There was definitely too much testosterone at this table. I patted Max's hand in hopes of calming the situation. "Sit down. I appreciate what you just said, but it's my choice, isn't it?" I was surprised when he slowly dropped down beside me. Max nodded his agreement.

"Enough." Dad's one word shut everything down, but I could feel tears welling up in my eyes. "It is still my table, and Gio and Max are family. I said we will shut this discussion down until we know what we are facing. Sean never opened his eyes today."

"Yes, he did, Dad," Paddy countered.

"No, he did not, Paddy. You thought you saw it, but you didn't. I was in the room with you. They are afraid he is falling into a vegetative state. That's the truth. We need to be realistic this time and not pretend everything will work out."

A pin could have dropped. The stillness was frightening as we heard what we all feared. Max grasped my hand under the table and held it tight. Gio covered his mouth. Jane, and my sisters-in-laws' faces paled. Tom and Paddy masked their sorrow.

"If that is the case, Judge, and it comes to that, the Taylor Trust will pay for the care he needs. I promise that. I know he has insurance, but sometimes more quality centers won't be covered. We will cover the best in care." Max's slow, soft words were unbelievable, but I knew he meant every word. Without thinking, I placed my head on his shoulder.

Dad swallowed hard. "Thank you, Max. That makes my decisions much easier, and it is very appreciated."

Jane ran out of the dining room to the solitude of the kitchen, and Meg trailed behind. Paddy's wife Linda stared at me as though I needed to say something, but Max had done the talking. I had nothing to add. My thoughts were that I was selfish, but I knew I wasn't. Guilt seemed to live constantly in my thoughts these days, and I opened my mouth to say that I would step up. Surprisingly, I closed my lips firmly. Paddy continued to glare at Max. There was an uncomfortable undercurrent surrounding the two of them. I wondered if Paddy as Max's inside man had discovered something in one of the federal cases, or even in our personal adventures. Max had thought Paddy was watching him. Was he?

Paddy had a full fifty or sixty pounds on Max and at least three inches. My oldest brother's build was much like our late grandfather. The man had been a bit scary, but what I could remember of him was his hug that swallowed up a child like me. He had been a huge teddy bear, but Paddy when prodded was a grizzly, fast to attack. And he never forgave or forgot.

"How about cannolis and coffee?" Gio's attempt at tamping down the solemn feeling within the room was met with quiet murmurs. "Good, I'll make a nice pot." He stood and patted Max's shoulders. He leaned down to whisper. "Sometimes, it is better to stand down or to walk away. As a former hitman, I have experience in this arena. Max, don't take the kill shot. This is family." Gio headed into the kitchen.

Paddy quickly nudged his chair back and walked out. Tom followed suit. We heard the front door open and close.

Linda frowned. "He's just upset."

"We're all upset," my father suggested. "There's no reason

for him to plan for any of us to take on a Herculean task. He's not thinking. We just have to wait."

My sister-in-law knew her husband's mind better than any of us. Linda also understood how Paddy's brain glitched, placing his thoughts on a one-way track. He only had one speed, and if something got in his way, that something, or in this case someone could become roadkill. "I'll go check on him." Linda offered me a sympathetic glance as she left the table.

That left Dad, Max, and me. He smiled my way. "Max, thank you for your generous offer. If it does come to that, and it won't put any burden on your family, I will be the recipient of your charity. I've always worked off loans, but this time–"

"It's not charity. It's what family does for each other. I'm learning how to do that." Max gave me a side glance.

My dad nodded. "Charlotte, your brother goes off like that. You know that, right? I won't have that happen to your life again. You seem happier than ever. Going into family law really has changed everything for you."

"Dad, it is what I want to do, but it's just not my practice. I, we need to–"

"Max, get your sorry ass out here." Paddy reentered the room quickly with Linda, hanging onto his arm. Her attempt at slowing down a rolling tank was futile.

Max stood up slowly. "Now what, Paddy? Will it make Sean wake up if you beat the hell out of me? Will it make it all better?"

"No, but I'll feel better. I know what you're doing, and it has nothing to do with our investigation."

Dad stood and headed over to his ill tempered son. "Slow down, Paddy. You've said enough. Just keep any secrets to yourself."

Paddy pointed at Max. "He came back here and made a place at our table."

Tom stood in-between Max and Paddy. "Look, Max is my best friend and has been for years. We welcomed him back."

Paddy's demonic smile frightened me. "You don't know, do you?"

Tom shook his head. "You need to go home. Linda, take him to cool off."

"What is going on?" Jane held the coffee pot in her hand. Gio and Meg had their hands full with plates of cannolis.

"I think Paddy is calling me out, but I'm not sure why," Max said calmly. Gio placed his tray on the table and stood behind us.

"No one knows what you're doing except me. I figured it out. You played your hand when you said you wouldn't allow Charlotte to care for our very own brother. She loves Sean. Of course, she'd want to sacrifice, but it would take time away from you."

Max slid his chair back and moved around the table. "You want her to sacrifice her life? That's ridiculous. She's done enough, and you know it. You never worried about your father after your mother died. Tom told me. You didn't even like coming into this house. You had your life. You had your career." Max looked around. "The judge said this is a mute point. No one knows yet how Sean will do, or what he will need. Even if Charlotte wanted to, she's petite; she's half of Sean's size."

"Why did my brother want to talk to you, Max?" Paddy screamed, his face growing red. His eyes were glassy with tears. "He wanted to tell you who killed Conor, and who shot him. He made them wait to take him to the hospital. Those minutes probably changed the course of his life, you spoiled rich kid. It's all about you. I've done everything you've asked of me, but–"

Surprisingly, Max didn't back down. His back was ramrod straight, his fists balled tightly. "That's what this is about. You think I'm taking charge of your family. For your information, Sean wanted to tell me because I know whoever it is. He didn't tell you because he knew you'd overreact."

"The hell I would. So, who is it?"

I tried to temper my tone, but I knew it sounded shrill and offensive. Why was Paddy so offended? What had he done for Max? Those questions would have to wait. "Sean wasn't able to tell Max. You know that, and you also know he couldn't remember when we were there with him in the hospital. We told you. There's been no secrets. A reporter said there was a curse over our family, and I'm beginning to believe it. I think someone is out there watching us and wanting us to suffer. You aren't helping."

Paddy came closer, pushing Tom out of the way to tower over me. "No secrets, little Charlie? Seriously? I can't believe you just said that. You're disgusting." What was going on with my brother? Surely this wasn't just jealousy of Max? Was something else creating the tension between them?

"That's enough, Paddy," Dad interrupted. "Go home and cool off."

Paddy began to laugh as we all looked at him as though he had lost his mind. "You all really don't know, do you? Really? You've been very good at fooling everyone, Max."

"Paddy, what do you want from me?" Max's hands relaxed as if he knew what was coming.

"Our sweet little sister says she doesn't have any secrets. Well, apparently our family doesn't know that little Max here has been screwing our Charlie."

And just like that our non-relationship was out in the open. I could feel Gio's large hand on my back for support. Thankfully, my sister and sisters-in-law were smiling. My father's face fell a bit. Tom was incredulous. He just kept exchanging looks between Max and me. We had betrayed him.

Paddy's stance was unchanged. Silence took over a room that was usually filled with conversation and laughter. My family didn't have one word to say? That was a first.

Paddy laughed in our direction. He pointed at the man I loved. "Max, I bet you've told the other guys that you're fu-"

"That's enough," Max said forcefully, and my brother's smile disappeared. "I think you're misrepresenting what is going on, Paddy. Charlotte and I are close. We were going to tell you all today that we have been spending a lot of time together, and we even had a date last night that I think went very well. Not that it's any of your business, but Charlotte was home here by midnight. As for your terminology, Paddy. Don't you ever use either of those terms when speaking about your sister. She's a grown woman who very much makes her own decisions, and she's to be respected, cherished, and loved. Your words are foul and demeaning, and frankly, if that's how you feel about women then maybe we should go outside."

Paddy flew past Tom and grabbed Max by the edge of his sweater, pulling him closer. They didn't remain in the house but began blows on the front porch. Max was able to get in two quick rights on Paddy's jaw before my brother brought Max down. Tom, Gio, and Dad grabbed at the two men to pull them apart. Max watched from the floor of the porch as three men held Paddy back.

"He sucker punched me," Paddy complained.

"No, he got off a couple good shots. You're damn lucky. Now, go home. I'll talk to you later." My father hadn't requested, he commanded with his outstretched arm pointing the way to the car. Linda took Paddy by the hand and began her own scolding all the way down the sidewalk.

"More cannolis for me?" Max joked as he laid there, one hand rubbing his jaw, the other his side.

For the first time since Sean's shooting, Dad laughed out loud. "Yes, Max, more cannolis for you. But first, you and I need to have a discussion. Alone and now."

"Shouldn't I participate?" Both men stared in my direction.

"No," they answered in unison.

Now that the show was over, Max and Dad took their coffee and dessert into my father's office. The rest of us sat at the dining room table as Gio regaled us with stories of the old days of the River Quay bombing and the mob activity to distract us. But my eyes were laser focused on the closed door across the length of the house. Tom was doubled over in laughter at one point, and I relaxed a bit. It was a welcome relief from the sorrow and stress we had been experiencing.

When the door finally opened slowly, Dad and Max eventually came to the table. Everything seemed fine, and Max was in one piece. Both men were quiet and reserved, but that could be the litigator in each of them. I asked with my eyes if everything was okay. Max just nodded and smiled.

Innocuous conversation highlighted the next hour. Max nudged me.

"Gio looks tired. I should get him home, and I'm sure your Dad wants to see Sean one more time tonight."

"Okay, so I think announcing to them that we were seeing each other went well, don't you?"

Max's eye roll was a sight to behold. "Oh, yeah. My jaw says it went really well. I told you Paddy was following me.

I wasn't paranoid. I'll call you later." He stood, and in front of the remaining family, Max bent down and kissed me on the cheek. "I'm going to get Gio home, Judge. Thank you for dinner."

"Gio made just about everything, and you brought the cannolis. I'm just happy you survived, Max." Dad retreated from the table to walk them out.

"Charlotte Rose O'Donohue," Jane chided.

Tom held his face in his hands. "I don't want to hear anything."

"Oh, about Max screwing me?" I finally lashed out. Jane murmured something about wanting all of the details.

Tom brought his head up to see me. "That was inexcusable. Paddy owes you and Max an apology, and all that crap about stopping your life was just ... crap. Paddy can't do anything to help Sean, and he couldn't for Conor either. This is killing him just like when Mom died. He acts out on his grief, and sadly, he took it out on you. Man, did you see the shots Max got on the big bear?"

I nodded. I thought for a second before I asked the questions that were nagging at me. "Why didn't anyone stop Paddy? Why did Max have to be the only one to champion my defense?" My questions were met with silence for a minute.

"You're right, Charlotte. I'm sorry," Meg acknowledged.

"Me too," Jane mumbled. "I guess we didn't know what to say or do."

"Or, the hard reality is none of us wanted to step up to mess up our lives to care for Sean, or buck our eldest brother," Tom added. "I'm sorry, but I don't know how I feel about you and Max doing whatever you're doing. I can only warn you again that my old friend, the player, is dangerous. I've told you that before. I'm afraid you'll get hurt, Charlie."

"I'm afraid too, Tom, but he gives me something I haven't felt in a very long time, maybe not ever. It's not what your dirty mind is thinking. It's companionship and support. We are adults, and this time if I get hurt, I think I'll be able to handle it better. We seem to be very good together in a crisis. We may be rotten when things are more normal. Who knows?"

"Or what if your relationship works out?" Jane leaned over to grab my hand. "Max is a stand up guy, and he has been for all of us through this crisis. I believe he really cares about you."

"Me too, Charlotte. He does care about you. His words were beautiful." Meg's hope filled smile buoyed my confidence.

His words were lovely, but ... I chuckled. "He talks for a living, Meg."

"Look who dropped by," Dad led two men into the dining room.

"Wow, Brody, I haven't seen you for the longest time, and now twice in one week," I commented.

"I know, Charlie. I just wanted to stop in like the old days and see everyone. This is Doug Myer. Do you remember him from Judge McIntire's staff?"

Tom stood up and shook hands. "I remember you. Weren't you in our high school class too?"

"Yes. I just saw Max Shaw. I thought he'd never come back here."

Tom nodded. "He thought that, but his job brought him back. Sit down, and let's catch up."

Paddy's cannolis went to Brody and Doug. They provided the light entertainment we so desperately needed, but I saw Dad peeking at his watch. He wanted to see Sean again tonight, but it was getting late. Even the judge couldn't get in if it was past visiting hours.

"Charlotte, I have been thinking about you since the other day. Would you like to meet for drinks one night next week?"

I almost spit into my water glass. I hadn't had a date in so long, and now Max and I were doing more than dating, and here was Brody asking me out. "Well, maybe we could meet for happy hour at the bar and restaurant on the corner from my office? I'm in the Waldo area."

"Oh I know. Your father said you'd rented a nice office. I'll call and see when you're available. Will that work?"

"Sure, Brody. I'd like to catch up and see what you're doing."

"Wonderful. It's a date."

"Well, we will meet. I'm not really dating anyone right now."

"Again, wonderful."

No, I'm just falling in love with someone. That's not really a big deal considering everything else happening in this family. And why did I have the nagging feeling that Paddy's problems with Max had less to do with my honor and more to do with some secret that the two of them were sharing? One thing was for sure, I needed to keep my head on straight. I'd have to take one crisis at a time, and I needed to watch every move in whatever strange chess game was being played before my eyes. Being a pawn on the board while master players moved the pieces was never an enviable position.

Chapter Six

Charlotte's Office

"For me?" Phoebe Lawton opened her arms to gather the large bouquet of dark red roses.

"No, sorry, they're for your boss." Max looked straight into Charlotte's office. "Where is she?"

"She's visiting with an old friend down at the corner restaurant."

"Really? I thought we could begin the weekend a little earlier, but I guess she began without me."

"Did you text or call?"

Max sat down and placed the flowers onto Phoebe's desk. "No. We haven't seen each other since Sunday so I just thought–"

"You assumed she'd just be here, didn't you? I've seen this movie before." Phoebe shook her head dismissively.

"Really, great sage?" Max folded his hands together and stretched his legs out in front of him for story time. "Enlighten me."

"Honestly?"

"Yes, honestly. Obviously, you have a story to share."

Phoebe bit her lip as if in thought. "It's a story as old as time. Powerful man keeps gaining more power and fame, and the little woman sits by her phone waiting for his calls. Then, the little woman is noticed by another man, or she is involved in a job that makes her heart sing. Woman isn't there when the man has time for her. The next thing you know, man becomes disappointed."

Max chuckled. "How does this story end?"

"It depends. One very powerful man I knew worked hard to provide for his growing family. Well, it wasn't that large compared to other Irish families. One side of their family has twelve kids. Can you imagine?"

Max's forehead creased. "No, I can't. I haven't really thought of having a family."

Phoebe ignored the comment but put it aside as a mental note. If Charlotte ever asked her, she would tell her the truth. "He loved his wife very much, but he thought he was doing the honorable thing by putting his head down and working hard. The next thing you knew, he wasn't home. He worked late. He missed his own daughter's twenty-first birthday. He completely forgot it. That's when the little woman changed. She got a job at a department store. She had her own money and a discount. She also ran into an old friend. In fact, the friend had been a former boyfriend."

Max shifted uncomfortably in his chair. "I think I know the plot of this story."

"Maybe, maybe not. One night the honorable man came home late, and the woman had her friend over. Oh, they were just visiting, but he saw her laugh like she hadn't for a very long time. That old friend had reawakened a joy within the woman that her husband couldn't provide because he was just too busy being him. He had no room for her unless it was to meet his needs."

"I'm a bit confused. I haven't figured out if I'm the old friend or the powerful, honorable man."

"Exactly, Mr. Shaw. It's in your court to figure out who you will be, which role you will play. Will you take her for granted or will you bring her joy?"

"I'm assuming that the woman and man in your story stayed together? Everything seemed picture perfect."

"Yes, of course. He changed his schedule a bit, and gently requested she quit her job. He turned a blind eye when the woman and his personal assistant used his credit card for lunch and copious amounts of shopping. The couple was very happy until the day she died."

"Ah. I figured. So, what don't I know?"

"Charlotte was asked out for drinks with Brody. I remember him from the judge's staff."

"I know, and Tom and I were in high school with him. He came asking for a job."

"Really? Did you give him one?"

"No. I remember what he was like back then, and he's the

same guy. I don't think he's grown over the years. Besides, I didn't think he'd fit on my team."

"He was good for the judge, but there was always something about him. He would pass by me to get to Judge O."

"Yes, one on one he seems fine, but he's not a team player, Phoebe. I want a team. That's how I worked in Atlanta, and I believe it will work here. Besides, I need people I can trust. There's something about Brody that bothers me. Maybe he has his own agenda?"

Phoebe smiled and nodded her head in agreement. "Perhaps you are feeling a bit jealous?" Before Max could answer, she continued. "You are the boss. A prosecutor's office is very different from Judge O'Donohue's."

"Besides, Brody doesn't have the trial experience I need. I'm sure he's a nice guy. It has nothing to do with jealousy, by the way. I don't operate like that. So, they're on the corner?"

"Yes, Mr. Shaw. You need to understand, Brody has been there when the family needed him. He is well-liked. And your operating procedures? You may need to change those. By the way, I hear you got a couple of shots in on Paddy. Is that true?"

Max rubbed his jaw. "I went on offense, but he took me. I knew going into it I'd lose, but–"

"You had to do it for Charlotte, didn't you?" Phoebe watched his reaction when she mentioned her boss's name. Max softened. His lips curved in a smile that was loving.

"I didn't like what Paddy said."

Phoebe nodded. "Well, I know a certain woman who really appreciated your defense of her and for mentioning she shouldn't put her dreams on hold again. Thank you for what you did just for her. Someone needed to wake them all up."

Max was uncomfortable with the praise. He really wasn't a member of the family, and Charlotte and he were just friends. They were having a good time. His intercession had been out of bounds, but someone needed to stand up for her. As he stood up, he presented the flowers to the woman in the chair. "Phoebe, these are for you. Enjoy your weekend."

"Well, aren't you the charmer?"

Max flashed his signature smile. "I try."

"Max, just one more thing."

"Yes?"

"You've probably been warned by others, but here it is from me. Don't hurt our girl. Got it?"

Max was suddenly serious. "Understood. Gio and Judge O have made that abundantly clear. For what it is worth, it isn't my intention to hurt Charlotte. Ever. Thanks, Phoebe."

Max removed his tie and tucked it into his pocket as he walked down the block. When he entered the bar area of the restaurant, he looked over the top of the crowd. A Friday night during Happy Hour was always crowded, but he seldom participated. He saw Brody in one of the booths taking a drink from his beer. Max made his way through the crowd.

"Well, hello, Brody." He looked over to the other side of the table. "Charlotte? How are you? I haven't seen you in days."

"Hi Max. I'm good. What are you doing here?"

Max slid in on Charlotte's side of the booth as Brody looked stunned by his intrusion. "I was headed home, and I stopped by your office to see how your brother was doing. Phoebe told me you were here. I haven't been to Happy Hour in a long time, and this way I can visit with you and with Brody."

"We are so lucky." Brody's voice trailed off as Max smiled.

"So, how was your day?" Max's question was directed at Charlotte.

"Busy, what about yours?"

Max smiled. "The same. Brody, I was thinking. I'm pretty sure you'd be a perfect fit at McLuskey and Bruce."

"I really wanted to work at the federal level. That's what I'm used to doing."

"I understand, but you haven't prosecuted a case at that level. You were amazing with Judge O'Donohue, but you need the experience. My team has to be able to step in for me."

A server stood in front of the threesome. Max ordered a bourbon for himself and added another beer for Charlotte and her companion.

After a few minutes of awkward small talk and the delivery of the drinks, Max's mood darkened. "And how is Sean?"

"In and out. He can feel pain, but he sleeps more than he is awake. Did I tell you that he still has a bullet lodged in his body?"

Max threw back his drink. "No, I didn't know that."

Brody picked that time to reach across the table to hold Charlotte's hand. "I'm so sorry, Charlie."

"Thank you," Charlotte whispered. She added a smile, but she could almost feel the heat from the flaming eyes of the man next to her. His focus was on her hand and that of Brody's. She pulled back slowly. "Brody, Dad really appreciates you keeping in touch."

"I miss working with him. He taught me so much, and it really was the experience of a lifetime just being around him. Frankly, I hung on his every word when we were working together."

"When you were working for him," Max corrected.

"Well, yes, but I thought we were a team."

"Phoebe is my assistant and paralegal now," Charlotte volunteered. "I bet you miss her too."

"Phoebe and I weren't as close. The judge was like a father to me, and I cherish the few years I worked for him."

"So, Brody, I feel terrible about not having a place for you. Where do you want to work? I'd be happy to help you find a suitable position." Charlotte rolled her eyes at Max's charming demeanor. She wondered what his game was this time because Max Shaw never did anything spur of the moment without calculating the outcome and benefit to himself. What was his payoff?

"I said I really want to work at the federal level."

Max moved a little closer to Charlotte. "Why not work for another judge?"

Brody noticed Shaw's movement. "I really wanted to work in your office. By the way, how did you get that appointment? We all heard you were very happy in Atlanta."

Max smiled. "I received the appointment the same way everyone does. The president and the attorney general thought I'd be a good fit when the position was open."

Brody winked at Charlotte. "The rumor at the last alumni get together was that Max knew someone. Frankly, I was shocked when you came back to Kansas City. I thought you'd shaken the dust off of your shoes never to return again."

Max chuckled. Strategically, his arm touched Charlotte's. He could see Brody's intent gaze on their physical proximity. "I thought I wouldn't come back, but I did want to connect with old friends like the O'Donohues." Next, he threw his arm over Charlotte's back, bringing their bodies closer than ever. He took it all in, watching Brody's subtle reaction. The man across the table seemed surprised. His bottom lip slacked and a vein on the side of his neck throbbed. Max understood Brody to be a man who was making a move on Charlotte. He wondered what reaction he would receive if he told the old friend that Charlotte shared his bed and made love to him in the middle of the night when neither one of them could sleep. Instead, he smiled with his secret intact.

Brody directed his attention away from Max. "Charlotte, do

you remember when we went to the zoo for that charity event? We had such a good time. It was so late we had breakfast at that dive off of Main Street."

The body warmth from Max's jacket was almost too much, but Charlotte was getting used to having hot flashes when the man was near. "I remember. That was a great night, and you were so nice to go with me when my ex backed out."

"We always had a good time together. We should do that again."

"Maybe we could get a group together? I think that event has already passed for this year," Charlotte replied quickly. She felt Max's hand drape over her left shoulder. His thumb casually formed circles just above her breast. Thankfully, she was wearing a sweater over her blouse. "Yes, a group."

Max noticed the disappointment in Brody's eyes. Brody liked Charlotte a little too much, and it wasn't in a brotherly stand-in position. The man was nice enough, but Max was not in the business of sharing or liking that many people who were just nice. He usually found them shallow and non-confrontational in a very boring way.

"I wouldn't mind going," Max said coolly. "Of course, it would depend on what you all were doing."

Brody tilted his head and looked inside his beer. "If you can't make it, you can't make it. We all know how busy you are. Do you even find time to date? Have you met anyone here in the city yet? I've heard about your conquests in Atlanta."

Max removed his arm from around Charlotte and held Brody's gaze. "I don't know what you heard, but I don't ever consider a woman a conquest. I have been busy." Max began to add more information and realized it wasn't necessary. The man sitting across from him didn't need to know about his personal life. Charlotte wasn't a pawn to move around the board just to make him feel like a big man. She was his, and until Charlotte and he spent more time together there wasn't any reason to cry it out to the entire city. Their announcement of their closeness had created enough chaos within her family.

"I bet Charlotte might know someone who might want to go out with someone like you." Brody's smile was even more smug and confident than when he had been conversing with Charlotte before Max's arrival.

Charlotte laughed out loud. "I think Max can find women on his own. Gentlemen, I need to head to the hospital." She searched for her purse under the table, pulling it up, and grabbing her keys. She glanced outside. "It's raining again. I don't know about you two, but everytime it rains, I think it's going to flood."

Max looked down at his watch. "I should go too. It was great catching up, Brody. Charlotte, I'll follow you out." Max got up and waited. Brody was left with his beer as Max placed down money for the server.

As Charlotte began to slide out, her arm accidentally nudged her glass of beer off of the table. The liquid splashed Max's pants, eventually landing on his well polished shoes.

Charlotte remained in the booth looking up. She began to laugh. She was usually the recipient of slush, ice, muck, water, food, and glitter at the hands of Max, but this time ...

"I'm so sorry," Charlotte said, but her laughter was louder than any sympathetic words.

Max merely looked down. "You are not. I know you aren't, and I know why. We will discuss this later."

"It was an accident, Max," Brody added as he offered a napkin.

Max shot a glance at the intruder. "Yes, of course." He didn't accept the offering but shook each leg dramatically.

Charlotte pushed Max back to make her exit. She came over to Brody and kissed his cheek. "Brody, it was lovely catching up. I'll tell Dad I saw you, and again thank you for your friendship. I'm sure Dad appreciates it so much. Goodnight."

Charlotte said nothing until they were under the awning across the street. She hit Max with her purse.

"Ow, what was that for? You've already thrown beer on me."

"Really? You're going to ask that? And that was an accident unlike a certain glitter incident."

"Which was also an accident," Max added quickly, his own voice cracking as he grinned.

"Give me a break. I haven't been to a Happy Hour ... who believes that?" Charlotte continued to walk back to her office.

"I have to get my laptop and briefcase." Max followed without uttering another word.

Charlotte entered the building and headed into her office. There was a coldness she'd never experienced before. "Max, do you feel that?"

"Feel what? Is someone in here?"

Charlotte nodded. "I think ..." She barely heard a whisper.

"Can you hear me?"

"Um, Max, could you wait out here at Phoebe's desk?"

"Why?" Max seemed confused and then dropped into one of the chairs in the room. "Do you need to talk to one of your ghosties? Is that what's going on?"

Charlotte glared back at him. "Yes, and stop calling them that. I'll be just a minute."

She closed the door to her office and paced back and forth. "Is someone here?"

"I am."

"Hello. Who are you and what do you need?"

"You."

Charlotte's goosebumps had goosebumps. Her head began to throb. "Who are you? You need to tell me so we can talk properly."

"Not necessary. The man is lying."

Charlotte sighed. "Really? Which one? I've had a few men in this office. You, whoever you are, need to be more specific." She sat in her chair and noticed Phoebe had left a message in the middle of her desk. "I'm waiting."

"One of your men is lying. I know a liar."

"Okay." Charlotte read the note from her assistant. "Is there anything I can do for you?"

"No."

"Great," Charlotte answered sarcastically. "My office is haunted by some strange spirit. Fine. I'm gone for the night."

There was no answer as Charlotte turned the doorknob to leave. It seemed stuck. She tried again, but the door wouldn't budge. "Oh come on."

"Now you are here too."

Charlotte jerked on the door. "Let me out. Now! I'll have you exorcized."

"Charlotte? Are you okay in there?" Max's voice stopped Charlotte's panicking.

"Could you open the door from your side?"

"Yes." Max calmly entered the office. "Are you finished with your meeting?"

"I am now. The door was stuck."

Max examined the door. He glanced up at Charlotte who was holding up a piece of paper. "You brought flowers? The note says Phoebe thought you'd be going to break up my visit with Brody."

"I brought Phoebe flowers. Yes, I did." Max stood tall and proud. "And I wanted a drink."

"You never want a drink at a bar, but you do like to be in charge of a situation, don't you? Brody is a very nice man, and he has been devoted to my father. He asked to talk, and I didn't think it would do any harm."

"He likes you very much and not in a brotherly way."

"Are you describing Brody or you? It wasn't that long ago that we were just friends, and you were just like another one of my brothers, but somewhere along the way–"

Max brought Charlotte into his arms. "Things do change." His eyes searched her pale gray eyes before his mouth was on her full lips. Before Charlotte could protest, Max's attention brought that warmth only he could to every cell in her body. She threw the note into the air and locked her arms around his neck. It really was no use to rebuff him when she wanted him so much, even if he could be a liar.

Max's lips moved down her exposed neck. He pulled away her cardigan and began to unbutton her blouse.

"Stop it," Charlotte demanded as she slapped away his hand. "If we start this, I'll never get to the hospital. It's hard to say no to you."

Max smiled widely. "That's the way I like it. We could drop your car at the house, and I'll drive us there. We can visit for a bit, make sure your Dad has eaten, and if not, we bring him with us. Deal?"

Charlotte's eyes became thin slits of suspicion. "Which house?"

Max laughed. "You caught me. Your dad's house is where we will leave your car. Trust me now?"

"Promise? I'm not sure when you're telling the truth or not."

Max crossed his heart and added a wink. "You can't tell? That's good for me, but I assure you I've been honest with you more than with anyone else on the face of this earth."

"Good. Keep it that way, buddy." Charlotte playfully patted him on the arm. They walked hand-in-hand to her car. It was a happy moment, but it soon passed as Charlotte thought about which man was lying to her. The warning had chilled her. The spirit wouldn't identify themselves, and that was never a good thing. In fact, she wasn't sure she'd ever experienced that before. She'd only been held captive one other time when she was younger. That had ended very badly.

A new experience brought a world of different questions. Why wouldn't the spirit tell her who they were, why had the ghost been so nasty, and why was some man in her life lying to her?

Chapter Seven

"Dad, tell Max about that U.S. marshal's testimony in your very last trial." It was an entertaining story I thought would offer my father the opportunity to laugh. All through dinner at one of his favorite downtown grills, Dad had been sullen and distant. I figured the news on Sean wasn't something he wanted to discuss yet.

"I'll tell Max that one on another day. I'd rather talk about what happened last Sunday." My father's gaze fell on Max and me. Naturally, almost too naturally, I had sat next to Max instead of my father when we arrived at the restaurant.

"What do you want to discuss?" Max's direct question was obtuse, but honest. "You and I had our little talk. I thought you and I were fine."

"Yes, we are fine after our discussion, but Paddy said some awful things, and I talked to him. Hopefully, nothing like that will happen again." My father directed his attention toward me. "Charlotte Rose, you are an adult, but as I've said before you'll always be my baby. I don't want to see you hurt."

"Who says I'll hurt her?" Max had a touch of indignation in his question. "I'll answer my own question. Everyone thinks

I'll hurt Charlotte. I've always had great respect for you and your family, Judge, and I told you privately ..."

My father's hand flew up to stop him. "We don't need to get into that, and I know how you feel about our family, but I think I know you, and I obviously know my daughter."

This time Max held his hand up to stop my father. "Judge, I had a nice conversation with Phoebe earlier. Actually, she talked, and I listened. It was similar in nature to the one you and I had privately." Their exchanged knowing glances told me I'd probably never discover what was discussed in Dad's office.

My father smiled. "That does sound like Phoebe Lawton. What brilliance did she lay on you?"

"Well, she told me a story of a very powerful and career obsessed man who worked very hard for his family. She said that the man's wife found herself lost because he wasn't there. He worked too hard, so she went out and got a job. I have a feeling Phoebe didn't know the details of the negotiations between the powerful man and the wonderful dutiful wife, but she made it very clear that things did change."

I remembered when Mom had a job for a brief time, and then she didn't. Where was Phoebe and Max headed with this?

"What did you learn from Phoebe's fable?" Dad asked.

"I learned that I've been working so hard at being successful, it might be the right time to begin to enjoy and to evaluate what my future could be. I'm learning every day what

I could have, and Charlotte is teaching me that there is more to life than just that downtown office. Does all of this make sense?"

Dad nodded. "I'm worried about my daughter, but I'm also fearful that I'll lose you Max. We will all lose you, and you'll lose yourself. You really are one of us, and Gio too. After all of these years, to be reconnected with the little old gangster, believe it or not, is a blessing. We talk about the old days, and we work hard on your house. We feel needed in more ways than one. And, I'm afraid my daughter will have her heart broken again. Charlotte, I wanted you to know my concerns."

"Dad, we've agreed that if the day comes when Max and I don't have feelings for each other, we'll part as friends."

Dad shook his head. "You say that now, but we all know it's not that easy. Life will change if that happens." Dad took in a deep breath and smiled. "But, I loved how you shut down Paddy. Charlotte will not be Sean's caretaker."

"And I will make sure whatever your son needs that isn't covered by the insurance, will be taken care of by my trust. You have to allow me to do that." Max was adamant. I touched his arm proudly.

Dad nodded. "I appreciate that so much, Max. Are you sure your mother and father will be in agreement?"

"Oh, they have nothing to do with the money. Dad is fine and was never allowed any control. Old man Taylor and my great grandfather took care of that. Mother has her own trust.

This is all on me. It is what I want to do with the money."

"Okay, Max. Thank you. It does take a weight off of me. Now, you two, how does this work? Will Charlotte move out of my house?"

Max began to answer, but I stopped him by placing my hand on his arm. "Dad, I want to continue to live at the house, but–"

"But, your old man needs to turn a blind eye when you come walking in around five in the morning after spending the night somewhere else?"

Fortunately, the lighting in the restaurant was low or my father would see my lovely shade of crimson rising from my neck. "I guess?"

"I know," he assured me. "I just hope you two know what you're doing. It won't be easy. Your personalities probably won't blend, and your backgrounds are vast wastelands of different. You're both strong-willed and driven. Charlotte, you can't always let this one have his way." Dad pointed at Max.

Max shifted uncomfortably. "And I won't always let her have her way."

"You should, if you know what's good for you, Max." My father winked in my direction. "Charlotte, you're the baby so even at your age, there will be expectations from your sister and brothers, and even from me. I'm counting on you both not to be reckless."

"Yes, Judge," Max answered quickly as though my father was a commanding officer.

Dad shook his head. "You know I like the two of you together, but this will be a challenge. The world has changed. Your mother and I, well, she let me kiss her before we were married. That was it. Neither one of us really knew what we were doing or what we had gotten ourselves into, but we managed."

"You must've figured it out. You had six kids." I thought a little humor wouldn't hurt the conversation.

"I don't want to even think about any of that. I was the same way with Jane. I don't know why we have such different standards for men and women, but I'm old fashioned."

"In a good way, Dad. I appreciate what you're saying, and don't think for one second that I don't have Catholic guilt sometimes."

My father looked up to the ceiling. "I don't want to even hear that. I'm going to pretend that the two of you are talking for hours or playing cards."

"Word games," Max joked. "You know I like words."

"You do like words, and you use them to your advantage. Just don't blindside me, please," Dad insisted.

I nodded. "Seriously, we like spending time together. Max has a huge–"

"Charlotte?" Max nudged my leg under the table.

"Before I was interrupted, I was going to say we watched a movie the other night on his large television. We even turned off our phones." My eyes narrowed at Max. "Get your mind out of the gutter."

Dad chuckled. "I'm not sure I can take too much more of the two of you, but you do make me laugh. I need to get back to the hospital."

Max went for the car. The rain was heavier than before. I could feel my father's eyes on me. "What?"

"You're happy with Max."

"For now. Max has his own demons, and he has the affinity to keep secrets hidden for far too long." And he could be lying to me about something.

"The devil always does, right?"

I nudged my father playfully. "What exactly did you and Max talk about in your office the other day?"

"That was a private discussion. You don't need to know everything."

We shared a lovely minute of knowing smiles before Max pulled up. As we drove back to the hospital, Dad insisted that we would both be at Sunday dinner. Max stared ahead at the road. I was beginning to realize that if he said nothing, he was saying so much. He would be there because Dad asked him, but he didn't want to be there with Paddy. I didn't want to feel the entire family's judging eyes, although I now knew each one of my siblings had seemingly done far worse than what we were doing as consenting adults.

For the first time, they allowed all three of us to visit Sean. He had been moved out of ICU and into a private room. Max stood in the background while Dad and I took positions on either side of the bed. The equipment emitted the only noise in the room. Dad began to talk to Sean as though my brother could respond, but there was no response.

This had to be the first time that Sean didn't answer with some stupid comment when I heard the voice.

"Charlotte, I'm here with him."

I bent my head down so neither Max or Dad could see how upset I was. Conor was in the room.

"Charlotte, I'm here behind Dad. Look up."

I slowly moved my head and smiled at Dad. Conor was there. I had no words. I couldn't speak out loud with two spectators involved.

"Charlotte, Sean is here."

Oh Lord, where? Was he with them or was he still here?

"Charlotte, danger, Max."

Not again. They needed to be more specific. I reached for Sean's hand and held it for support. At one second I was comforted that Conor was here with our brother, but in the next, I was frightened for the future, perhaps a future without another brother.

"Charlotte, are you listening?"

"Yes, you will wake up Sean," I said out loud. Dad and Max looked at me as if I'd grown two heads. "I just needed to say that."

"Charlotte, you are listening. Good. I can't tell you that Sean will survive. I can tell you he has love surrounding him.

His angels are here. Charlotte, be careful. Watch the storm. Max will know."

Speaking with the dead became tricky when attempting to decipher some meaning for their words. Conor could be speaking of the real storm building outside or the one of tragedy swelling around our family and Max. And Max knew, or would know ... know what? What were you up to Conor, and why didn't anyone know?

I kissed Sean on the head and left the room so Dad could have time alone. I knew Max would follow, and I soon felt his hands on the back of my neck.

"What was that about?"

"You wouldn't believe me." I couldn't face him. My head was beginning to throb and my hands were shaking.

"Try me, love."

"Conor was in the room watching Sean." I turned to face Max. I needed to do something drastic. "I think maybe we should cool things. I really do think you're a target because of me. This is dangerous for you. We need to break up."

Max didn't flinch. "We haven't even started. Let me worry about it, will you?"

"But what if it's because someone is trying to hurt me?"

Max leaned against the hall wall. "What if someone is trying to protect you?"

I was confused. "What?"

"I've been thinking about all of us. I have several theories.

This could be revenge against your dad for a judgment, but to carry this vendetta for so long is very improbable unless someone was just released from prison. Maybe Conor was in the wrong place at the wrong time, and Sean was too? Maybe Conor and Sean did something in the past that we aren't aware of, and everyone else is immune? Maybe it has something to do with Conor's secret? I could still have some nut after me, and we blamed my biological father for no reason, except for his staffer who apparently did that on his own. We also have those two thugs, and we have no information on the root cause of their involvement. And then there's the scenario where you have a stalker. I'm still working on that one."

"Oh wow. You could've gone all night without telling me that."

"So, it's probably not a curse, and I should know because being a demon I know my curses." He pulled me against his body until I wrapped my arms around his waist. "I also know my curves. I like yours, and I miss them."

"We are in a hospital."

"Then let me go."

I looked up into his handsome face, his dimples showing as he smiled. My hands had already stopped shaking and my episode of panic had passed. "I don't want to yet."

"Good." He kissed me quickly and then reluctantly released me. I hung onto his waist briefly until Dad joined us.

"Charlotte, I want to stay tonight. I just have this feeling.

I'll be okay. When Tom dropped me off this afternoon, Meg had packed me a snack bag."

"Then, I'll stay with you." I just needed to get these shoes off.

"No, go home. Thank you both for getting me to eat, and I promise I'll call you with any news or if I need a ride home."

Max touched Dad's arm. "Please call me. I'll come and get you, no matter what time it is."

Dad agreed. We said our goodbyes and headed to the parking garage. It was raining hard, and it seemed like the cool breeze was ushering in fall in full fashion. I wrapped my arms around my body as we walked. Max's jacket was soon covering my shoulders, and he grabbed one of my hands in his.

"It is getting cool," Max admitted as he opened the car door. Instead of shutting the door, he leaned down to kiss me. There was a pop in the garage. The light near the car shattered, falling onto the concrete next to the parking space. "What the hell?"

"My God, if you had been standing–"

"Stay in the car." Max headed to the damaged lighting system. He took a couple of photos and looked around on the concrete floor. I watched from my insulated position to see him squat down across the lot. He picked up an item and stuck it in his pocket.

Then, as if nothing had happened Max returned to the car, sent a text message, and drove quickly out of the garage.

"What was it?"

"A weird accident."

"Then, why aren't we stopping to inform hospital maintenance?"

"Because, we are getting out of here."

"Max, what did you pick up? Do not say nothing. I know you're hiding it in your pocket. There's more than enough secrets to go around. We don't need another between us." He stared straight ahead again. "Maxwell!"

When we finally stopped at a light, he looked over at me. "You're staying the night at my house. I just sent an emergency text to Nate and the police. They can investigate the garage. I found a shell casing, Charlotte. Someone took a shot at us or me, but when I bent down to kiss you–"

My hands covered my face. "What is going on?"

"I have no idea." He pulled down one of my hands and kissed it. He continued to hold it as he sped through the streets of Kansas City.

"Conor warned me. I just didn't understand." I looked out the window at the ribbons of rain-stained streets. My tears clouded my view. My thoughts were as dark as the night. I needed to figure all of this out before it was too late. "How do we live like this?"

"Honey, I've lived like this almost all of my adult life. We will solve this mess."

Had the man read my mind? "You sound very confident."

"I'm adamant and determined. Let's just get home."

Home. Rose was certain that Taylor House was my home. Perhaps it was the safest place for me?

"Max, are you lying to me?"

"No." Max continued to stare straight ahead.

"Now you are."

Max shook his head. "Charlotte, just stop."

I grabbed my phone and hit the number.

"Who are you calling?"

"Paddy. We need to protect Dad."

Max nodded. "Tell him as little as possible, please. I'm wondering how the shooter knew we were at the hospital and when we would leave?"

Paddy answered. "We just left Dad down at the hospital. Paddy, I need you to go and be with him, or send an officer to protect him."

"What's happened?"

"Paddy, just do it. Don't ask questions. Will you do it?"

"My keys are already in my hand. You will call me to explain, right?"

I could hear him running. "I promise, now just get your butt there."

Nate was at the house when we arrived. He had a gun in his left hand and an umbrella in his right. He shielded me from the rain as we ran into the house.

"The police are already investigating the garage. Your dad has the FBI there. You know how they swarm a place. I've checked the security system, and Gio's friend has this place wired like a prison. How is Judge O?"

Max threw off his coat as we entered the hallway. "He wasn't with us and knows nothing about the shot. Charlotte called Paddy to stay with him. Nate, could you go back out and grab the items in the back seat? Charlotte has her laptop and briefcase, and I have my workout bag and briefcase."

"Sure, boss. I put the coffee on too. Throw me the keys." Max did as he was told and turned to look at me.

"Let's get you out of those clothes. Come on." He led me upstairs to his bedroom.

"I'm fine. I'm not as wet as you."

Max searched in his closet and threw two pieces of clothing out at me. I held up a Navy sweatshirt and sweatpants with a goat down the side. "These are stylish."

"Hey, they're warm. You've been shaking since we left the garage, and don't tell me I didn't see what I saw. You really need to move some clothes over here."

I took off my shoes and walked toward the bathroom. "You're beginning to talk like me."

"Am not." Max was pulling off his own wet clothing. He pulled his own sweatshirt over his head.

I laughed. "See?"

I closed the closet door for some reason and changed quickly. I fingered through my hair to pull it off of my face. There was no use in styling it when the ends began to curl from the rain. The frizz would come next. When I opened the door, I was alone. Max had hung his wet clothing on a door hook in the bathroom. I made my way down the steps, but stopped to look inside Rose's sitting room.

"Rose? Can you give us any help? Please? Your boy is in trouble, and I think I am too."

There was no answer. I heard Nate and Max in the kitchen. The FBI discovered a piece of evidence. I headed in and was greeted by a cup of coffee placed into my cold hands. "What have they found?"

"A piece of paper. It could be from the shooter or from anyone who has parked in that garage." Max was looking at his phone as though it would buzz at any minute.

Instead, my phone buzzed. It was Paddy. "Is Dad okay?"

"Yes, Charlie. He's fine. He's worried about you and the boy wonder. Some FBI agent filled us in. This is what you get when you're around a man like Max."

I bit my lip. Paddy was wearing on the only nerve I had remaining. "I'll call Dad in just a bit. We are safe, and the FBI is coming to the house to pick up the shell casing."

"Which house?"

"I'm at the Taylor House." If I called the home by name maybe Paddy wouldn't bristle. Eventually, he'd figure out it was Max's house, Max's security, Max's bed ...

"Figures. He has you where he wants you. I wouldn't be surprised if he's the one doing all of this. Maybe he shot Conor–"

I placed my coffee cup on the island and walked quickly into the sitting room. "Paddy, this needs to stop right now. You are being ridiculous. Besides, I'm where I want to be."

"You said he was the devil."

"And maybe I was wrong. You know, when people meet you the first time, they don't exactly think of you as a fluffy bunny. Our main goal is to keep everyone safe and to find out who is using our family for target practice. This place is secure, and I'm not alone."

Paddy moaned. "Fine, but you have to consider one thing. This all began with Max's return, even the murder of your client who was discovered on the floor of your big house sale, remember? Max gets shot at, and now all of us. We let him into our home and all hell breaks loose."

Paddy might have hit on a small nugget of sane thinking. "Paddy, are you staying at the hospital?"

"Yes, of course. Who else is going to do it?"

I shut my eyes. Lord, give me the patience to deal with my jerk of a brother. If I only had a dollar for every time I had uttered that phrase in my life. "You are wonderful. I'll talk to you tomorrow. Goodnight."

Before he could condemn me to hell again for staying the night at Max's, I ended the call. I could see two agents coming to the front door, but Nate was already on his way to greet them. The two men met with Max in the dining room and the small piece of evidence was exchanged. They asked a few questions and were soon on their way.

"I could sleep out in my car," Nate suggested.

Max shook his head. "That's not necessary. We will be fine. Go home."

"When is Gio's mob suite scheduled to be completed?" Nate's laughter was infectious.

Max didn't seem to be amused. "It'll be finished before Christmas." Max was distracted, as if he were a hundred miles away.

Nate glanced in my direction and hunched his shoulders. "I guess I'll go. Yell if you need me. Goodnight, Charlotte."

"Goodnight, and thank you." Max continued to study the air. As Nate headed for the door, he finally followed and set the security alarm before his friend had begun walking down the sidewalk.

Max watched as Nate's form disappeared into the rainy night. "Do you need anything?" He walked past me as though I wasn't there.

"Yes, one thing." He continued into the kitchen and shut off the coffee maker.

"What?"

"I need you to tell me what you are thinking. You seem to be a million miles away."

"Only a little over a thousand." He finally turned to face me. "I'm trying to think of what has followed me here."

We were all on the same page. When in the world would anyone think that Paddy, Max, and I would all come to the same conclusion? Maybe it was the end of the world? Maybe that's why Rose had no great words of wisdom? Maybe we would see her in person on the other side of life?

"Let's just leave this until tomorrow." I pulled at his hand. He didn't budge. I used both of my hands, arms, and body weight. "Come on. You're like a stubborn mule."

Max lips finally formed a thin smile. "Fine. You're the stubborn one. Let's get you to bed."

"And you too." By the time we arrived in the bedroom, Max had returned to planet earth. He pulled back the linens and pointed.

I happily slipped in expecting he'd be joining me, but after a quick kiss he turned to leave. "And where are you going?"

"I have a few work related things I need to take care of, and I promise I'll be in bed within the hour. You are very bad for my career."

"How so?"

"You make me want to do other things." As he closed the doors, he blew me a kiss. I was left alone in a king-sized bed, in a magnificent master suite as rain softly touched the window. Everything would be perfect if I just had the handsome man next to me. I yawned. Despite my mind racing with thoughts of lies, warnings, and a cantankerous spirit who held me captive for a few minutes, I was ready to sleep. As I snuggled into the bed, my eyes closed. Tonight, all the romance I was living was in my dreams.

Chapter Eight

Max's Office, Taylor House

Max threw his pen onto the desk. "What the hell am I missing?"

He made note after note. He wasn't here when Conor was murdered. Maybe Sean's shooting had nothing to do with his own brother's? Maybe Sean figured out who his brother's killer was at the wrong moment? Maybe it was about his family? It wasn't like they didn't have their own threats and challenges. His own sister and a cousin had been in dangerous situations. But what if this was about Charlotte? Who could she have pissed off so badly that they wanted her dead?

"Charlotte only makes me mad," Max whispered. She was only a few feet away, sleeping in his bed, and here he was sitting at his desk analyzing theories. "What is wrong with me?" Max ran a hand through his hair. "Charlotte ..." When had she invaded his heart and made a home there? She was so much different than anyone he'd ever dated. She was a relationship. He'd never had one of those.

Max constantly thought about her during the day. He wondered if she was biting that bottom full lip that was always amazingly pink even without lipstick. She seldom used any makeup, but her smile made her entire face glow. He wished her hair was longer, but her short cut made her look younger than she was.

Max smiled. Charlotte had to stretch to kiss him. Her hand always lingered around his waist. Her curves fit into him perfectly, making him realize that he had disliked all the other women who had thin legs, flat chests, and no hips. Until Charlotte, he never knew they weren't his type. She was. He needed to protect her; he had to protect her.

Max looked at his phone. It was nearly one in the morning. He wondered if he should do what he was about to do. What was the worst thing that could happen? Quite a bit.

He closed one eye and frowned as he hit the contact list and made the call.

"What do you want, *Poop Head*? I would've thought you'd be in bed doing whatever you do."

"Nice to hear your voice too, Paddy. How's Judge O and Sean?"

"Dad is sleeping in a chair, and I'm having my seventh cup of coffee. Hey, we have some FBI geeks hanging around. Thanks for that."

"No problem. Any police?"

Paddy took another drink of his caffeinated beverage. "No. The U.S. marshals checked in, and I guess they figured I was enough. What do you want, boy wonder?"

"I've been thinking about this entire mess."

Paddy scoffed. "This entire mess that you've created? When you asked me to join in your little investigation, I didn't realize it would put my brother and sister in jeopardy."

Max wondered again why he made this call. "Just listen. Conor was murdered when I was long gone. I'm thinking that Sean's shooting could've been completely random. Maybe he suddenly figured out who killed Conor, and it's not related at all."

"Do you hear yourself? That sounds ridiculous."

"It does. Why did he want to tell me?"

"He knew you wouldn't kill the guy like I would. You are a pretty boy with finesse. I'm not."

Max nodded on the other side of the call. Paddy finally accepted the truth. He would've gone charging in like the bull he was. "Maybe someone did follow me from a previous trial, but why hit your family? If the threat is from my past, they wouldn't know anything about your family, or of the relationship between all of us."

"And present," Paddy added thinking of his sister somewhere in Max's house, in his bed. "What about that pretty girl who came to town just a few weeks ago? Is she the jealous type?"

"No, besides, she's in Europe on one of her beauty queen trips."

Paddy cleared his throat. "You aren't still seeing her, are you?"

"Not that it's any of your business, but no. I didn't even know she was coming to Kansas City."

"We're back to a whole lot of questions, and absolutely no leads or answers. It has to be about that real estate scheme."

"It does look like that, but why go after Sean and Charlotte?" Max questioned. "Paddy, it might even be about my assignment here, but I'll talk to your dad tomorrow. Maybe he'll allow me to go through his files, and I can cross reference with whomever is out of prison, or maybe look over his records. Maybe it is a former juror with an ax to grind?"

"I've already begun looking into that, Max. Dad kept copious lists of every person who entered his courtroom over the years. Why don't you look through your past cases, your ones in Atlanta, and what you're working on now. It could be your assignment. Maybe check in with your boss? Maybe check your staff."

"What about your dad's staff? I met up with Brody again. I turned him down for a position, and he's very friendly with Charlotte."

Paddy began to laugh. "Wow, are you jealous of Brody? What a joke. He's a good guy. Dad and he meet for lunch now and then. Besides, he was with Conor when he died. They were out for drinks with friends that night. His statement is on file if you need to look it over, but you're going down the wrong path there. I think he's secretly had a crush on Charlotte for a long time, but he tried to date Janie first. It was weird since she was older than him and already living with Brad. They were out of town then so nothing came of it, and Jane can be really rude when she needs to be. She shut him down. He's just a family fixture, and he was Conor's pal."

"Okay. He was always a hanger in high school. He always wanted to be part of the group, but he really didn't add anything to the party." Max noticed his calendar with a red circle around next weekend. "Crap. Paddy, I have to be in New York City next week at a charity function for my mother's foundation."

"Take Charlotte with you. I can't believe I just said that, but get her out of here."

Max couldn't believe Paddy had just said that either. "You think she'll be safer with me in New York?"

"I'm not the sharpest pencil in the box, but at least she'll be away from here. I don't want to lose any more of my family."

"Paddy, I'll try. You know your sister. She has a mind of her own."

"She does, but it seems you're pretty good at convincing her to do your bidding. By the way, Max, thanks for stepping up to care for Sean. You were right about my baby sister. She's done enough for all of us. Make her go with you and treat her like a queen. Just don't send me the bill."

Max's mood finally lifted. "I'll try, Paddy. What do you think about Sean?"

"I don't know. I can't believe we won't have the idiot around anymore, but my mind says he'd be better off–"

"I understand." There was a brief moment of silence before Max heard Paddy clear his throat. Hearing a hardened man like Paddy O'Donohue choke up was uncomfortable.

"Max, considering our last encounter, you know the one where you sucker punched me–"

"I had to get the first punch in."

"I would've done the same thing, well, I've kept your secret about your assignment here, but does my sister know?"

Max stared out the window into the darkness. "She only knows you're my inside man. My staff doesn't even know the gravity of this investigation. Your dad does though. We've talked about it."

"Good, but Max, if all of this is about that secret, Charlotte deserves to know. If she gets hurt, I'll take you out myself."

"I understand, and thanks for not mentioning it the other day when you wanted to pummel me into the dirt. When you mentioned secrets, I thought you were going to spill."

"I wasn't even thinking about it, Max. That's our professional lives. You've got a hell of a mess."

"Thanks for the understatement, Paddy. I'll let you know if I figure anything out."

Paddy cleared his throat. "Max, I won't blame you if you just tell me to go to hell, but I need to ask you something."

"You can ask, but I might not answer." Max looked out of the window into the darkness. He could only guess at what Paddy might ask.

"Max, there's not a day that goes by that I don't hear about your attributes. If Linda isn't telling me to get a haircut because you look so well groomed, then it's Janie commenting about your suits. I get it ... you're a good looking guy with a trust fund, and a powerful job."

Max couldn't wait. "Just ask whatever you're going to ask. What the hell do you want to know?"

"Fine. You're an impatient ass. Here it goes. What is it about Charlotte?"

"What?"

"Why my little sister? You can have any woman you set your mind on, but why Charlotte? She's nice, sweet, and not your type."

Max chuckled. "I wasn't aware you knew my type."

"You guys all have types. My sister lives in sweats on the weekend, and she hates wearing heels. I've only seen her in makeup a handful of times. She knows college basketball better than me, and she's a great friend when you need one. She's pretty, cute, and funny as hell, but why her?"

Max leaned back in his chair. Only the judge had asked the same question and insisted on an immediate answer. "Paddy, your sister challenges me and checks my behavior like no other woman I've ever met. According to Charlotte, winning isn't everything, and there's way more to life than prestige and money. I guess ... I didn't know I've gone unchecked and unchallenged for far too long. It was a lonely existence." Max smiled as he thought of Charlotte biting her lip in concentration, then looking up at him when she'd been caught. "And Paddy, I need her if I'm going to be a better man."

"Ah, I get it now. Thanks for answering me. Don't hurt my baby sister."

"As I've said before, it isn't my intention. Sorry about the late call. I need to get some sleep."

"And I'll do the same. Goodnight, and tell Charlotte before she figures out that something else is going on with you. She's a smart woman. Your assignment might be what is churning up this storm. Charlotte could help. If you don't, I'll be spreading the story line that you're the one who killed Charlotte's client in your old house, killed Conor, and shot at Sean."

Max sighed. "Paddy, you make my ass tired."

There was laughter on the other side of the call. "It's something I do quite well. Tell my sister."

"Yes, sir."

After they said their goodbyes, Max looked out the large window behind his desk. He remembered a fishing trip with his dad. He had just left active duty. They'd met in Key West, chartered a captain and his boat, and fished for three days. They drank, ate fresh lobster every night, and talked about everything under the sun and moon. At the time, his father had a serious threat against his life.

"Maxie, if I'm ever in the position where you think I'd be better off if you turn off the machines, don't hesitate. Just do it. Don't let me linger."

"Dad, I couldn't. There might be a chance you could come back."

"No, I don't want to," Edward Shaw answered defiantly. He had poured two more shots of tequila and toasted his son. "Living is a lot of work after a crisis happens. Max, son, promise me. This is what I would want."

"Fine." Max's surrender that one night ended the discussion. He wondered if Sean would want the same ending, or if he could live with limitations that would change his and his family's lives forever. Max began to walk slowly to his bedroom. He stopped in the doorway as a cool breeze passed by him.

"Damn drafts," he murmured. Every hair on the back of his neck was standing up. Entering the room, he stopped at the end of the bed and gazed down at the body in deep sleep. His eyes lingered on her lips. Kissing her was so easy.

Charlotte was a very smart woman. He smiled. After dating models, an actress, debutantes, and several pageant queens, Charlotte was unexpected. Paddy was correct in his description of her. She was cute, but he saw so much more. How could she be absolutely beautiful in his sweatshirt, her body fully covered, her mouth now open, and one arm flung over her head.

"What have I gotten myself into with you? You make me think of planting a garden, signing up for the neighborhood watch group, sleeping in on Saturdays, and having a family."

As Max slowly crept into bed, Charlotte changed her position. She turned closer to his pillow and almost moved into a fetal position. He kissed her forehead. "But only if I do it with you. It wouldn't be a life without you." For several minutes he stared at the woman next to him. He swung an arm protectively over her as she molded her body against his. Max fell asleep instantly.

Chapter Nine

I woke up. Max had been next to me, and then he wasn't. I headed to his office. "I thought I heard you talking to someone. Who was it? Is it something with Sean?" He was just finishing a phone call, and it was nearly four in the morning.

"Nate says hello. Nothing with Sean, but I did call Paddy earlier."

"You did what? What were you thinking? Do you really have a death wish?"

"I was thinking he and I could get a handle on all of this." Max was looking down at some paper on his desk. "I made note after note, and I'm nowhere closer to figuring this out than I was a few hours ago." Max looked up at me and smiled. "Charlotte, I think you're right. We should cool whatever we have going on."

I walked with determination and stopped at the side of his desk. "Oh no! I suggested that last night, but I was just talking nonsense. I'm invested in this, whatever we have. Are you trying to get out of this with me?"

His eyes lowered, avoiding mine at all cost.

"Max, look at me, please, and answer my question."

He did as he was told. "I think we should stop not because I want to hurt you, but to save you."

I sat down slowly in his lap, hanging my arms around his neck. He shifted my body and brought me closer to his chest. "I feel the same way about you. I thought earlier I should just walk away to protect you from whatever curse is surrounding me."

Max shook his head. "Stop that. You aren't cursed. If anything, you're admired by a few too many people."

I kissed him on the cheek. "You are jealous of poor Brody, aren't you?"

"Poor Brody, my–"

"Stop." I placed one finger on his lips. "Brody just wants to be one of us. He wants to be liked, to be needed. He's harmless."

Max bit at my finger playfully. "He likes you. He counted that as a date until I showed up."

"Don't be silly." Max was right. Brody apparently wanted to date me. Heck, he almost purchased my house. I'd almost suspect the sweet friend, but Brody was Brody. He'd never hurt me or any of my family. "Is your work or your theories that important that you shouldn't get a few more hours of sleep?" I nuzzled my nose against his. "Is it?"

Max smiled. "I slept for a couple of hours. You were snoring."

"I don't snore," I answered adamantly.

Max kissed my cheek. "Fine, you were breathing deeply."

"You look tired." I ran my finger around his lips.

"Charlotte, you make me smile."

"You have a lovely smile. You should do it more often."

"I wouldn't be much of a prosecutor if I'm smiling at the defense all the time, now would I?"

"Okay, you don't need to smile then. Too many female jurors would fall in love with your adorable dimples. Come on, come to bed. That bed is too big for me." I began to lift off of him, but he stopped me.

"Wait." Max's eyes were pleading. "Charlotte, I came here to do a job, a very special job."

"Okay, and you're very good at it."

Max shook his head and began to frighten me. The man who had no problem talking his way out of a bag was having difficulty finding the right words to address me. "Charlotte, I told you Paddy was assisting me, but you need to know I was assigned here for a special project. I can't go into too much detail, but you should be aware–"

"That you have a huge secret? I kind of figured that out all on my own. You can't tell me?" Maybe this was the lie?

"No, but I would if I could. Just know it might be the reason why people are shooting at me. So, I want you to come to New York City with me next weekend. I know this is late notice, and I know Sean's health remains a concern, but we will fly out on a private jet Friday afternoon, and I promise to have you home for Sunday night dinner. It's a charity event for my mother's foundation, and I really don't want to go alone."

I suspiciously studied his face. His eyes gave him away. "There's a hidden agenda. I bet you've always gone alone to this thing, right?" He offered no answer, but I had mine. "Wait, did Paddy think this up? This sounds like something that the big bear would suggest to get me out of the city. I'll only make an exception for your job, but no other secrets, remember?"

"Fine, yes, Paddy thought it up, but I think it's a pretty good idea."

I scrambled off of his lap. "I don't know. I'm not sure you're ready for this step."

"I'm not sure? Don't I get to decide if I'm ready to introduce you as, as–"

I quickly pointed at him and laughed. "Ah hah! You can't even say it, and you haven't decided what you're going to call me. Max Shaw, you are so bad."

"My date? I was your plus one for that family wedding."

I continued to shuffle back to the bedroom. Right now it was a good thing that the bed was so big, and my attire looked as though I was a nun in hiding. I flipped my hand back at him as I stomped away.

"Oh, come on. Do you really want to go with boyfriend and girlfriend?"

"It's better than this is the girl I can't commit to, so I'm ... what did Paddy say again? Right. I'm just screwing her."

Max caught up to me, turning me around. "I have never said that in my life, nor have I ever appreciated it when other men used that verb when they were discussing their women. You need to get that straight."

I accepted that. "Okay. Let's just get some sleep. I had a terrible dream, and I'm afraid today will be a bad day. I also have a headache, and that's never good."

I could feel Max's eyes on me as I snuggled under the sheets and turned my light off, bathing the room in darkness. It was several minutes before he was laying next to me.

"Charlotte Rose, you are the most maddening O'Donohue. I will introduce you as the woman I'm seeing. When they ask who you are, I'll tell them you're mine."

"And I'm your woman," I said in my best caveman accent. Max chuckled.

He held me tightly, and soon I heard his even breathing. At least I was his for now.

Chapter Ten

I heard someone calling my name. I wasn't dreaming. I looked next to me to see Max sleeping soundly. Touching his hair, I felt content. I hadn't even known that word before Max. Despite the murder attempts and Sean's health crisis, I was strangely happy. I heard my name again. I sat up in bed and looked out to see daylight. It was morning and the sun was shining on a Saturday. When I looked at my phone, I cursed. It was only six in the morning.

I carefully got up, went to the bathroom, and heard my name again. The house was quiet. With fall here, the air conditioning wasn't running, and the heat hadn't come on. I padded quietly down the hallway so I didn't bother Max.

"Rose?" I looked down the stairs. I heard my name again, but the voice seemed to be coming from the south side of the house. Max was just beginning to rehab that area.

I allowed my mind to open. Standing against the hallway's wall, I focused on my breathing until I could hear my heart beating. I had only done this a few times. When I was experiencing terrible headaches in high school, a doctor had recommended meditation and biofeedback. I was completely relaxed and open to another level of life and energy. It was frightening to think that if you could allow the good spirits in, you could also welcome ones who were in distress because of their own misfortunes in life. The whisperings were coming from one of the bedrooms. I entered, but I left the door open for a quick getaway.

"Hello? Who is in here?"

"What are you doing here?"

It was a man's voice, stern and authoritarian. "I'm a guest here."

"Not mine."

"You called me. You knew my name."

"Charlotte Rose, how fitting."

I butted my back against one of the walls of the room. This spirit knew my middle name, and was sarcastic. I felt my skin crawl. "Who are you?"

"I own this house."

"Not anymore. Max owns this house."

"Danger, Max. Ha."

"Are you manipulating what's going on?"

"Of course not. I'm entertained."

Well, this was an interesting banter, but I didn't want to participate. "I'll tell Rose."

"She knows me very well."

"I see. I don't think you should stay."

"I've been here. No one has ever heard me."

In an unusual circumstance, I began to see him materialize. He was fluid at first, but his features soon became clear. He was a tall man about Max's height with jet black hair, graying around the edges. His mustache was thin. He wore a light suit, more for summer than for our season. "You know me. Who are you?"

"I told you. I own this house. Happiness has disappeared. Danger is here, and I am here as well."

"You were Rose's awful husband, weren't you?"

It was as though he wanted to strike me, but he was stuck in position, held by something or someone. He was confined by one of those pesky rules from beyond. Maybe sometimes the energy shielded me from harm?

"I am still Rose's husband. My home."

"I'm assuming you'll disappear when we have better times, so we won't have to deal with you much longer."

He began to laugh. I inched my way to the open doorway. *"Be careful. My house has secrets. Tell the boy wonder, his life has been easy. Not anymore."*

I hesitated. I wanted to respond, but that would just give him the justification he wanted. Rose and I needed to have a discussion. I'd never run into a more malevolent spirit in my life. Well, there was that one time at the funeral home several years ago, the two times I was kept from leaving, and ...

Easing out of the room, I began to run down the hallway back to the safety of Max's arms, but was frightened by the body I hit.

"Honey, what is going on?" Max held me in his arms. "You're shaking, and you're so cold. I guess I'll have to try out the heater. It's drafty on this floor."

"No, it's not that. I'm cold because I just met someone in the south bedroom. He's not very nice."

Max pulled me back so he could see my face. "Someone is in the house?" Max whispered.

"No, it's your evil grandfather, well not your real grandfather. That's Gio."

Max appeared to be bewildered. "Do we have other ghosts? Okay. Can I get some coffee before you tell me about all of this?"

"Sure." As we headed downstairs, I felt the cold. I felt a shove. "Max!"

Thankfully, Max caught me before I missed the step and ended up in a huddled mess at the bottom of the staircase. "I've got you."

"He pushed me. Your nasty grandfather pushed me. I will not put up with that." I looked backward to the upstairs area. "I won't talk to you. Play with someone else, you nasty man."

I heard laughing, but Max saw a raving maniac. "Let's get that coffee, and maybe we should get you breakfast. Maybe you have low blood sugar like me?"

I kept peeking back to the second floor. Rose and I would have words, heck I would talk to Gio about this one.

It was fortunate that Max and I hadn't finished our scrambled eggs when Gio came in with a box of danish.

"Good morning you two." His smile vanished as he saw our faces. "Rough night?"

"Max was shot at as we were leaving the hospital, and did you know Rose's husband is upstairs? He's obnoxious, and he threatened me."

"He shoved her," Max added casually. He held up the carafe of coffee for approval, and Gio nodded.

Gio touched my arm and looked me over from head to toe. "You seem okay."

"Thanks to Max, and you seem unphased by the information I just shared with you."

Max poured the coffee for Gio and watched me. "I think I'll go up and take a shower. You two can batch this out since I don't hear all of these people. Lucky for us this house is a big one." He came around and kissed me on the cheek and patted Gio on the arm. "Good luck."

I waited until I knew Max was out of earshot. "When were you going to tell me he's around? He's awful. How do we get rid of him? Frankly, I don't need him here when I have one at my office that tried to keep me as a prisoner."

Gio's eyes widened. I shook my head. "Nevermind about that. How do we get rid of Mr. Taylor?"

"Honestly, I haven't figured that one out." Gio sunk his teeth into an apple pastry.

"Oh great! Max can't stay here with that menace. Rose has been wonderful, but we may need an exorcism or something.

I don't think the holy water I have will be enough. Oh, and he knows about the danger we're in too. He doesn't seem to like Max."

"Of course not. Max isn't his in any way. I'll talk to Rose. Maybe she'll have an idea."

"I hope you get more out of her than I do."

"You're just frustrated. I listen. Now, what about this shooting?"

"It was in the hospital parking garage. The shot took out a light. The FBI is around."

"I saw them. I had to show my identification just to get in. They didn't seem impressed that I had my own key."

"Max is making himself crazy trying to figure this all out. He even called Paddy in the middle of the night to go over things with him. Oh, and now he wants to take me to New York for some charity event."

Gio smiled. "His mother's event? My, that's interesting. Charlotte, if you think your ghost was nasty just wait until you meet my daughter."

"Oh great. Is she fond of shoving people down the stairs?"

Gio cocked his head. "I think she'd probably use poison, and only if she thinks you're taking her son away from her."

"Well, crap. Do you want to tag along and be my food taster?"

Gio laughed out loud. "Sorry, but not on my life or yours. You're on your own with Olivia. Don't give her an inch."

Chapter Eleven

"I could get used to flying privately. That was the best flight I've ever had. Unbelievable. Did I tell you I brought the black dress I wore at my cousin's wedding? I hope it's okay. You seemed to like it. I don't know what I'll do with my hair. I've brought enough makeup to paint an elephant."

Max threw me a side glance as we walked through the airport. "Charlotte, you'll be beautiful. Don't worry and stop being so nervous."

"But I am. Everyone, including a ghost, has warned me about your mother. I can't help myself. Did I tell you she sent a card and flowers when Mom died?"

"Did she? I didn't know that. Good. I called Tom back then to see if I could help in any way. It seems I'm only good at donating money."

"That's not true. You are very thoughtful and caring. Do you know who is picking us up or do we take a cab? How does this work?"

As the doors of the airport slid open, a cold evening breeze hit me. The fall season had arrived in New York City earlier than at home. Max looked around and heard a car's horn. We saw a man's hand waving at us from a very impressive dark sedan. "That's our ride. Please try to relax."

Obviously, Max really didn't know me. I couldn't relax to save my soul right now. We approached the vehicle and Max placed our luggage in the trunk. The door was held open by a suited man who smiled broadly at Max.

"Palmer, is that you? What are you doing in New York?"

"Working for your mother, Boss." The two men greeted each other with a quick hug. "I'll explain to you during the ride." He nodded toward me. "Miss."

"Palmer, this is Charlotte O'Donohue."

Palmer winked at Max. "Well, this is very special. It is wonderful to meet you."

Max rubbed his hands. "It's getting late. We better go. I believe Mother has reservations for us."

"Yes, she does. I've been ordered to deposit you at the restaurant."

I listened during the ride to the Upper West Side of New York City. Palmer and Max catching up was very entertaining and enlightening. Through their stories, I finally realized something I figured my father probably knew but didn't share. Max's move to Kansas City wasn't really a promotion. Atlanta was a larger city with higher profile trials. There was a limit to how long he would hold the post. He had moved laterally, and had been inserted into an office that had been left in disarray by a prosecutor who had political ambitions. But, I had the feeling Max was still holding back. Was all of that part of the secret? As far as I knew, Max didn't have a political bone in his body, except for his father's DNA. I began to keep a running list of what the secret wasn't.

We pulled up to a valet who ushered me out of the car.

"I'll call you when we are ready," Max said to Palmer. He placed a supportive hand against my lower back. "Take a deep breath and smile. You are about to meet her, and she's nothing like Gio."

"Probably nothing like Rose either?"

Max shrugged. "I don't know, but you do. Probably, from what Gio has told me about her."

"Max, maybe I could just go to a hotel? I'm not really hungry."

Max smiled as he leaned down to look into my eyes. "Liar. I heard your stomach growl."

"Fine. I can pick up something. This is New York City. There's food everywhere. Let me go to a hotel, please." Max nodded negatively despite my pleas.

"Charlotte, just be yourself."

I laughed loudly. "I'm afraid that's what I'll do, and you should be afraid of that too."

Max opened the door and pushed me inside. As we entered, Max informed the hostess of our reservation. His mother was waiting. With every step I took, my stomach knotted tighter. I was hungry after the flight, but my nerves were creating an acid reflux attack from hell. I kept repeating that she was just a woman. How bad could she be? I soon realized my estimation of her had been woefully inadequate.

"Darling Max." He leaned down and kissed his mother on each cheek in the French way. She merely glanced at me. "And you must be dear Charlotte." Her voice dripped with fake manners.

"Yes. It's lovely to meet you."

She extended her hand out wide. She was offering places on either side of her, but I thought she looked more like a flight attendant directing passengers in case of a crash. That was certainly a possibility tonight.

"I've ordered appetizers. I hope you like oysters, Charlotte."

I detested the slimy suckers. I smiled and uncharacteristically said absolutely nothing.

"I'm not sure if your father will be in attendance tomorrow night. I request one thing a year from him. I'm sure he'll try harder now that he knows you have flown in with your little friend." She looked straight at me. "Charlotte, you're the daughter of Judge O'Donohue? Well, that is interesting. I recall your mother very well. She was lovely, but common. I don't believe your parents ever joined a country club, did they?"

Before I could answer, she continued speaking to Max, literally turning to the side to face him completely. She offered me a view of her back. Max's eyes were trained on me, but he listened intently to his mother.

A wine sommelier appeared at the table, but Mrs. Shaw ordered. I stopped him before he could leave. "Excuse me, I would like a sweet white maybe a Moscato, please?" He nodded before leaving.

"But we're having a cabernet, dear."

"I don't drink reds, unless they're sweet. They give me headaches."

The woman pursed her lips as though she was sucking on a lemon. This was going to be the longest weekend of my life. This was supposed to be a trip to keep me safe? I had gone from being shot at to being thrown into a shark's feeding path.

Thankfully, I was distracted by a man staring at me. He stood across from me, on the other side of our table. Max and his mother didn't notice me or the man. Oh good grief! I didn't need this here in the middle of a restaurant and in front of Max's mother. At least this spirit couldn't lock me inside the restaurant or shackle me to the table.

I smiled at the man and took a drink of my wine. The man blew me a kiss. His playful demeanor was charming. He waved and pointed over to another table where an elderly woman sat alone.

"Charlotte Rose, you are a brave one to come to this city with Max Shaw."

I couldn't answer out loud. Instead, my thoughts answered him. "Really? Why?"

"You've met his mother. She's a real piece of cheesecake."

I giggled into my wine glass. "That's a new one."

"Actually, dear girl, it's an old one. It's lovely to meet you. I think you'll do very well."

"As what?"

"Legacy, child. Love too. I'm very impressed."

"I appreciate that, but I don't understand. We don't know each other." I took another drink of liquid.

"You never heard of me? I doubt that. I'm the head of an American family. You will fit in well. The boy has my eyes, and I like him very much." He pointed toward Max.

I nearly spit out my wine. I quickly raised my napkin to my lips as Max and his mother looked over with concern. "It went down the wrong way. Excuse me for a minute." I quickly left the table, but I smiled at Max as I walked by to assure him I would return. But, there probably was a back door I could access for a quick escape.

Thankfully, the restroom was empty as I looked at myself in the mirror. My eyes had tears in them. This was Max's biological grandfather. "Mr. Hughes?"

I heard him immediately. *"Yes, my dear. I am here. My wife is the one alone. Will you please visit her and express my love still today?"*

"What if she isn't receptive?"

"She will be, Charlotte. In my life, I would've offered you money to do this for me. I have nothing to offer you now."

I sighed, wiped my eyes, and pulled back my shoulders.

"Okay. I'll do it. I'm sure she knows how you felt."

"How I feel. Charlotte, there are loves that transcend. You have that, but I'm not sure you know it yet."

I smiled. "We will see about that one. It's too early to tell with your ... with Max. Wish me luck."

"Irish or old fashioned American?"

"Either and both." I opened the door and slowly made a path to the elderly woman who had apparently finished her meal and was enjoying her coffee with a small piece of cheesecake. Cheesecake.

"Excuse me, Mrs. Hughes. I'm–"

She reached up and grabbed my hand. "Charlotte O'Donohue. How lovely. I saw Olivia enter, but I managed to be unnoticed by the grand dame. Please sit." She extended her hand toward the chair. Her other hand remained clasped tenderly around mine.

"I have to get back, but I'll visit for just a minute. I didn't want to bother you."

Finally, Mrs. Hughes released her hand and waved it in the air. "Bother? You are no bother. My husband told me to come tonight. He said we have family in common." She glanced over toward Max. "Is that him?"

"Yes, ma'am. Your husband told you?"

"You must think I'm batty."

I struggled to stifle my laughter. I patted her hand as she held on. "Mrs. Hughes, I hope you're open to this, but your husband spoke to me here in the restaurant."

"I hope he didn't talk your arm off. He was always one to go on and on. I think that's why my son is a politician ... lots of words."

I smiled. "Max is a great speaker too."

"Max. It's a nice name."

I looked over at the huddled mother and son and realized they didn't even realize how long I had been gone. "Mrs. Hughes, your husband has a message. He loves you still today. Your love transcends."

"Oh my. See? Just words, but those are lovely. Thank you, Charlotte. It seems I don't hear from him as frequently as I used to, but I suppose the closer I get to him the lines of communication aren't as clear."

I shook my head. "I'm not sure about that. I wonder how all of that works, but I believe it is a blessing to hear them beyond their time on earth with us."

Mrs. Hughes pulled her hand slowly away from mine and fingered her wedding ring. "It is a blessing." She began to dig into her purse and pulled out a tissue and a small card. "Charlotte, this is my private number. You are welcome to call."

I looked at the card and wondered if–

"You will call, won't you?"

I nodded. "Mrs. Hughes, your son is causing–" The server arrived with Mrs. Hughes' bill. She took it in hand and began to eye every charge. I noticed that an attendant was delivering our appetizer to our table. "Mrs. Hughes, I need to go back. It was very nice to meet you."

"And it was lovely to meet you, Charlotte. I know we will be seeing each other in the future."

With any other person, I might take that as a threat, but in this case her warm smile comforted me. If I talked to her again, I could breach the subject of her son and his threats against Max. I stood up quickly and said my goodbye.

The oysters had arrived, and my two companions hadn't even dropped a word in their conversation when I returned. Max offered a look that was asking me if I was okay. I smiled back, but my stomach growled. Luckily, small rolls were placed on our equally small plates. Salads arrived. I didn't remember ordering anything from the menu. In fact, we never looked at the menu. Lord, Olivia Shaw had ordered for us. And I thought Max was a control freak!

Thankfully, over an hour later, we were served filet mignon, vegetables in a puff pastry, and grilled asparagus spears. I didn't say one word throughout the entire meal. But I ate. Occasionally, Mrs. Shaw glared at my chewing. My eyes pleaded with Max, but he was just as quiet. She talked, and we listened. She barely ate any of her dinner. So that's how she stayed so slender.

When I had the opportunity to look over at my new friend, her table had been cleared, and she was nowhere to be found.

We were served coffee and a lovely liquor of chocolate,

caramel, and mint while we waited for whatever she ordered for dessert. I studied her. She did love her son in her own way. I could see facial similarities, but the nose and mouth they shared were Gio's. Her neck was long. Her posture was perfect which made me sit up straighter. On her ear lobes, long liquid gold earrings hung, posted with a large ruby in each. Her matching necklace hit above her collar bone. On her left ring finger sat what looked to be a wedding band and wedding ring. Really? She still wore what Edward Shaw had given her so many years ago?

"Charlotte, I'll want to review what you've brought to wear. I know that sounds a bit overbearing, but this event is quite important to me, and I don't want to be embarrassed. You understand, don't you?"

What? Did she say something? I was watching the wait staff and searching for my dessert. But as my mouth opened, Max stepped in.

"That is overbearing. I've seen Charlotte's dress, and it is lovely. It suits her very well. We have no intention of embarrassing you, Mother."

Max drug out the last word, making it last at least four syllables. "Oh good. The dessert is here."

His mother's mouth clamped shut. In fact, she was fairly quiet the remainder of our restaurant visit. Palmer was called, and the three of us sat quietly in the sedan for the trip to Mrs. Shaw's home.

I hadn't been in the city since I was in high school. Conor and I had gone with one of our aunts for a short summer vacation. She'd even taken us to a Broadway show. We visited the usual tourist locations, but for the two of us our favorite part of the trip was the ferry ride to the Statue of Liberty. Conor became obsessed with our family tree after that. Our relatives on both sides of the family passed through Ellis Island.

While Max and his mother discussed tomorrow night's party, I enjoyed the buildings passing by. As we came closer to Central Park, I saw a couple climbing into a horse drawn carriage. Sadly, there wouldn't be any time for Max and me during this trip. Mrs. Shaw had organized every single minute of her son's life for the next two days. My only hope was that I could blend into the wallpaper in some vacant corner.

We arrived at her building. Palmer unloaded our luggage, but Max insisted that we could handle them. He sent the man on his way for the night, much to the dismay of his mother. There was only silence in the private elevator. The doors opened to an expansive living area with an amazing view of buildings and lights. Dark cherry wood furniture with the same coloring of Max's bathroom towels of light plum and gray highlighted the decor. It was a fantastic mix of old and new. The chandeliers were modern. The chairs were elegant with high backs and rounded arms, but the table accents were glass and tile.

"This is absolutely stunning." I thought maybe Mrs. Shaw would appreciate the compliment, but she ignored me. She was more intent in retrieving any messages on her phone.

"Her designer would thank you," Max whispered. "Let me show you."

"Maxwell, don't you think Charlotte would prefer her own bedroom?"

I wanted to laugh, but Max was stoic. He looked like a little boy caught in some very large fib.

"I thought she would stay with me."

Mrs. Shaw walked slowly toward us. "Since this is the very first time you have brought a friend to my home, I would appreciate you respecting my wishes."

"Mother, for the love of God, I'm in my thirties. Charlotte isn't a friend here for a sleepover. She's a grown woman."

I touched his arm. "I'm fine with my own room. In fact, if I can't sleep I have work to do."

Max leaned down and spoke through clenched teeth. "I'm not fine with it."

"You'll live. We're still their children." I directed my attention to his mother. "I would be very happy with whatever arrangement you wish."

Mrs. Shaw smiled. "Wonderful. Max, you know where your room is. I'll show Charlotte to hers. This way, dear."

Max headed down one hallway, and I was led to another. It seemed as though we were running out of building when she opened the door and turned on the light to a lovely corner room. "I hope this will do for your short stay. It has a private bath. There are towels and toiletries, a blow dryer, probably anything you might need. If you want to work, this is the perfect room. The desk has a fantastic view of the park. I believe the passcodes for the internet are in the drawer."

"This room is very different from the living area. Did you decorate it yourself?"

Mrs. Shaw narrowed her eyes. "Yes, I did. How could you tell?"

"It looks like you. That bedspread is elegant yet cozy. The mix of velvet and velour pillows is sweet but very romantic."

"I was going for romance. Here, let me help you." She took my briefcase in her hand and placed it over on the desk. "Charlotte, how is your brother? This must be devastating for your father, and of course your family."

I bit my lip. I hadn't thought about Sean in a few hours. I'd been so overwhelmed by Max, his mother, and the city, I'd put his tragedy aside. "He is still holding his own. Next week they'll make a decision. He'll probably go to a facility. Dad is tough, but I see he's becoming more lost every day."

"I understand completely."

I rolled my luggage toward the bed, but Mrs. Shaw stepped in. "Let me do that. There's this little dressing area by the bathroom." She took it from me and waved me in. "Right here. You have the closet and this area for the bag and shoes, worn clothing. Now, let me see the dress."

Dang her! Boy, she was good. Her little nice act had all been a ploy to see if the backwoods girl had enough fashion sense to stand next to her little boy at a big people's event. I said nothing but went to my luggage and pulled out what I planned to wear.

Mrs. Shaw reviewed it, eyeing it up and down. She placed one finger to the side of her mouth. "Well, yes, that's nice. What size are you dear?"

"It depends. I can wear an eight on a good day, sometimes a ten or twelve."

"Really? My, you're a little chunky."

And you're a freaking toothpick! I smiled. "I like food."

"Well, your mother had hips and breasts too. It must be an Irish thing."

I wanted to hit the wall with my head. This was definitely not a safe trip. If she didn't kill me, I might just have to do away with her. I could hear the phone call in my head. Dad, I'm in jail for murder. There's no need to worry about the curse anymore.

"I suppose it will do, but I may have something else in mind. What shoes did you bring? Your feet aren't huge as well, are they?"

Huge too? I could see the headline in the morning's newspaper that a Midwest girl shoots a socialite for no reason except she had hips and boobs and the other woman didn't.

I removed my strappy heels from the bag. "I'm wearing these. I can stand in them for a few hours."

"Those heels aren't very high."

"No, Mrs. Shaw, they are not. I don't like high heels. Yes, I'm much shorter than your son. I don't care." I stared at her without blinking.

"Fine. Look like a short elfin child." She passed by quickly. "If you need anything through the night, you can call Max."

Once she was gone, I shut the door firmly and locked it. I jumped up and down. I stomped my feet. I threw a silent temper tantrum and then threw myself down on the most luxurious bedspread I'd ever felt.

"Max." My scream was muffled. I heard a light knocking. It was him.

I opened the door slowly. "What?" Max seemed stunned by my growl.

"Yikes. What did she do?" Max entered the room and sat on the bed. "At least she gave you a nice room. She made my cousin Alicia sleep on a cot next to the kitchen once."

"She called me an elfin child. I have huge hips and breasts, and I'm chunky."

Max's hands pulled me in front of him. "I like your hips and breasts very much, and I wouldn't change one inch. As for the elfin child comment, I'll talk to her in the morning."

I pulled out of his grasp. "Oh no you won't. I won't have you fight my battles. She's just a bully, and I have this feeling she's testing me. Do you know she was all nice and caring as a ruse so I would show her the blasted dress? By the way, it's not good enough. I'm not good enough."

"This was a mistake, wasn't it?"

Max's question took me aback. "No, not really. It's probably good that I'm going through this. This is part of who you are. Maybe I'll understand you better after this trip." I began thinking. Or, you can visit me in prison.

"Charlotte, what are you telling me?"

"Nothing yet. Let's just see how this weekend plays out."

Max stood up and took me into his arms. "Look, I've never begged a woman to do anything, but this once, I'm begging you to hang in there. Give me a chance, please."

"I'll try." I reached up and brought his face to mine. "No wonder you're the way you are. Your mother is a pain."

"Are you insinuating I'm a pain?"

"No, of course not." I batted my eyes until he laughed. I thought I was safe after he kissed me for far too long and slowly made his way to the door.

Max turned back. "Were you okay at the restaurant?"

"Yes, sure."

"You were gone for a good ten minutes, and who were you talking to?"

Darn, he had noticed. "A lovely woman who thought she knew me. We tried to figure out who she thought I was, and if we knew someone in common."

Max seemed to be scrutinizing my answer. He was suspicious. "Interesting. Well, I missed you. I thought you were attempting an escape."

I kissed him on the cheek. "If I were doing that, I would've taken you with me."

Finally, he seemed to relax. "Yes, please, always take me with you, Charlotte. Good night."

I closed the door behind him and collapsed on the bed. "Congratulations Charlotte Rose, you are getting awfully good at lying." I muffled my screams into a satin pillow that smelled of lavender.

Chapter Twelve

Two hours into the event at a modern art gallery, I found my little vacant space where I could disappear. It was a lovely corner with a small table for my glass of champagne and the small plate of food I had managed to retrieve. These people didn't eat. They just drank and talked. Above me on my left side was a piece of art that looked like something Dad's dog had thrown up. On the other side of me was an emergency exit door.

It was entertaining watching Max as he pivoted from one donor to the other. I saw several people from film and television, others were anchors from major news networks. I was impressed when the vice president of the United States walked in with all of his security. At one point, several secret service agents checked out my exit. They approved.

Max's mother flitted and floated throughout the room. She was making excuses that her daughter couldn't attend this year. Taylor was in Milan. Milan, really? If someone in my family couldn't attend because they were out of town, they were usually in Omaha! Heck, I was lucky to go to Lawrence, Kansas for a basketball game now and then when Meg didn't want to go with Tom. I didn't fit in here at all. I wore my dress and my shoes, and I looked fine. Max said I was stunning after the makeup artist and hair designer his mother had brought in finished my look. Even they had recognized that I would be uncomfortable with layers of color. Instead, they gave me a sexy smoky look to my eyes and added a light coral lipstick. Part of my hair was up, the other hung down in short curls. I'd never had my hair this long, and it barely touched the top of my shoulders.

"Can anyone join this private party?"

I looked up to see the director of the FBI staring down at me. "Mr. Shaw, I mean Director Shaw."

"Wow, Charlotte, the last time I saw you was your high school graduation. I have visited your father since then, but you were away at college."

"He really has appreciated your calls since Sean was shot. Thank you so much."

He motioned for me to scoot over on the bench. "I have no words for what is happening to your brother and to your family. We are doing our best to figure this thing out."

I nodded. I gulped. I wanted so badly to cry. No, I wanted to go home. I felt so out of place here. "I know."

"Has my son left you over here? That's unacceptable."

I smiled. "I told him to do his thing, and I'd be fine right here. He needs to do his schmoozing, and I'm just not that social."

Director Shaw nudged my arm. "Yet. You'll get there."

I shook my head quickly. "No. All of this is way too much. Why are you here with me and not out there?" We both viewed the crowded room. Guests were shoulder to shoulder, drinks in hand.

"Well," Max's father began, "Olivia brings me out like a comfortable pair of heels when she needs me for her charities or a special event. She doesn't usually bring her boy toys to important soirees where she'll see people she knows."

"So she uses you?" I began to apologize as soon as the question had left my mouth.

Director Shaw chuckled. "No, you're right. Don't apologize. Yes, Olivia uses me. It's just easier to say yes than to explain why I can't." He pointed at my glass. "It looks like you could use a refill on your champagne, and I'll see if they've opened the dessert bar. Are you a chocolate or fruit kind of girl?"

"Yes."

He laughed. Actually, Max laughed exactly like him. "I'll be right back. Don't move."

As he walked away, I noticed Max and he had the same shoulders and their gate was similar. How was that remotely possible? Wait, didn't mother cats sometimes nurse puppies? Max had imprinted with Edward Shaw.

The nation's second in charge left, and a well-known Broadway actress arrived. Edward Shaw returned with champagne and a full plate of delicious morsels. "I'm very fond of nuts, but whatever you want."

I took my glass from him and investigated the sinful delicacies. Now, this was a guilty pleasure. "I'll have this little chocolate thing. You Shaw men really know how to treat a girl." And tempt me into sin.

"So, has my wife punted you into Times Square yet?"

I smiled slightly. "Nah, just to the edge of Central Park. I'm tough. I can take it, at least that's what I tell myself." I took a bite of my treat. "My gosh this is good."

"She knows her desserts. Enough about Olivia. What's this about you and Max?"

"Too early to tell. I'm seeing so many different sides to him, I'm figuring out who the real Max is." I munched away.

"I'm not sure that's possible," Edward Shaw admitted. I could tell he bit the inside of his mouth to prevent further elaboration. "I believe the question for you will be if Max is worth it. He's a full time job."

"He is high maintenance, and I'm surely not. Your, well Max's mother brought in a makeup artist and a hair professional to make me suitable for tonight."

Director Shaw nudged my arm playfully. "He's never brought a woman to his mother's or to this event."

"Really? That's interesting."

"What does your family think of you two together?"

"Dad and Gio are thrilled. Paddy not so much."

Director Shaw slapped his leg. "I remember Paddy the bear. I liked him, but I can see where he might want to beat the crap out of Maxie."

"Maxie. That's cute." I'd heard other people call him that, but when it was from Edward Shaw's mouth, it was so much more personal, so very loving. I pursued another treat and settled on a chocolate covered strawberry. I decided against discussing the Sunday afternoon fisticuffs with the head of the FBI.

"He's my boy. So, how's this thing with Gio?"

"Gio has been a godsend for all of us through Sean's health crisis. His food alone keeps us all going, and Dad and he have struck up a friendship. With Gio around, Max is becoming more like–"

"A real human with feelings and everything?" Edward Shaw's eyes brightened. "I hear most of that is due to you. I thank you for that."

"He says I make him laugh. I'm not sure if that's good or bad, but I can't be serious for more than thirty minutes at a time."

"Well, Maxie needs you. I see a joy in him that has been missing for a long time. Any questions for me?"

"Yes. You're sure I can ask anything?"

The director nodded. "Go for it."

"Why does she still wear your wedding ring?" Mrs. Shaw stood in our view.

"I've wondered the same thing. I'm not sure. We could've lived apart and just gone on, but she wanted the divorce. She backed out of it, and we ended up with a separation. She never signed the blasted papers. It really never changed anything. I think I'm her crutch, her security blanket. She has her dalliances, but she disposes of them as often as you take your trash out each week. Believe it or not, we had some good years."

"Maybe you weren't wearing the right suits?"

"Excuse me?" Edward Shaw's smile warmed my heart. For an older man, he was tremendously good looking with his salt and pepper hair. His eyes twinkled every time he smiled. His wrinkles only enhanced his handsome face. But the man seemingly knew heartbreak and tragedy. I bet I knew several women my age who would date him in a heartbeat.

"She didn't approve of this dress or of my shoes."

The man shook his head. "I'm so sorry." His attention was drawn by a throng of guests circling around someone who had just entered. Max's mother moved rapidly from her location to join the group. "My view is blocked. Who just walked in? Can you see, Charlotte?"

I stood up on top of my bench and stretched my neck. "It's a man. He's attractive, and he looks familiar. I think he might be a governor or a–" I plopped back down next to Max's father. "Director Shaw it's a senator. It's **the** senator."

"Like hell. I warned Olivia." The good-natured man I had been enjoined in pleasant conversation disappeared. His strong jaw clenched, and his eyes darkened. "Max doesn't need this. Charlotte, we need to get to our boy before he does something stupid, and let me tell you he is capable of that."

I slugged down my champagne and stood quickly. "Let's go."

Max's dad placed my arm in through his as we made our way through the gallery. I noticed his security detail pushed toward the entrance of the gallery as we got closer. I pointed in Max's direction. I could see his head. We headed there quickly, and we divided to stand on each side of him. Max placed his left arm around me and was stunned to see his father on his other arm. "Hello you two. I was just speaking with Justice Freidman. He and his wife are making a large donation. Dad, you'll have to take him to lunch when you're back home."

"Sure, great, son."

Max kissed me on the cheek. "Where have you been? I thought maybe you'd perfected your invisibility act to get a hotdog somewhere."

"No, but that sounds really good. If you add a beer or two, I'm your girl."

"You're my girl anyway." He kissed me again, and despite the attention I was suspicious.

"Have you had anything to eat, Max?"

"I don't remember."

His father moved to look at his eyes. "He's drunk, Charlotte."

"I'm not drunk Charlotte. I'm drunk Max."

"Okay, son. Let's get you some fresh air." Edward nodded at me. "Charlotte, he isn't acting right."

I agreed. Max Shaw was always in control. He would never act this way at any public event. We began to pull on him, but he balked. "What's going on that you two are teaming up on me? Is one of my old girlfriends here?"

"What? How many old girlfriends do you have?" I asked quickly.

Max's dad kept moving us through the guests. "Focus, Charlotte. That isn't our mission right now."

"Sure, okay, but I want details later."

Max shook his head. "No, you don't, love. They weren't really girlfriends. One-night stands maybe, or two-night stands. Would you call that a weekend stand? I'm not sure. So, where are we going?"

"For the hotdog and the beers," I suggested.

Director Shaw motioned to me that we needed to follow a path to the right, away from the senator and his friends. He pointed to his two agents.

"Dad, have you met Charlotte? Of course you have. You're talking to you, her, sorry. I only had a couple drinks. My body feels weird, and I have a headache. What's wrong with me?"

"You didn't eat, Max," I chided. "Keep moving."

Max's father continued to lead the way. Now, I only held Max's hand as the pathway became narrow. Mrs. Shaw noticed our threesome and pushed through.

"Where are you three going? You can't leave our event."

"Max isn't feeling well," I suggested. "He needs some air."

"Hi Mommy. Have you met Charlotte?"

"What is wrong with him, Edward? Is this your doing in an effort to embarrass me once again?"

"We need to get Max out of here. It's not all about you," he said as he shoved past her. One of his agents was attempting to open up an exit.

Olivia Shaw grabbed at Max's tuxedo and pulled him back. "I need him here."

"That'll be the first damn time." I saw Director Shaw's growl affect her. She was visibly hurt as if he had struck her physically.

The crowd shifted. A man came up from behind Max's mother and placed his hands around her small waist. "Edward, it's good to see you away from Washington."

We were face to face with **him**, the senator. Max's biological father was a mirror image of the man I cared for so much. He was fairer skinned; Max had a darker skin tone probably due to Gio's DNA. I focused on Max. He smiled, but then became serious. "I'm going out to get some air."

"So, this is Max?"

Why did I want to punch the man? I didn't know anything about him except for our suspicions that he had his staff member break into Taylor House to retrieve Max's real birth certificate naming him as his father, his sperm donor. He might be the one who ordered shots fired at us. We still didn't know for certain.

"I am Max Shaw." I held tighter onto his wobbling body.

"I'm Senator Daniel Hughes. It's very nice to meet you." The man stuck his hand out.

Max looked at the hand. His eyes set on his mother and then at me. "Senator, it is lovely to finally meet you. It's well over three decades late, but some things take time." Max lunged forward and hugged the man to the surprise of all of us. As the closest person to them, I heard Max whisper in the man's ear.

"If you hurt anyone I love, I will personally take you down." He pulled away with a smile. "Have a lovely evening. Mother, I'm leaving to get a hotdog with my father and my love."

Max led us out, but stopped to lean against the side of the building as soon as we exited. Director Shaw spoke briefly to his protection detail. I heard him mention a drugged drink and one agent proceeded back into the building. As he walked away from the remaining two, he had a smile from ear to ear, and my heart had grown three sizes larger.

"Max, do we need to get another location to sleep tonight?" If his mother had invited the man to the event, I really didn't want to see her again.

He pulled me up against him. "First, let's get that hot dog. I need some real food."

"The tavern where we used to watch hockey is just down the block. Can you make it? My guys can get my car." Director Shaw continued to study his son.

"I don't need the help. Let's just walk slowly. My head is fuzzy, and it's still throbbing." He reached out to his father and looped his other arm behind him.

By the time we reached the bar, Max was feeling better. Either the air was sobering him up, or whatever was wrong with him was passing. We were considerably overdressed for the establishment, but we received applause as we grabbed a booth in the corner. The bartender remembered the Shaw men and brought us three Irish beers immediately.

"Max, it's not Thanksgiving. What are you doing back here?" the man asked. We were given menus with real food listed.

"Another mother event."

"Yikes. You may need a couple of beers. Let me know when you're ready."

"We need water, please," I suggested. He nodded and Director Shaw stopped him before he left and pointed toward his agents. They were given a table near the door and menus as well.

As I reviewed the food choices, I took a side glance at Max. He propped his head up with his arm on the table as he moved the menu closer to his eyes. He didn't look well. This might not be a little alcohol on an empty stomach.

Max dropped the menu onto the table. "I wanted the hotdog, but I think I want the stew or a ham and cheese on rye."

The man beside me had a point. I needed something deep fried. "I want the fish and chips."

Director Shaw placed his menu down. "Charlotte, I'm with you. I'm having the fish and chips. They used to be the best. Are you a vinegar or tartar sauce girl?"

"Tartar. Dad prefers malt vinegar."

The bartender returned with three glasses of water and a beer for each of us. "Are you all ready?"

Max looked up at him. "Are the fish and chips still good?"

"The best, Max. We've missed you since last Thanksgiving."

"It's good to be back. We need three orders and a couple sides of coleslaw or potato salad. Whatever you have left tonight."

He wrote our order down. "I'll bring both, and an order of mac and cheese."

I leaned past Max to add to our order. "We'll need some coffee in a bit, please."

He nodded and headed to the kitchen.

"Well, that was interesting." Max's dad uttered the understatement of the night. "What happened to you?"

Max ran his hand through his hair and swiped at the perspiration on his brow. "I hadn't eaten anything before the party. I just had this feeling that something was going to happen. I don't remember much, but when we arrived, Mother pulled me in different directions to meet some of her adoring fans. I lost Charlotte, and I never had a chance to grab any food. But, the drinks were coming around. I have a problem with sugar processing. It's nothing serious, but I guess I need to pay more attention."

"Or, you've been under a lot of stress and just let go," I muttered before I enjoyed a drink of my own cold beer. "This is good." But I wondered. My suspicious thoughts went straight to someone adding something to Max's drink in order to embarrass the impressive United States attorney or even his elitist mother.

Edward Shaw saluted me. "Simple pleasures are always the best, Charlotte. Max, could someone have placed something in your drink?" I wasn't the only one with diabolical suspicions.

Max murmured he didn't know, but his father had voiced my speculations out loud. I lifted my hand and softly brushed back the hair from his forehead. "You aren't yourself. Someone could've done something."

Edward nodded. "We could have you tested, but I'm not sure it would show–"

"Why? That's ridiculous. Let's toast." Max joined in as we all touched glasses. "Mother will kill me."

"No, she won't. You're the only one who shows up for her for these things. Your sister never comes anymore." Edward Shaw pulled at his bow tie and removed it. Almost in a similar motion, Max performed the same task.

"Dad, she's in Milan."

The man sitting across from me smiled. "And what is she doing? Nothing. She didn't come last year or the year before. Your mother marches you out like a prized dog in Madison Square Garden. She talks about you to every guest she greets. Trust me, she won't kill you."

I became more comfortable by the second as I slipped off my shoes under the table. I slanted my body to lean up against the side of the booth and to see Max. Even though it was dimly lit in the pub, I noticed the color returning to his cheeks. "You know, you threatened a senator."

Max seemed surprised I had heard him. "Hopefully, he'll try to arrest me, and everything will come out."

Edward Shaw watched us intently. "What did you do, son?"

"I warned him off. He knows where we stand. That's one thing I do remember."

Max's father grabbed his head as if he were in pain. "Never poke the bear. I've taught you better than that. We don't know where we stand with him."

"I can handle it."

"Can you? You were almost shot last week. You've been the target of a presumed hit, and there was that lady who set fire to your house. Why add another enemy?"

"Because I'm not so sure he's not running this entire circus," Max fired back. "Think about it. He has the power, the money, and the resources."

"And that's exactly why you don't threaten someone like that. I can handle myself. I can always retire, but you have your career ahead of you. Charlotte, tell him."

I wasn't about to get in the middle of this father and son bonding time. "I won't. Actually, I thought it was very romantic, yes dangerous, but it was sweet."

"Sweet?" Edward Shaw seemed to be on the edge of a nuclear explosion. "You two are crazy."

It was my turn to diffuse the situation. "Which brings me back to our lodging. Do we need to clear out of your mother's apartment?"

Max touched my hand tenderly. "I'm not sure, but I'd definitely think twice if she offers you an apple to eat."

Great. "And I bet the car will turn into a pumpkin too, right?"

My mixture of fairy tale metaphors humored my companions, but I was deadly serious. The clock struck midnight, and any thoughts of a kingdom on a hill disappeared. But, I had heard words tonight that made my heart quicken, and that was enough for now. I'd deal with the evil queen later ... or not. Fleeing was definitely the smarter option for this invisible woman.

After our delicious meal, the coffee and two pieces of apple pie arrived. I took a bite and slid one piece in Max's direction. Edward Shaw dug deep into his and announced he wasn't sharing. "Max, we need to talk about that research I did for you."

Max looked up from his pie and glanced toward me. "Charlotte, Dad has information about Conor. I told you I'd find out."

I nodded. "I know. I trust you. No matter what, I want to know."

"Dad, go ahead," Max answered seriously.

Director Shaw took a drink from his coffee cup and sat back in the booth. "Fine. You told me you thought Conor was like you in some respect, that you hit roadblocks when Nate was searching for information. Max, you were right. Conor was a special investigator for the justice department."

I leaned in. "What? How did that happen? Did you know, Max?"

Max finished his sip of beer and shook his head. "No, but once I began to see a pattern of no information I figured he was undercover for some department. Dad confirmed my suspicions. What else, Dad?"

Edward Shaw touched the side of his mouth with his napkin. "Charlotte, your brother was away for a few years while you were in college."

"Yes, I guess. I thought he was in college too."

"No. He was for a bit, but he was recruited. He was investigating at the time of his death. Max, we should probably wait—"

"No, Dad," Max interjected quickly. He grabbed my hand. "Charlotte needs to know. I think I know what you're about to say."

The man on the other side of the booth had a slight smile on his lips. "Fine." He looked into my eyes. "Charlotte, your brother was investigating a problem with several judges in your city. Max is now in Conor's place only on a different level."

I stared at the director and then at his son. "Now, you're the undercover investigator?"

"That's part of my assignment. Of course, I can't go into details with you, but yes, I'm looking into several problems at the federal level. They wanted someone who knew people. They knew my relationship to the area, to some of the judges–"

I pulled my hand away. "Like my father? Are you investigating my dad?"

Max winced. "Don't go jumping to conclusions."

"I knew this was a bad idea, Max," Edward announced.

I laughed nervously. "You think?"

"Charlotte, stop. Listen to me." Max grabbed my right hand and placed it firmly in his. "All of the judges were reviewed. The prosecutor I replaced is under investigation. Everyone. It's my job."

"You weaseled your way into my family for your job?" I searched Max's eyes for an answer. "Are you using me?"

"God, no. Don't even think that. Look, I talked to your dad from the beginning. He gave me the answers I needed. Other than that, I'm not going to say anymore. You and me, well, you and I, our relationship has nothing to do with my job. Do you understand?" Max's lips stopped moving.

I looked over toward Edward and saw a sympathetic face, an honest one. "Should I believe him?" I nodded toward Max.

Edward smiled, his frown lines deepening. "I think you should. My son may be a lot of things, but he will never lie to you."

Despite a twinge of guilt about my own untruths from last night, I glared at Max. "Really? Never?" A certain ghost had told me differently.

Max appeared to be uncomfortable. "If I can help it?" He braced for impact, but I waited.

My thoughts turned to Max's return to the city. He thought I was a murderer. He ingratiated himself with his charm, his good looks, his love. He said that word tonight. If he was promising to not lead me astray, I needed to do the same.

"Max, that woman I was talking to last night at the restaurant was Mrs. Hughes."

"What in the bloody–"

I put my hand up to his lips to silence him. "I know, but I had this feeling I needed to talk to her, and she needed to speak with me. We had this feeling."

Max's brow furrowed. He removed my hand and whispered. "Feeling or did you hear a voice?"

"Voice. She did too."

Max's eyes raised in supplication. "Lord. She can hear too?"

"Her husband."

"Her husband? Charlotte, this is unbelievable."

Director Shaw cleared his throat. "Excuse me, but could you two fill me in on whatever is going on?"

Max motioned for another round. "Dad, Charlotte meets new friends in the darndest places. You'll never believe who she talked with last night at the restaurant."

Oh boy, this was going to be interesting, but I was discovering that being with Max would never be boring.

Chapter Thirteen

"Are you packed?" Max stood at the entrance of my guest room the next morning. His bag was in his hand as was his briefcase and laptop. "I figured we would leave early and have brunch before we head to the plane."

"I packed last night after we came back here." I zipped up my luggage and placed it on the floor. "That sounds like a wonderful plan. I'm ready to go to Kansas City where I'm safe?"

"Yeah." Max smiled. "It does seem safer there, doesn't it?"

"You know, I was thinking. If your sugar is that off, you need to visit a doctor."

"That's why I originally had those blood tests. But, I was thinking. It really isn't too wild to suggest that someone put something in one of my drinks, is it?"

I grabbed my purse and laptop. "Not exactly considering what has been happening to both of us. Actually, that was the first thing I thought, and your dad had his suspicions."

"So?"

"So, it is possible. Anything is possible including a blood sugar problem. Seriously, you really could've just let your hair down or maybe your subconscious wanted to embarrass your mother."

"Wow, you think more than me."

"Sometimes, well all the time lately." I paused and sighed. "On the other hand, maybe it was an attempt to embarrass you or your mother by slipping something into your drink. We may never know. But one thing is for sure. I'm ready to go home."

"Me too." As Max led the way, I was comforted by the fact he considered our next destination as his home.

Max stopped in the hallway. "When are we going to discuss in detail your little talk with Mr. and Mrs. Hughes?"

"On the plane. When we're up in the air you'll have nowhere to go."

We made it to the front door before Olivia Shaw addressed us.

"I have reservations for us at my favorite restaurant."

Max's head hung in despair. We'd almost made a clean escape. He turned slowly. "Mother, we are leaving early. I think it's best."

"Best for you two maybe, but not for me. Did little Charlotte convince you that your bad mommy hurt her?"

Max began to respond, but my hand touched his arm. I'd had enough, and when I was done, I was done. "Mrs. Shaw, you have been rude to me and very opinionated despite the fact you haven't attempted to get to know me. You judged me, and I'm sure you have already deemed me as unworthy. I appreciate your hospitality and your lovely home, but I don't convince Max of anything. As you can tell, he doesn't speak for me either. I can't say it has been the best experience of my life, but thank you." I pushed past Max, but stopped. "Oh, and thank you for your son. Max, I'll be in the hallway so you can say goodbye privately."

I made my exit and stood up against the closed double doors that today separated our free departure. I could just get on the open elevator and leave without Max. Damn, that was stupid. I couldn't hear them now. But it was for the best. Whatever they said needed to be private without an outsider listening in. When I saw the knob turn I stepped away.

Max smiled shyly as he stood beside me. "We're waiting in the car for her."

"We're having brunch with her?"

"Yes. She promised she'd be good, and she wants to talk."

I wanted to scream, but I needed a ride home. I chose to be silent during the ride down and as Max and Palmer loaded in our luggage. I didn't wait for assistance as I opened the car door and scampered in. I began to text Dad to see how Sean and he were, and that we would be late for dinner, but at least I would be there for the night no matter what. I needed a little distance from Max and the comfort of knowing my mother was looking over me in my old bedroom.

Max entered the car and reached over for my hand. "Charlotte."

"Yes?"

"I don't want to leave this way."

"Well, we are. She's very good at getting her own way."

Instead of addressing my comment, he became quiet. He knew what

I was thinking even though I wasn't even sure. At least he thought he knew. I was thinking my little bedroom back home was so much better than the most expensive room on this street.

Olivia Shaw entered the car after Palmer assisted her. It was a cool morning, and she wore an elaborate wrap cape with a stunning brooch at her neck. A matching fedora hat finished her look. That seemed fitting for a woman who was probably just as ruthless as a crime king. I was amused by that analogy considering Gio was her biological father.

"Charlotte, you'll love this place. It used to be a Russian tea room, and they kept so many of the decorations, but they upgraded the decor of course."

"Of course," I muttered. So, this family just ignored confrontations? We harbored. We fretted and planned. Fights in a family needed to be settled or they festered until the next get together.

"They serve the best mimosas. Of course, they use the traditional orange juice and champagne mixture, but they add a touch of brandy. I think you will love it."

"Really?"

"Yes, I believe the brandy is from Ireland. They have several healthy options for you in case you're trying to lose a few pounds."

I closed my eyes. If I just couldn't see her perhaps she wasn't really there? Max said nothing. I pulled my hand discreetly away from his and clutched my purse to my apparently too ample chest.

Max's mom was correct about one thing, the restaurant was amazing. Their homage to the tearoom was nostalgic in the lobby, focusing on red and gold colors. Once we were seated, I noticed that the dining area looked more like an upscale apartment than a restaurant. I could understand why Olivia Shaw felt at home here.

She ordered mimosas and the signature coffee for the day for all of us. I was determined to order the most caloric option on the menu just to see her faint, but instead she and I ordered identically. The brunch's eggs Benedict menu item was traditional, but came with mixed fruit, and potatoes that were baked in garlic and parsley. Max ordered an omelet that featured sirloin steak. That was a new one for me.

I sipped my drink as Mrs. Shaw babbled. I knew a nervous babbler when I heard one. She was amusing. Suddenly, we were hearing about the silk-screened scarf Max's sister had purchased in Venice, and she was planning for another month in Italy. Mrs. Shaw was worried that her daughter wouldn't be home in time for Thanksgiving. That seemed to be a trigger word, and I nearly spit my mimosa out as Max explained he'd be staying in Kansas City for the holiday.

"What? You know you must be here."

"Mother, I've told you before I'll be staying at home."

"Max, you have to come. We agreed years ago that attendance was mandatory."

"Things change. With Sean's situation–"

"Sean O'Donohue means absolutely nothing to you." She waved her hand in the air as if she was the queen dismissing the lowly page.

Max's jaw clenched. "Their family means everything to me. You won't be alone. You'll have your latest gentleman on your arm and your favorite chef's perfect turkey on the table." Max looked at me. "Hopefully, I'll be sitting next to Charlotte, wearing comfortable jeans and sneakers so we can throw the football around later. We will pass around copious plates of food like mashed potatoes and gravy, mac and cheese, green beans, candied sweet potatoes–"

"Don't forget Dad makes at least three different varieties of pie," I added.

"He does? Like what?"

"Last year he made pumpkin, pecan, and a Dutch apple. I'm not a big fan of apple, but it was so good."

"And you wonder why you're not a smaller size?"

I tried to place my glass softly on the table, but it clinked against my water glass. "Mrs. Shaw, I don't wonder, and I don't appreciate your comment." For the first time in my life I knew for sure my fate was to spend eternity in hell.

Her mouth shut firmly. She seemed to plead to Max with her eyes. Max didn't come to the rescue. Instead, he leaned over and kissed me on the cheek.

"I'm sorry, Charlotte." Despite the apology, Mrs. Shaw held her head high. You had to give it to her. She probably apologized only once in a decade, if that. It was at that moment that I amused myself. If Max was the devil, in some cultures, didn't that mean Olivia Shaw was the queen of darkness and evil?

I smiled slightly. "Thank you."

"Charlotte, Max has never brought anyone here. Oh, I've seen him with dozens of women." It seemed as though the queen was a little nervous.

"Mother." Max squirmed in his chair.

"Well, a few, but he has never had someone come to last night's event or brought her into my home. I suppose I'm not very good at this."

"You think?" Max asked. "You keep pushing Charlotte's buttons, and you're intentionally being rude." He took a drink, his eyes still focused on his maternal unit.

"Charlotte, Max, what I did last night was inexcusable. I should have had the senator stay away. His invitation went out with the others, and I didn't realize that my personal assistant didn't pull it. Actually, it is all my fault. I added him for the first time. I thought that maybe you would want to meet him, and that he would want to meet you."

"You were outrageously mistaken, Mother."

Max's eyes were dark and sad. This family had everything one might want. They had a certain amount of fame, money, and definitely power, but they weren't on the same page. They kept passing each other in the night, and the night was bleak and stormy. I almost felt sorry for the woman sitting across from me. Almost.

"Max, you'll miss the wonderful food the chef prepares."

"I won't."

I held up my napkin to my mouth to hide my amusement. Thankfully, our food came to the table, and we were too busy eating to pursue any conflict.

"Maxwell, your father says you're still working on that mausoleum."

"Mother, it's a large home, but I'm bringing back some of its beauty. Gio and Judge O'Donohue help out quite a bit. You should see it."

His mother scoffed. "I will not return to that place or that city for any reason ever."

"What about my funeral?"

Mrs. Shaw and I dropped our forks. "That's an awful thing to say, son."

"You should visit and see Gio."

I watched the drama unfold. I could tell the usually effervescent conversationalist was thinking of an excuse.

"I have met him a few times, and I've talked to him on the phone. I have no need or want to come to that city. That is the end of it."

I wanted to ask if she'd come for our wedding or the birth of her first grandchild, but figured that would be inappropriate. Besides, Max still had a lot of demons to dispose of in his life before I was sure we could do this for more than just two days a week. Had he even mentioned marriage? I couldn't remember.

Instead, the devil did the deed. "Surely, you'd come to my wedding, Mother."

Olivia Shaw almost choked on her mimosa. She dabbed at the edges of her mouth. "What? Are you two ... " She looked at me and then returned her questioning eyes toward Max.

"We aren't anything," I quickly answered. "I think Max was just trying to find out how restrictive your travel plans back to Kansas City really are. Right?"

I nudged him. Max held my gaze briefly. "What Charlotte said except for the part that we aren't anything. We are something to each other. You just can't make a blanket statement, Mother. You always do that. My life is changing, and you need to understand and welcome that. Dad does."

"Your father doesn't understand anything except for law enforcement. Besides, now that the secret is out, your real father could assist you substantially with your career. Have you ever thought about the future? If you went into politics–"

"No, and I thought you hated politics." Max cut her off before she could continue. "I'm happy doing what I'm doing."

Olivia Shaw shook her head. "That is another thing I don't understand. Why did you take that position there? Atlanta was much bigger, and you could've spent your entire term there. You went after those real estate schemers all because someone you knew lost everything. Max, you'll never get ahead if you keep taking these charity cases. Your bleeding heart gets in the way every time."

So, my devil was an angel afterall! Apparently, Max's past was lined with good deeds. Again, there wasn't a week that passed that I didn't learn something new about Maxie. That endearment created a cute, vulnerable Max rather than the man who seemed to always be in control. But what did Max need that he didn't already have?

"Mother, I want justice. I want criminals to pay for their crimes. I don't consider that a bad thing."

"Of course you don't. I understand, but you can't help everyone. Well, excuse me Charlotte, but I don't understand why my son feels the need to help pay the hospital bills for her brother. Surely there's insurance."

Max's entire body clenched. "Mother. Stop."

"Wait, what?" I looked between the two of them. "Max, what is she talking about?"

"He's paying your brother's bills. Apparently, the hospital recommended a week ago that your brother should be moved to a facility. Max swooped in and said he'd pay the expenses. The insurance company had cut off your brother's care at the hospital and wanted to move him to a rehab center covered by the insurance."

I grabbed Max's sleeve. "You said you'd pay for his extra care through the trust, but you didn't say anything about this. Dad doesn't know, does he?"

Max placed his fork down deliberately. "No. Please don't tell him. Judge O has so much on his plate. The police chief called and told me the insurance company insisted Sean be moved. He wondered if I could talk to your dad. Even the hospital didn't want to tell the judge, so I began the negotiations. It gave your dad some time, but next week we search for the proper place for Sean. Whatever the insurance won't pay, I will. There are better rehab centers than the insurance will cover, and then when he comes home, the trust will pay for everything."

"There goes that bleeding heart again." His mother's remark didn't phase me. I was too busy looking differently at the man sitting next to me. He was the same man who held me in his arms during a bad storm. I had been bracing for this moment, but I was losing. I wasn't falling in love with him, I was already there with my heart and soul. I loved Max Shaw for who he was and what he did. That part of him made up for every commitment phobia, and the fact that he had a mother who could quite possibly make God lose his temper.

In front of the entire restaurant, and possibly to spite his mother, I grabbed his face with both hands and planted the most fierce kiss I could manage while seated. "I love you, Max. You don't have to answer. I just wanted you to know that."

"Irish impulsiveness," Mrs. Shaw muttered. "Her mother was the same way. That's how they ended up with all those children, well that, and the rhythm method."

Max and I shared a laugh and completely ignored her. She was right. I was just as impulsive as my mother, and I planned to live my life like that. My mom had the love of a good man, a wonderful family surrounding her when she passed, and the knowledge she had lived a life full of joy, tears, lots of good food, and love ... so much love. And my mom had danced in the rain. She'd taught me to do the same. As I glanced at Max, he smiled. The softness soothed my heart and soul. I realized then and there it wasn't about the rain or the storm, it was about life's challenges and loves.

My thoughts had finally been collected since my announcement. "And, Mrs. Shaw, my mother had hips because she loved food. So do I. Oh, and those hips grew each and every time she gave birth to one of us. I plan on doing the same thing. My mom wasn't even Irish so it's not an Irish thing; it's my family's thing."

"I see." That was all she said. Max looked down at his watch and suggested we head to the airport.

Again, inside the car, conversation was limited. Max checked his phone. Mrs. Shaw checked hers, and I watched for the tourist sites. Even though I had proclaimed my love, Max hadn't responded. I knew he wouldn't. I wasn't sure he ever would. Yes, my heart would break again. But, this time experience was on my side. This time my lovely memories would outnumber the bad ones. I would heal faster, at least I hoped I would.

Before we entered through the doors of the airport, I thanked the evil queen and stepped away from the mother and son duo. I couldn't hear again, but I didn't need to. If Max wanted me to know, he would share the conversation.

When he arrived at my side, he was smiling. "Well, Charlotte O'Donohue, formerly snotty nose sister, formerly Charlie, you held your own quite well. As soon as we're up in the air, I'll give you a special treat."

"Ice cream?"

"Something way better than that." His brow arched devilishly, and his caramel eyes sparkled. "Now, let's go home."

We held hands as we walked through the airport. "Since it's a private plane, is the pilot giving me a set of those little wings? Is that my treat?"

Max shook his head and chuckled. "Have you ever wanted to be a member of the mile high club?"

Sometimes, he was too much. "Max, I've never actually been eager to become a member of any club."

"I think you'll enjoy this one," Max said as he added a wink.

My entire body was warmer by at least ten degrees. "I think I'd rather have the wings and ice cream."

Chapter Fourteen

"We can't just make out the entire trip back to Kansas City. Stop it." I pushed Max back into his own seat.

"Why not?" Max kissed me one more time on the cheek before he secured his seatbelt. "What do you want to do?"

"Talk."

We managed to have a short conversation about Mrs. Hughes and her husband, and how I was too impetuous. Max was right. When I needed to know, I needed to know. I'd told the matriarch that hearing those voices from beyond was a blessing, but had I lied? Their messages sent me down very different paths from the life I could be leading. Stubbornly, I would head into situations undaunted. They pushed me to ask questions. Whatever road I was on was uncovering a web of secrets and indiscretions based on love. But who was the spider weaving this deadly web?

And then there was Max. He was curious about the spirits who contacted me, but I could tell his belief was shaky. But he believed me.

"I still don't understand how your ghosties work."

I laughed. "This flight isn't long enough, in fact, I'm still learning. No one else in the family can really help."

"Family." Max took my hand and kissed it. "Charlotte, do you want a family?"

"Yes, of course." Was he asking me to have one with him? My heart quickened unexpectedly. I shouldn't get my hopes up, yet I was.

"How big of a family?"

"Five or six kids would be great." I waited for the explosion.

"Two."

"Four." We were negotiating?

"Two."

"Three." We were negotiating.

"Fine."

I gave him a side glance, and the man was smirking. "You are such a–"

"Poop Head?"

"Exactly. Do you always have to win?"

"Always. It's best that way. You should know that by now."

By the time we landed, I'd almost forgotten about his shrew of a mother. I knew she existed and could make life hell, sort of like the plague. It was out there, but not near me at the time, and there were treatment options. Before we even arrived home, we made a visit to the hospital where Dad and Gio waited for us.

"Sean opened his eyes today," Dad said proudly. "His eyes followed the light too."

I looked over at Gio for confirmation. He nodded. I hugged Dad tightly. "That's the best news. So now what?"

"They'll keep him this week. Phoebe has been helping me, as has the hospital, to find a rehabilitation facility that will meet his needs. I want you and Max to look at the choices. Jane, Paddy, and Tom have weighed in. We're all in agreement except for Paddy, but he's always contrary."

"May we see him?" Max asked quietly.

"Of course. You two should go in. I'm feeling so good, I thought you could take me home. I'm not going to stay the night."

That was a big decision for my father. I knew he was haunted by the night Conor died. Dad had returned home with Sean and me. He'd been confident that his son was holding his own. But Mom stayed behind. We had just gone to bed when her tearful call came that he had passed.

As Max and I walked into the hospital room, Sean's eyes opened. It didn't seem to be a reflexive motion as his eyes followed me. "Sean, I'm so happy."

He blinked and looked at Max. He began to try to say something, but he still had the tube down his throat. "Sean, it's okay. You can tell me later."

"Nnno."

Sean's blood pressure numbers began to rise. "Sean, stay calm. It has to be later. You need to heal. Please calm down or they'll kick us out. Soon, you'll be able to tell us or write it down. There's time."

"Nnno time." I understood him even though his words were garbled.

Max leaned down. "Have you remembered who it was?"

Sean blinked twice, but then shook his head back and forth.

Max looked up at me as confused as I was. "Sean, rest. We're happy to have you back, and until we can solve all of this, we will all be careful."

Max left me alone in the room. I told Sean about New York and how nasty Mrs. Shaw really was. We heard rumors, but experiencing it first hand was truly an experience I wish I had been spared. He tried to smile when I recounted how I told her off. "I have had years of experience telling you to go away or shut up, Seany. It just came off the tip of my tongue naturally." I added an Irish accent to my joke. "Mom would've killed me and told me I was better than that."

Sean nodded his head ever so slowly.

Dad came in to say his good nights and walked me out. "Max wants to talk to all of us. The doctor is there, and I've given him permission to speak to him."

My heart began to pound. Fear took over after such good news. Max stood in the middle of the room, speaking with the health professional.

He offered me a slight smile. "We're all happy Sean has opened his eyes, and now he's attempted to speak, but no one can know."

The doctor lowered his head and nodded in agreement. I was incredulous. "But the family needs to know. We can all help him recover."

"No, Charlotte," my father said. "Listen to Max. It's for the best given our situation."

Max focused his eyes on mine. "If the shooter discovers that Sean is awake, he'll come for him. We have to pretend he's still in a coma. I'll arrange for around the clock security for him at the new facility. Any therapy will come to him. No one out of this room will know Sean is tracking and beginning to speak slowly."

I collapsed onto the couch. Gio grabbed my hand. "But everyone needs to know. We need him as much as he needs us." Dad came to my other side and held me in his arms.

"Charlotte Rose, I know, but Max has a point. If he thinks he can pull this off, and we can get the help Sean needs, then we need to try. If the shooter hears that Sean is awake, and if that person thinks Sean has told anyone of us who shot him, he'll finish the job. Whoever this is won't stop. I agree with Max completely. Your brothers and sister only know Sean needs to be moved out of the hospital."

"And I'll cover all of the extra costs. I want this solved as much as I know Sean does," Max said calmly. "We'll just have to keep him isolated. The doctors will think of something, maybe a virus–"

"Right. We keep everyone away from him." I understood completely, but my heart was breaking. I saw Max wince as I uttered my final statement. Sean needed us, all of us. Paddy could rile him up in a good way, Jane would want to help with his speech therapy; Tom would tell him all of the events he was missing. He'd tell him to work harder to get his butt out of that bed, and I was missing my goofy brother. I missed the stupid things he said, and the crazy way he lived his life.

Max knelt down in front of me, placing his hand on my knee. "Charlotte, we can make this work. We can keep Sean safe and have him improve at the same time."

I nodded as I wiped away my tears. "We'll be lying to all of them."

"For a good reason, love." Max had used that word again. It wasn't a verb. It was used as a noun, and that was good enough for now.

Chapter Fifteen

"The prosecution rests, your honor."

"Thank you, Mr. Shaw. We will recess for the day. Court will resume at nine am."

As the gavel pounded, my body flinched. I managed to finish my day a couple of hours earlier and headed over to the federal courthouse to see Max. Carolyn personally escorted me. He was brilliant. Watching him reminded me of several movies about court trials. His articulation and inflection was perfect and calculated. He lowered and raised his voice at the proper moment for emphasis. He really was the boy wonder.

Max threw a glance at me and waved his hand, but continued to give orders to his second chair. He organized his papers and placed them into his briefcase. As he closed it, he turned to walk toward me. "This is a nice surprise. What's up?"

"I finished early and thought I'd watch the great Maxwell Edward Shaw."

"Were you disappointed?" He hustled me out of the courtroom and into the hallway. "Wait here." He visited briefly with an officer standing at the end of the hallway. When he returned, he looked relieved.

"What was that about?"

"A part of my evil plan. Come up to the office with me, and I'll treat you to a happy early dinner."

"That sounds amazing. I've missed you." I stretched and kissed him on the cheek despite the formality of this place.

"I've missed you too. As soon as this case is over, I'm going to take some time off."

As we entered the elevator, I laughed. "Yeah, you nut. It's called the holidays. We all get them off."

"No, I mean it. I'm thinking of taking a break between Thanksgiving and New Year's."

"Again, federal holidays are in there."

"Wow, I can't catch a break with you."

I maneuvered closer to him. "You could, if you ask nicely."

The elevator door opened onto his office's floor. "I will. Later."

Max walked briskly into his office after retrieving a few messages from Carolyn. I stayed behind to hear the latest gossip from the office.

"Charlotte, I hear New York was amazing."

I laughed. "From Max, Mr. Shaw? It was amazingly dreadful."

Carolyn smiled knowingly. "No, he said you were amazing."

"Did he? That's nice to know. He's acting suspiciously. What's he up to?"

Max's trusted assistant checked something on her computer. "I have no idea what you're talking about."

"My father's personal assistant and paralegal knew everything. Max had a little talk with one of the officers in the building. I couldn't hear a thing."

With a wave of her hand, Carolyn motioned me into the supply room. I followed as she shut the door. "Well, there's something going on at the courthouse. I've heard so many rumors, but it focuses on one of the judges."

"Really? That's unusual."

"It gets more interesting if you know that the judge's nephew used to be the U.S. attorney. Max replaced him."

I began to consider different scenarios. "I knew him, well I know the judge. It's Judge Linus Parmeter. I didn't realize Max replaced the nephew. I just thought the man had moved on."

Carolyn understood. "I know. That's what they made it look like, but the nephew was under FBI surveillance."

"Wow, this is all coming together. I bet Max's dad told him something."

Carolyn touched my shoulder. "And by the way, his father absolutely adores you."

"That's nice. I wish his son did." My voice faltered as I allowed my greatest fear to be heard out loud.

"Oh, Charlotte, he does. Max has a very dynamic personality, but he does adore you. You seem to be holding your own."

I was beginning to realize I needed a girlfriend to share my inner thoughts. I found paralegals and assistants instead. "I told him I loved him, and he hasn't addressed it. Why is that?"

"You've met his mother, honey. The facade that is the perfect boy wonder hides a really messed up little kid, and now with all the secrets coming to light about his family, you need to have a little patience."

I frowned. "I'm not very good with that."

The door opened, and there he stood. "The staff was worried there was an emergency. Is there?" His arched brow warned me that our cover had been completely blown.

"Is there any point in telling you that Carolyn was making me a copy?"

Max shook his head. "Charlotte, once again you have proved that you are a terrible liar. Carolyn, Ms. O'Donohue and I are leaving for the day with or without that copy."

"Alright, Max. Remember, I'll be late tomorrow. I have that doctor's appointment."

He snapped his fingers. "I remember. You are okay, aren't you?"

"Yes, it's just a checkup."

Max pulled me out. "Good. Let's go. I'm starving."

I waved back. "I guess I'll get that copy the next time I see you."

Max leaned down. "Give it up, Charlotte."

"I'm playing out my scene, and I'm practicing my fibbing."

I managed to grab my laptop and bag as we exited quickly.

An hour later, Max and I were seated outside on the Country Club Plaza at a restaurant that I could never afford. Despite the first frost of the season hitting this morning, the afternoon was stunning. Our table near the firepit was the best on the patio. Max watched me as I reviewed the menu.

"Max, why did you pick one of the most expensive restaurants?"

"It's not as bad as New York. Do you want a drink?"

"No, thank you. I just want coffee."

The server stood waiting for our order. "I'll have a bourbon, and the lady wants a coffee. Could you put an order in for the crab cake appetizer, please?"

The server hurried off. "Max, are we celebrating?"

"Yes. We survived New York and my mother."

I pretended to search the menu again. "My mouth was running as if it was in a marathon. I said some things–"

"To my mother or to me?" He smiled at me, and I melted. He was too handsome for his own good. And he was so good at deviling me.

"I was too honest with your mother. I was rude."

"And–"

Now, he was just being obnoxious. "And I'm not sure what you want me to say."

Thankfully, the server appeared. Max asked him about the fish, and I was still attempting to find something that wasn't over forty dollars.

"I'll have the bass, grilled with the citrus aioli. I'd like the scalloped potatoes and the beet salad. Charlotte?"

"I don't know. What would you suggest?" I looked up to the server in desperation, but he selected the most expensive item on the menu.

"Could you give us a few more minutes?" Max asked. As the man left, Max leaned in. "Charlotte, what's wrong? You always know what you're eating."

"I have a problem spending this much money. Usually, we're at a normal restaurant."

Max loosened his tie and one button of his shirt. His eyes were dark, sending a slight shiver up my spine. "Charlotte, I like a great dining experience with good food. I don't look at the prices. I want quality clothing and even my bathtub needs to be perfect in design. Your brothers call me a snob. I don't really give a damn. You need to get used to me treating you, and treating you very well. Now, you're going to get really mad."

Max waved for our server. "You know what I want, and the lady will have the lobster tails, the scalloped potatoes, and …" He looked over the menu and winked at me. "And the coleslaw with pineapple. Thank you."

The server removed our menus, but I took a quick look at the cost. "Max, that's outrageous, and you are right. I don't appreciate you ordering for me."

Max smiled slightly. "Be mad, but your father said you haven't been eating. Why is that? It has nothing to do with my mother, does it?" He clasped his hands on the table as though we were having a business meeting.

The crab cakes came as did an early refill of my coffee. Caffeine would be good for me. I had work plans for the evening. "No, I just haven't been hungry. I'm trying to save every dime so I can get my own place again."

"Why is that?"

"When you know who comes home, Dad doesn't need to be worrying about me anymore."

Max stabbed one of the small cakes and dipped it into the remoulade sauce. "Here, try this."

I ate it off of his fork as though we were newlyweds. "That is so good."

"I know, right? Your dad doesn't worry about you being in the house. He loves it. He doesn't mind having dinner ready for you, or making sure your favorite bagels are there in the morning for breakfast. Finally, when I take you out, do not look at the prices anymore. Got it?"

I nodded hesitantly. "Max, I've been looking at different scenarios. I still think part of this insanity has to do with my family or with me."

"What do your little spirits tell you?" He popped another one of the appetizers into his mouth.

"They aren't little spirits. They're our family. I'm still hearing there's danger for you."

"Let me worry about that. Now, I want to get back to that lovely mouth of yours and what you said."

I rolled my eyes and sat away from the table, dropping my shoulders as if I was totally bored. "I will apologize to her if you want me to."

"You know damn well I'm not talking about what you said to my mother. You said something else to me."

He did remember, and he did want to discuss it. This was my worst nightmare. The friendship was nice while it lasted, and the relationship or whatever we had was lovely. The sex had been even better. "I did?"

Max laughed loudly. "Liar. Let's just get it out, and then we can move on. I want to know if you meant what you said."

"I realize that we're supposed to be honest with each other even though we keep having all of these secrets creep into our lives, but my honesty was probably premature. You asked me to be patient, and I'm lousy at doing that."

"I remember. When you were little, you always wanted to be older so you could go with us big kids. You always seemed to run so you could catch up to the group."

"I didn't want to be left behind," I said slowly. Max reached for my hand across the table, and I gave it freely to him.

"I know. That's why I would come back for you."

Taking a deep breath, I steeled my nerves. Hopefully, we could stay for the main entree. I really did want those lobster tails. "I said I loved you. It was in response to hearing about your thoughtfulness toward Sean and my father. You are doing a very sweet thing."

"It just had to do with an action and not me? It was what I did, and not because of who I am?"

"Well, no, but yes. You're confusing me. I hate attorneys."

Max chuckled. "You're an attorney."

"Not like you. You are evil."

Max's thumb rubbed naturally over my hand. His touch, even fleeting, set my body on fire once again. "I know. I'm the devil."

"Yes, sometimes you still are, especially in the middle of the night," I scolded.

Miraculously, our meals came, and I was saved once more by a minor distraction. I knew he wouldn't let it go. Max Shaw never surrendered until he received what he wanted. First he wanted my heart, and now he was going for my very soul.

I relished each and every bite of those lobsters who gave their tails to me. The remainder of the dinner was just Charlotte and Max eating. We enjoyed a dessert together and a short walk around the shopping area. Max followed me home and came into the house to make sure I was safe.

"Do you want coffee?" I took my jacket off and deposited my things in the chair next to the stairs.

"No, I'm good." I noticed Max looking around. "Does your dad have a security system in this place?"

"Not a great one but just motion lights. All the doors have deadbolts."

"I'll have Bobby Mack and Nate come over and put in some upgrades."

I turned on the kitchen light, and Mickey yawned as though I'd interrupted the best slumber he'd ever had. "You lazy dog. I know Tom came over earlier and took care of you, but you need to go out again. Come on." I opened the back door to the fenced in yard.

"I thought your nephew was helping with the canine?"

I came back to Max who was now sitting casually on the couch. He had removed his necktie and thrown his suit coat over onto Dad's chair. "That was just for a short time. I made a schedule, and so far everyone is doing their part."

"Of course you made a schedule, and they better be." He patted the cushion next to him. "Sit down for a second. We need to talk."

Oh no. Now what? Had the dinner and nice conversation just been the good before the ugly? "Okay, but I have work to do tonight."

"It won't take long."

I sat down and kicked off my shoes for the first time today. Max moved closer, allowing only a few inches between us. His arm draped over my shoulders. "So, Charlotte, you love what I did, not who I am?"

"Max, let's not talk about this anymore." Should I mention he had called me his love?

Max's lips found that small area behind my right ear lobe that was most susceptible to his attention. "But, I want to," he whispered. "Does that feel good?"

"Yes."

"Good." He moved his mouth slowly from my lobe to the side of my cheek until his warm lips rested on my mouth. "Charlotte."

The air in my lungs completely left my body. When he whispered my name and made it sound like a love song in a musical, I couldn't stand it. Even my toes were tingling. I needed to get him out of the house and head up for a very cold shower. Damn him.

His other hand touched my face in slow motion, stroking my cheek. He pulled me up against him as his other arm pushed me forward until I was wrapped in his arms. Slowly, one of his hands cupped my bottom. I rested partially on his chest. "Charlotte, tell me the truth. I'm not letting this go."

"Don't make me. If I do, this entire fairytale is over, isn't it?"

I mumbled, barely able to form another sentence with the frontal offensive he was putting forward.

"Try me. Just tell me the truth."

Why not? Everything else was crazy right now. I was juggling my work, dealing with my family, keeping a secret from my siblings, listening to dead people give me warnings about Max, worrying about Sean's future, wondering about Conor's murderer, and who was targeting Max and maybe me, and attempting to keep life normal. Sure, go ahead and screw up the only good thing in your life right now. Why the heck not?

As he kissed me, he wasn't being fair. He massaged my lower back and pulled my blouse out of my slacks. His hand slid down my bare skin under the waistband. I moaned from his touch. "Max."

"Tell me, Charlotte. Did you mean to say it or was it just the moment?"

My hands coveted his face, finally lacing at the back of his neck. I shifted as he attempted to pull me even closer. I looked into his eyes, and I saw my future. I blinked, and I only saw my friend. My hands fell from him and pushed back against his body. I shot up from the couch. "I can't do this, Max."

"What?"

"Oh don't look so innocent. You know very well what you are doing. I can't do this. I have so much chaos. You do too, but you handle it very well, and you're not the one who is going to get hurt. And why do you always have to do this seduction thing? It isn't fair."

Max sat up and held his head between his legs. "You're giving me a headache."

I began to stomp, jumping up and down. "I hate you for what you make me feel."

His head popped up quickly. "What?"

"I hate you. You make me feel like I want so much more with you. Only you. Fine. Are you ready for the truth?"

Max nodded. He appeared to be laughing at me. "Please don't say that old movie line. I can handle the truth."

"And we'll still be friends when you walk out of that door? I don't want to lose my friend, not when I need you so much."

Max stood up. "Just say it!"

"I love you, Max Shaw!" I screamed out so loudly that Mickey began to bark from outside. "God help me. I tried not to, I honestly did. Well, as soon as I began to like boys I've always had this mammoth crush on you. You were older, and you were Tom's friend. I pretended to be drunk when I kissed you that first time. Then we ended up making love, and you were so wonderful. You carried me in so many ways, not just lifting me into your arms. You left me breathless. My mother told me to only fall in love with a man who could do that to me. You checked all the boxes. Oh, and then you fixed me breakfast. Why did you do all the right things? You're just a player. You've had dozens of women. How have you had that kind of time? I'm sounding so stupid. I just can't handle rejection very well, so please say you'll still–"

Max pulled me to him. "Oh just stop talking. You scare me to death, Charlotte. God help me, but I love you too."

"Love should scare you, Max. Don't you think I'm scared too?" And then he kissed me, and my fear vanished as I returned the kiss voraciously. I was delighted that he seemed breathless too as his hands fell onto my hips. He pulled me down onto him as we both fell awkwardly onto the couch.

"Um, am I interrupting?"

My father stood over us as we acted like two teenagers

caught in the act. We were actually two grown adults caught in the act. I stood up quickly, straightening my blouse and hair at the same time. Max sat up, wiping lipstick off of his mouth.

"Dad, we were just–" I looked at Max, and he rescued me in the most wonderful way.

"I was just telling Charlotte I love her."

"Oh good. It took you long enough." My father seemed calm as he removed his coat and placed it on the front hall hook. Did he already know how Max felt? Of course he did. "I'm glad you're here, Max. I have some information for you. Is Mickey outside?"

He walked through to the kitchen as Max and I blinked at each other. "That went well."

Max got up and kissed me on the cheek. "It would've gone much better if he hadn't come home."

I slugged him in the ribs and headed toward the kitchen. "Dad, do you want coffee? I have work to do as soon as Max leaves so I need caffeine. Have you eaten? We have leftover–"

"Coffee is all I need. I ate a late lunch before I saw Sean. I'll just make a sandwich." He poured out food for Mickey and refilled the dog's water.

"I need to let Mickey in," I announced. I forgot all about the dog while Max was seducing me. The dog was waiting patiently and hurriedly headed in to greet his master.

Dad petted Mickey and pointed at the chairs across from him. "Have a seat. We need to plan."

Dad made himself a sandwich while I provided the coffee. My interest was piqued when my father shoved his cell phone toward Max. "I have the information on here. Take a look."

"What have you two been up to?" My eyes worked overtime to view the screen, but Max pulled it away. "Oh, come on. I'm part of the inner circle."

"Anyone home?" Gio's voice boomed through the house.

"I'm going to get that security system upgraded tomorrow." Max's complaint was understood as Gio walked in nonchalantly. We all stared at him.

"What? Judge O gave me a key. I bought an apple strudel from Strawberry Hill." He held up the bag proudly.

"I want strudel," I lamented, grabbing the bag to cut the delicious pastry.

"What are we doing?"

My father pulled the chair out next to him. "We're investigating a judge."

"Oh, the corrupt one?"

I hit the counter. "Oh come on. Gio knows too?"

Max grinned. "She doesn't like secrets."

"Oh, I know," Dad admitted. "I had to hide most of her birthday gifts at my office every year. She learned at an early age to peel the tape off of the presents without leaving a mark."

I smiled smugly. "I have skills. I keep telling you all."

I could tell Max was wondering about me, and why he had just admitted he loved me. He loved me. This was a time for a celebration. I gave each of us a slice of warmed strudel and sat back down. "So, what are you all up to? I already know about the judge's disgruntled fired nephew."

As all three men stared in my direction, I took a bite. "What?"

"How did you know that?" Max held the phone away from my prying eyes. "Wait, you were talking to Carolyn while you two were getting your non-existent copy."

"What copy?" My father asked.

"There was no copy, Dad."

He looked to Max for clarification. "Judge, it was just a ploy to talk about me."

"No, it was a ploy to talk ... forget it. So what about this nephew and the corrupt judge?"

"The judge was on the take. That's part of the reason why I really came here, to root out a few problems. His nephew was in on it, and I believe there's still a mole either on the staff or in the administration. Gio has checked with a lot of his old cronies, and they believe the goons that took shots at us worked for the judge, not the senator."

"That's a different turn of events. So, I want to go back to something. Your mother was wrong about your job here? Can we call and tell her? Can I call her?" I clapped with enthusiasm. Between the sugar from the strudel and the conclusion that Olivia Shaw was wrong about her very own son, I was on cloud nine.

Max continued to read his screen. "Simmer down, Charlie." He smiled as he glanced at me.

"You took that garbage off of her, and now you just called me Charlie. I'm not sure I trust you."

"You shouldn't." Max's eyes darkened. His side glance sent a twinge of dread and a strange sense of excitement throughout my body.

My father pushed his empty plate to the side of the table. "Max was in JAG, and he's an astute investigator. He shut down a smuggling ring, gambling, and drug operations while he was in the Navy."

Max looked at me through lash-veiled eyes. He seemed embarrassed by my father's praise. Again, the man surprised me. I touched Max's hand softly. "Have they found anything on the security cameras from the restaurants or bars when Sean was shot? Did they find anything to help nail the shooter?"

"The police and Paddy have continued to canvas the businesses. It's amazing how NASA can get such clear photos, and when we need a shot of a sidewalk there's nothing. One restaurant's CCTV caught a glimpse of the car stopping." Max gave Dad his phone back. "Your brother said the film isn't clear, but it appears that Sean is called over to a car, a car that he waved toward before he began to move closer. He came within five feet, and that's when the shooting began. There was no passenger so the driver was the shooter. They've attempted to enlarge the plate, but have been unsuccessful. It was probably an out of state vehicle."

I shook my head. "Or someone who knew where the cameras were, and the best place to take Sean down." My statement lingered in the silence. "I've been thinking. Tom, Sean, and I have never been settled with Conor's murder. I know Paddy has never stopped investigating, and, sorry Dad, but we've been asking questions and listening to information. I even collected interview statements from people who were there."

"When were you three going to tell me about this?" My father used his judgmental tone. He wasn't pleased.

"When we had something. Besides, Mom said to never tell you." I stopped and looked around at all three of them. "You all know I talk to her so why ignore it?"

"This may be silly, but have you ever asked Conor?" It was a strange question coming from Max, but one that made complete sense.

"I've tried, but he won't talk about it. He ignores his murder. I don't know why they can't talk about their deaths, but they don't. Perhaps it is easier for them to let go of us, than for us to let go of them?"

More silence followed. "Max, despite your father's revelation about Conor, I know you aren't telling me everything." When Max didn't answer and avoided my eyes, I had my answer. He wasn't that hard to read when he was vulnerable, at least for me. "Max?"

"This is an exhaustive investigation all around. Limiting our work to as few people as possible really slows us down."

He placed his arm casually over the back of my chair.

"And that means you are only telling me the basics, right?"

Before he could answer, Dad rescued him. "My dear daughter, I want all of your notes about Conor's murder." Dad's eyes were steel cold. "There may be something in there that can direct us."

"Dad, let me combine them first. We have witness statements from inside and outside of the bar. A couple of people were even able to give us exact times because they'd been dropped off by a rideshare service. Sean checked with the companies to confirm the times."

"It seems like you three did an intensive investigation." Max was interested in what we had accomplished; Dad was worried.

"We did. We hit wall after wall, and got on with our lives. But anytime we have an opportunity to speak with one of Conor's friends, we gain minute pieces of information. Tom always said one day we'd put the entire picture together."

Gio nodded. "You will. I know from personal experience that you can't hide forever."

Max crooked his head. "Exactly. We pull whoever this is out of his hole. Charlotte, compile your timelines, and see if there's any overlapping or inconsistencies just like you want to do. Gio and you sir, go over the information on those thugs who targeted Charlotte and me. Do we really think a federal judge would hire them? He or she would obviously have access to criminals. Maybe someone might owe the judge a favor over a reduced sentence? Maybe there's a larger circle of suspects? If this wasn't a Kansas City job, then where did these guys come from, and who paid for the hit?"

Dad and Gio nodded. I had one final question. "What about Sean?"

"What do you think, Charlotte?"

"I think we compile, construct, and create chaos. We wait, and then we announce that Sean is awake and talking."

Max nodded and smiled at me. "And we wait for someone to come out into the light."

Chapter Sixteen

Sean's Rehabilitation Facility

"It's very slow, isn't it?" With everything swirling around them, Max decided he would visit Judge O'Donohue. The man spent most of his days at the facility watching for any progress from his son.

From outside of the room, they watched through the glass as Sean's therapist worked his legs. Sean's eyes focused on the woman.

"Terribly slow. I lie to my kids. I keep them away. This is agony. I know they don't believe the garbage we've been telling them. Jane is planning a revolt. I just know it. Don't ever get on her bad side." Judge O'Donohue fixated on the bag in Max's hands. "What did you bring?"

"It's cold outside today so I brought you a reuben sandwich from Browne's."

"Now, I just need a good Irish whiskey."

One of the facilitators walked by the visitor's dining area and waved. The judge's fake smile remained planted on his face until she passed.

"If this isn't over soon, we'll tell the truth. Judge, you can't go on like this."

"I appreciate your concern, Max, but there's a lot at stake. I've lost one son, one may be like this forever, and my daughter could be in danger. I can and will go on as long as is required."

"Just like you did when your wife died? Tom told me all about it. You didn't sleep for weeks. You lost yourself completely, and then when she was gone you threw yourself into your work. We're all worried about you. I don't know what Charlotte would do if she lost you."

The judge was enjoying the first food he'd eaten for the day. Charlotte hadn't realized yet he wasn't eating. But it seemed she wasn't either. "Charlotte. How are you two?"

"Good, I think. We've both been very busy."

"That's not exactly what I meant. After the declarations of love, and what I walked in on, what now?"

"A little more time. We need a few things settled. Correction, I have a few things to settle. I won't have her thinking there's a curse, or that she's responsible if something would happen to me."

"Are you going to make an honest woman out of my little girl? I'll be very blunt. I have this fear that you don't really know what love entails. It's not just physical, and that seems to be the way you operated with other women in the past." The judge barely got the words out of his mouth before laughing. "I'm the father. I have to say things like that."

"I know, and you are always very direct with me. It does seem I have a problem showing love in other ways, but we don't have that much time alone. She and I need to talk, but not right now."

"After it's all over, will the attorney general place you somewhere else for another special assignment or a position in another city?"

"I've requested to stay here." Max finished half of his sandwich.

"That may kill your career, Max. Can you live like that?"

"I can. I have this feeling your daughter is going to give me a good run for my money." Max chuckled. "My money. She still won't order the most expensive thing on the menu even though she wants it."

"That's the Irish in her. I won't say we're cheap, but it's hard for us to spend. We work too hard to make it."

"Will she tolerate it, you know, the lifestyle?"

"Oh, she might get used to it, but she'll still look at the price tag. You'll have to convince her to purchase the steak at the grocery when chicken is cheaper."

Max nodded. "She's authentically herself."

"She has the spirit of her mother in her."

"I wonder what those spirits think of the storm we are in?"

Judge O'Donohue wiped his tired eyes with his hands. "I like to think they are at rest and have no idea, but with what Charlotte says, they do know. I hope they send us a little assistance so my family can have peace. A strong guardian angel or maybe even St. Michael himself would help the cause."

"Ah, Michael, I remember when he and I fought all those centuries ago," Max said, hoping his joke would lighten the judge's heavy heart.

"Maybe you are the angel we need?" With that the strong respected man of law broke down. His shoulders shook as he cried, and Max Shaw held him in his arms. Surprisingly, his emotions got the better of him as his own tears traced lines down his cheeks. The man he held was the most admired person he had ever known except for his father. He was part of the reason why he'd returned to this city. He wanted to be near him, to soak up the knowledge of law they both loved.

Now, he had fallen in love with this man's daughter. There was the possibility that they would be tied together for the rest of their lives if Charlotte and he did marry. Max Shaw had never thought of marrying any woman until now. He was even negotiating how many children they would have. He'd be a part of the family that always made him feel welcome and loved. Others might kill for that.

Max's mind began to race. The O'Donohues were well known in the city and very well respected. He knew that his money drew the outsiders to him over the years. They wanted a piece of that fame, or even a few thousand dollars of it. But there could be others who would do anything to just be near the judge, the gregarious and charming Conor, and the youngest single female of the family. It could be that simple. If it was, then it was way past time to put this behind them.

His corrupt judge theory would play out, and it would be tried in the public and in court. When Max's mission was presented by the president, he thought it would be cut and dry. They had suspected it might involve a corrupt judge, perhaps a state senator. Unexpectedly, the Martins' real estate scheme and the death of Max's friend involved a United States senator, possibly his biological father. People would eventually go to jail, and Max could continue to do his job unfettered by those who had placed a target on his back. All of this seemed so personal ... family, a friend?

Max could live with sentencing for the criminals when he could finally see who the bad guys were. For the family he loved, a betrayal of the worst kind needed to be placed to rest. The two men pulled apart slowly, both wiping their tear-stained faces.

"Judge, I need to call Paddy," Max announced as he stood, looking for the nearest trash receptacle.

Judge O looked up over his eyeglasses. "Really? You and he are best buddies, now?"

Max's smile was meant to be beguiling and to throw the man he respected off the track that he had a hunch. Instead, he figured the judge would know something was up. "I wouldn't say that, but Paddy is willing to do the devil's bidding if necessary. I'll call you later. Try to get some rest. And–"

"Don't tell Charlotte," the judge answered quickly. "That seems to be your mantra, Max. I don't like it."

Max shrugged. "I don't either, but that's the way it needs to be for now. I have to protect her from her own lovely self."

Chapter Seventeen

"Phoebe, go home. I'll be here for about another hour." I was intent on finishing my work on our investigation. I had cross-referenced statements and timelines, and I just had one more page to finish. I already noticed a discrepancy from one girl who dated Conor. She said she saw my brother walk outside of the bar after he'd received a text message. The police report had no such statement.

"Are you sure? It's dark already. We should leave together."

"It's dark because of daylight savings time, and it sucks every year when it becomes pitch black by six. Just wait until December when the sun is setting before five. I will leave my office door open." Hopefully, a nasty spirit wouldn't hold me captive.

Phoebe complained, but she was still throwing on her coat and grabbing her purse. "Promise me you'll be careful."

"I will be careful." I crossed my heart and added a cheesy smile. "Satisfied?"

"Does Max know what he's getting with you?"

"Yes, he has told me many times that I'm a snot nosed, obnoxious, little sister type. He's known me almost all of my life so he better know by now."

"You two will have fights that will be monumental."

"And we'll make up in the same fashion."

Phoebe threw her head back in laughter. "That's the spirit! Goodnight, Charlotte. Have a good weekend."

"Goodnight."

I heard the door shut, but Phoebe kept all of the lights on in the outer area. I'd lock up as soon as I finished this one sheet. Now I knew Conor had received a text message and went out into the open for some reason. Someone who had his phone number had lured him into a trap.

I turned to the police report and saw Brody's statement. They were standing at the bar when Conor went out to get air. Wait ... I looked over Conor's college friend's view of the night. He didn't mention Brody. Brody had left thirty minutes before the shooting.

No. That can't be. I frantically rifled through the papers in front of me. I called Tom quickly. "Tommy, I think the police report is wrong on Conor's murder."

"Charlotte, what are you doing?"

"Just listen to me. I've had this feeling that all of this is connected. I went back over our notes. Sean interviewed an old girlfriend of Conor's, and she said Conor received a text. He left the bar. Brody said he was standing next to him, but he actually left a half of an hour earlier. They apparently had an argument."

"You're babbling."

"No. This is a big deal. Brody was lying."

Tom had to go. His client had just walked into the office. I texted Paddy and recounted my findings. I then called him and had to leave a message. I finally called Max and left a voice message. Where the heck was everyone on a Friday night in November?

"Charlotte, danger, family."

Instead of hearing my elusive office ghost, I heard another friendly one. "Momma," I said out loud. "Am I right? Can you tell me?"

"Charlotte, get out."

I'd never received a direct warning like that. Sure, they'd yell at me to wake up in the morning, but this was different. I threw all of the papers into my bag, grabbed my purse, and messaged Max one more time. I told him I was headed for his house. Now that I had my own key and the security code, I felt safer there than anywhere else. The Taylor House had become a fortress with its high-tech alarms and cameras, and I had my own security system with Rose always guiding me.

"And now you know the man who is lying." My unnamed spirit added one more element of fear into my heart.

I rushed out of the office, locking it behind me. I ran into the night and entered my car safely. There was a soft rain beginning to fall. I only hoped the roads were still too warm to prevent the droplets from turning into ice. I called Max again.

"Max, I'm heading to your house. I think I know who killed

Conor. It was Brody. At the very least, he knows something because he lied to the police. He lied to everyone, Max. Max, where are you?"

Chapter Eighteen

Mulroney's Irish Pub, Midtown Kansas City

"Paddy, how did you find out about this?"

Paddy looked across at Max Shaw. He would never have thought that he would have an ally in the little rich kid or that he would work with him on a federal investigation. What had Charlotte called him? Oh yeah, *Poop Head*. "When all of this went down with Sean, I had a patrol car go by the house now and then and even head over to Charlotte's office. Almost three days a week, the same car was sitting down the block, and it wasn't one of your dad's FBI undercover vehicles."

Max listened to Paddy's loud voice over the bar noise. The pub was already packed on an early Friday evening. "We're looking at Brody, aren't we?"

Paddy wasn't surprised that Max knew the answer. "Yes. The car was registered to him. He even followed Charlotte from her office to your house one night. The patrol contacted me about it, but Brody must've seen them, and he pulled away."

"Damn. It is Brody. I figured it was someone close." Max remembered what Charlotte had said. He always wanted to be near them, to be part of the family, to be one of them. He glanced at his phone and saw the text and messages from Charlotte. "It's Charlotte, and she's heading to my house. We need to go, Paddy."

Paddy grabbed his phone and saw his sister's text. "Jesus, Max. We need to get to Charlotte." Max threw two twenty-dollar bills on the table as they rushed out.

When Charlotte entered the house, she called out for Gio and even Bobby Mack. No one answered. She locked the door behind her and began to turn on every light in the place. She was shaking not just from the weather, but from her realization and the ominous warnings from beyond. But why? Why did Brody kill his friend? And, if her suspicions were correct, Brody also shot Sean to keep him quiet.

Charlotte unzipped her tall boots and kicked them off in the hallway, hanging her coat inside the closet. She moved her bag with the papers and her laptop onto the small desk in the sitting room. Noticing the lights of a car pulling into the driveway, she figured Max had received her messages. She headed to the door to welcome him home with open arms and to receive a much-needed supportive hug.

As Charlotte unlocked the door, she heard Rose's voice. *"Charlotte, no, danger."*

Frantic, the usually in control woman attempted to turn the lock back, but it was too late. Someone shoved hard on the door, sending her flying into a lampstand.

"I'm home, Charlotte." But it wasn't Max. Brody stood before her, wet and smiling.

"Charlotte, run."

With Rose's direction, Charlotte ran. She fled through the dining room and up the old servants' back stairs Max had retained. She heard him coming. He was whistling like he didn't have a care in the world. The stairs led her just north of Max's bedroom and past the old dumb waiter. She knew he had a direct emergency line to the police next to his bed. She could lock the doors of the bedroom, call, and then lock the bathroom doors as a barricade.

"Why didn't I grab the gun in the fireplace?" Charlotte whispered, but Brody would've blocked her, and Rose had told her to run. As she neared the bedroom doors, the intruder waited for her at the top of the stairs.

"Charlotte, why are you running from me, honey?"

"Brody, you shouldn't be here. I'm not sure Max will like it."

"Why do you always have to run to him? I don't care about Max. We don't need to worry about him."

Charlotte's fear level rose. "Have you done something to him? Is that why I can't reach him?"

"Not yet, honey. He is very slippery. I've tried. Why are you so afraid of me?"

"Because you shouldn't be here," Charlotte screamed. "You're scaring me."

"You don't need to be scared of me. We're going to be very happy together."

"Brody, you didn't do all of this for me, did you?"

"Yes and no." Brody removed a gun from his overcoat pocket. "In the beginning, I just wanted to be the judge's favorite. I wanted to be part of your family, and when I noticed that Max was interested in you, I looked at you differently. You weren't just a little sister to me."

"Brody, I'm not your sister."

"I know. But now, we can be together. I have this feeling that Sean has talked to you, hasn't he?"

Charlotte looked around for anything to throw at him. Max, the neat freak, had nothing for her to use as a weapon. There wasn't one hammer or screwdriver left in the hallway. If she could just make it inside the bedroom, she thought Max had a gun in a drawer next to his side of the bed.

"Sean can't speak, Brody."

"You can't lie to me once we're together."

Charlotte was confused. "Brody, I'm not lying. He can't speak. He can't move. They work his muscles so they don't atrophy."

"I saw the judge today at the rehab center. The judge doesn't know, but I saw Sean. He looked at me. He told you, didn't he?"

"Brody, I don't know what in the hell you are talking about. Is my father and brother okay?"

"Of course, honey. I thought about how easy it would be to suffocate Sean, but I didn't have enough time. I never did like him. He just isn't like the rest of you. He judged me; made fun of me. I couldn't hurt the judge. Your dad will have to walk you down the aisle when we get married."

"Oh no," Charlotte murmured. "Brody, you aren't thinking right. We need to get help for you. Maybe you're in over your head? We can help you. You've always been so good to Dad and to all of us."

Brody came closer. "I don't want to use this gun, but I will if you won't love me, Charlotte. I want to be in your family and to take care of you for the rest of your life."

Charlotte saw no way out. She could go back down the steps, but he could beat her down the main ones and be at the door before she could reach it. She could retreat out the back of the kitchen, but she definitely wouldn't make it. She had to try something else. "Brody, what do you want from me?"

"Love, that's all. We'll get married and be happy. Your dad is going to be so pleased that we're together."

"But what about Conor and Sean?"

Brody's smile vanished. "Conor pushed me. I told him how I felt about your family, and he said I scared him. Besides, Conor was investigating my friends. I couldn't have him doing that. Conor was too smart. Then, your worthless brother Sean went looking. He broke into my apartment, and he found photos of Conor and me from that night. I was stupid, and I took photos when he left the bar, before I had to–"

"Oh God, Brody."

Brody brushed back his own tears. "I loved Conor, but he wouldn't love me. Your Dad loved me. Then he retired, and my career was over. I understood because the judge never does anything wrong, but I was lost. I'd drop by now and then just to stay in touch, and I tried. I was good to your family, remember?"

"When Mom died you were very good to us. Brody, you need to let me go."

"Charlotte, everything would've been fine, but my boss was in trouble.

Then they replaced him and most of us were offered other positions. No one suspected I was involved so I kept doing my jobs. I knew we were all in trouble when they brought in the boy wonder. Max Shaw just needed to do his job. I had covered up my involvement. There wasn't a record that I was working for all of them. Nothing would've happened, but then Max wanted you. I couldn't let that happen. You were my future, honey."

Charlotte tried to calm down. She was facing madness. She knew how to play after years of brothers fine tuning their harassment. "Brody, dear, I'll need some wine before we can sit down and talk."

"That sounds like a good idea. A little of Max's wine before we make love is the perfect plan."

Charlotte smiled nervously as it dawned on her what he really wanted. "I know where it is. He has a wine refrigerator in the kitchen. Will you come with me?" She held out her hand.

"Of course, Charlotte."

"Charlotte."

"Charlie, where are you?"

Max and Paddy's screams filled the house. Her plan had begun to work, but now Brody's face became an unnatural shade of crimson. "They're going to mess this up. Make them shut up! They're giving me a headache."

Max appeared on the landing of the staircase. He thought he'd heard a voice tell him to look upstairs. He did as he was told and saw Charlotte and a man who held a gun on her. "Brody, is everything okay up there?"

"Shut up Max. I'm not here for you. I just want Charlotte." He swiftly grabbed her arm and brought her to the top of the stairs with him. He shoved the gun into her rib cage. "Charlotte and I need some wine. We just need to talk and then you won't be able to take her away from me."

Max motioned for Paddy to talk to the madman as he retreated to the back stairs. Paddy waved at Brody. "Hey, buddy. What's going on?"

"Paddy? What are you doing here? Where's Max?"

"He's getting the wine, remember?" Charlotte told him.

"Oh, yeah. Paddy you need to leave. A brother shouldn't be around. We haven't had our first real kiss yet. Once Max gets that wine, she and I will want to be alone. Charlotte and I have so many things to plan."

Charlotte just prayed that Paddy would keep it together. From her precarious position on the second floor, she could see his furrowed brows and the color rising in his cheeks. "Paddy, do what he says, please."

"We have to sit down with the family and plan the wedding first, buddy. Dad won't like it if Charlotte fools around before marriage. Besides, Jane will want to stick her nose in–"

Brody's rage built. "She already did it with Max!" His screams made Paddy close his eyes briefly.

"Really? So it's true. We'll have to do something about him. Brody, I hate that little shit. I'd much rather have you as my brother-in-law than him. I wonder where he is with that wine? Max can't seem to do anything right."

Charlotte barely saw Max in her peripheral vision. She didn't want to draw attention to him. She looked away down the south hallway and saw Rose's awful husband. "Oh no, not you."

"Not who, honey?" As though a switch had been tripped, Brody was calm again.

"No one. Brody, I know some awful men, but you're different. I'm so happy you came for me. You're much better than any Taylor or Shaw man."

Paddy was watching her as though she'd lost her ever loving mind.

"The lady who used to live here years ago, Rose, had an awful husband."

"Charlotte, careful." Rose's voice was soft, and Charlotte could barely hear her.

"Her husband was an absolute ass of a man. I would never want a man like that."

The apparition closed in on Brody and Charlotte. He scowled with clenched fists.

"You play with fire," the spirit warned Charlotte.

"Do your worst."

"Charlotte, what are you doing?" Paddy yelled.

"Just go ahead you evil ass of a man."

Brody jerked hard on her arm. "You can't call me that. You love me."

"No one could possibly love you. Rose never did, did she? She had to go and find affection with a criminal. A dirty, filthy–"

The spirit created enough energy to wobble Brody. Charlotte assisted in the endeavor with a push to Brody's side but began to lose her balance. Max swooped in and pulled her away until they both toppled onto the hallway's floor. Max felt the cold stream of air flow over their bodies, and he thought he heard the anguished moan of a man in pain. Brody was pushed one more time and began to topple down the stairs. His gun went flying as Paddy stopped his body and pulled him up, slamming him against the wall.

Max ran down the steps to stop the overbearing big brother as Paddy's hands pummeled Brody's body. Max grabbed Paddy's left arm. "Stop. You'll kill him. We need him alive, and we don't need you in jail, Detective O'Donohue." Brody's unconscious body dropped onto the landing.

Paddy came to his senses. "Charlotte? Where's my baby sister?"

"She's upstairs, and she's fine except for a few scrapes. The police are here, and I need to meet them. You take care of Charlotte. She needs you."

Paddy sprinted up to the second floor and found his sister sitting on the king-sized bed. She had a towel on her arm and was wiping away tears from her cheeks. Her big brother sat next to her and lifted the covering to see a bleeding arm. "Brody is lucky the boy wonder stopped me. Does Max have a medicine cabinet in this place?"

"In the bathroom, in the far cabinet over my sink."

Paddy walked into the room after peeking into the massive closets. "Jesus, Charlotte. I could live in just one of the closets or even the bathroom. What do you mean your sink? Forget it. Wow, it echoes in here." He opened the cabinet. "Found it."

He placed the antiseptic tenderly on her wounds. "We'll have this looked at. I'm sure the boy wonder called for paramedics too."

Charlotte dropped her head onto her brother's shoulder. His arm protectively wound around her like a cocoon. "What was all that stuff you were saying, Charlie?"

"I was provoking the ghost. It's Max's grandfather, and he's the most dangerous spirit I've ever talked to."

"Honey, you might have a concussion because none of this stuff you're saying is making sense, but it worked out anyway." Paddy continued to rub his little sister's back. "We'll have your noggin checked."

Charlotte only nodded. Trying to teach her brother about the other side of life at this point wouldn't prove fruitful. He would suspect she was out of her mind. She continued to shake, but in Paddy's arms she was safe. Her brother had her. That's what they did as a family, they had each other. "So, do you really like the rich kid?"

Charlotte nodded again.

"I have to hand it to him. He's got a great place here. He must be spending a fortune on the renovation." Paddy held his sister tighter if that was possible, but he took a good look at the bedroom in front of him. Everything was absolutely perfect. "Don't ever bring my wife up here or she'll want me to get two part time jobs to make improvements on our house. Oh, and I want you to be my Secret Santa from now on if you marry the jerk. We should raise our gift limit to, well, I'll need a car that first Christmas." He felt the punch in his ribs and smiled. His baby sister was going to be okay. "Fine, maybe not a car. What about one of those refrigerators that controls the entire house? I hear you can program it to the perfect temperature for lagers." He laughed as a second punch hit. Yes, Charlotte was going to be just fine.

Chapter Nineteen

Couldn't anyone target my family during the day? Dad, Paddy, Linda, Jane, Brad, Tom, and Meg ran toward the danger and remained to look after me while forensics and a horde of police did their jobs. After Gio arrived, I lost the sisters-in-laws and Jane to a tour of the great house. Bobby Mack had driven him and stayed to review the security system to make sure the police didn't dismantle any of his secret features. Max, Paddy, and I were questioned. Dad served as my legal advisor.

Paddy and Max conducted a walk through for the detectives called to the case. The FBI and two U.S. marshals were on-site as well, adding their two or three cents to the mix. Eventually, Dad and I were left alone in the sitting room. He sat in one chair, and I collapsed in the other. As the best dad ever, he brought my slippers and a bag packed with a few items just in case.

He looked over at me while investigators paraded through the house. "I didn't know what to expect when I got here. I didn't know if he had hurt you, or–" My father stopped short of saying anymore. He brushed away the tears. "I feel so responsible."

I rested my head on the side of the highback chair. "You aren't. You had no idea Brody would be involved in some sort of corruption scheme, or that he would become obsessed with our family. You can't blame yourself for anything. You've been looking for solutions to all of this, not adding to the problem."

"But I brought him in."

"And he was a great guy for a long time, but he cracked. Dad, he didn't know what he was saying tonight. He was muttering something about a boss he has. He wasn't the Brody you admired."

Dad noticed Paddy and Max huddled with the detective in charge and an FBI agent. "It's nice to see the two of them working together?"

I chuckled. "I suppose, until the next time they get into a disagreement. Their relationship seems to be a lot like Sean and Conor. Remember?"

"Oh, I do. Before you were born, and when they were little, your mother called me in tears almost every day. Sean and Conor were wrestling. Sean broke Conor's nose when he punched him. Conor told Sean he could fly. Stuff like that."

I was too tired to laugh too hard, but I smiled. "Conor told him he could fly?"

"Yes. Conor had the blarney in him even at a young age, and Sean hasn't always been the brightest crayon in the box."

"Poor Mom."

"Indeed."

"Charlotte." I stopped talking. Rose was in the room. I noticed Max look up and smile at me as if he knew she was in contact.

"Dad, Rose is here."

Instead of acting shocked or upset, my father responded. "Thank you, Rose, for trying to protect my little girl."

"Welcome, family."

"I understand, Rose," I said out loud. "I made him mad upstairs, and he helped."

"I know. Charlotte, Max, yours."

I nodded. "Rose, is there still danger?"

There was a brief silence before the answer could be heard. *"Danger, always. Be careful. Love Max."*

I said nothing. My father knew something was wrong. "What did she say?"

"Nothing."

He shook his head in dismay. "You are such an awful liar."

"I've been told that before." My eyes searched the hallway, and eventually I saw Max thank the remaining officials. He closed the door soundly, resting against it briefly as though he wanted to shut the world out. I watched from my chair as the lights from all of the cars, vans, and assorted news trucks pulled away into the late evening hours. Max seemed to be inventorying each room to make sure no one was left behind.

He looked like a wreck as he walked over to me and kissed me on the head. "News at five, six, seven, eight, nine, ten, noon, four, five, six, ten ... How is the arm?"

I reached up for him with my good hand. "The paramedics said I should live."

"I'll have a doctor look at it."

I patted Max's arm. "I'm fine. I don't need a doctor. Relax."

Paddy rolled his eyes as he leaned over the back of Dad's chair. "Well, that was something. Max, in a crisis you are proving to be quite helpful."

"Thanks, Paddy. I'm glad I could be here for you," Max answered sarcastically. His eyes found mine. "This is going to be one big mess. They'll book Brody, and of course he'll be evaluated. I'm pretty sure he won't be able to stand trial due to mental incompetency. At least, that's what I would recommend if I were representing him."

Dad nodded. "I would do the same."

Paddy stood up. "Are you two kidding me? That guy might be one brick short of a load, but he should stand trial. He tried to hurt Charlie, he murdered Conor, and likely shot Sean. I don't understand any of this."

"Paddy, he's sick." I didn't want Brody to suffer. I wanted him to be put away for a very long time. If he never got better, then he could remain incarcerated.

"He was playing us. You all and your bleeding hearts need a good dose of reality."

Max's mother had said the same about her own son. My mind raced with Brody's words. Maybe Paddy was right. I looked up at Max. "Paddy might be right. At one point, Brody said he was working for his boss. The man you replaced was somehow a key to some of this. There's more to it than his obsession."

Paddy pointed at me and agreed. "Listen to her, Max. I know when someone is acting, and Brody is. Think about it. He acted like he was friends with Conor. He acted like he would do everything for Dad and our family. He acted like he wanted Charlie, but only after you had, well–"

"Let's say when we got together, Paddy." I settled his problem.

"We have a corrupt judge, a corrupt federal prosecutor working with the judge, Brody with a boss, and maybe a mole still in my office as a holdover from the previous staff. We have no idea who the boss or the mole is." Max sat down on the floor at the foot of my chair. "We are almost back to square one."

Paddy looked like he wanted to punch Max again. "You are telling me that the threat isn't over?"

"Exactly."

"And one more thing." All three men looked at me. "Brody saw Sean today at the facility, and he said Sean could talk, and he looked at him. Dad, he said he saw you." There was no point in sharing Brody's inclination to kill my brother or maybe even my father.

Dad seemed confused. "He didn't visit with me. If he was

there, how did he get back to Sean? Did Sean really see him or talk to him?"

Max shook his head. "We'll wait until morning to find out about that. Surely, if Sean could talk, the facility would've called someone."

Yes, they would've. Dad checked his phone and there were no calls. "I'll call in a minute and check in with the facility just in case."

I heard the group in the kitchen. Jane was commenting on the pot faucet over the stove. We did think alike. I smelled coffee. "So, now what?"

Paddy threw his hands up. "I have no idea. This is nuts."

Gio arrived just in time. "The ladies and I are making pancakes, sausage, eggs, and bacon for dinner. Would you four like to join us?"

Paddy headed for the kitchen with Dad, leaving Max and I alone for the first time the entire evening. He still sat at my feet. "You and Paddy, huh? I understand him helping you with your corruption investigation, but this buddy thing? When did that happen?"

"After our differences were settled, he and I began to meet to go over the little details that someone might have overlooked. You gave me the idea the other night. Paddy and I have been discussing all along the investigation that brought me here. You now know most of it. You, Tom, and Sean took all of those notes, and that's how you figured out Brody lied to the police. You are very good at this. Have you considered criminal law, maybe beginning as an investigator for a certain prosecutor?"

I roughed up his hair and stood up slowly, my good hand extending down to him. "Let me just make it past tomorrow before I change careers again, will you?"

As he stood, he pulled me into his arms. "I'm going to only say this once. Don't you ever make me that afraid again."

"I can't promise that. You might be scared when I drive home alone. You can't live like that."

"But I will." He kissed me desperately. "I don't want to lose you. I know that now more than ever."

"Max," I whispered against his cheek.

"Yes?"

"I'm starving, and I really need coffee. You know us girls with hips need to eat to keep our shape."

He released me and turned me around, patting my bottom softly. "Let's get you fed because I like this shape very much. I have plans for its future."

Chapter Twenty

Thankfully, it was Saturday. No one needed to go to work, not even Paddy and Max. It would've been the perfect November day to sleep in, but none of us would after all of the coffee we consumed. Sometime in the wee hours of the morning, Max pulled out the whiskey. At one point, Paddy had his arm around Max, suggesting that the boy wonder could adopt him. I wasn't sure what all of that was about, but I believed my brother had finally embraced Max as one of us figuratively and physically at least for the time being. At the very least, he had embraced Max's money. I would need to remind him that Max and I weren't a done deal.

The oldest married couples left first. They had children to check on. After revealing to the family that they could finally see Sean now that the threat was supposedly gone, Tom and Meg said they would visit him in the afternoon. Gio and Bobby Mack surveyed their new digs which were almost completed. Dad, Max, and I began to clean up in the kitchen.

"I want to see Sean as soon as I can this morning, just in case Brody was lucid. The facility said he was sleeping peacefully, but if Sean really did talk to him–"

"Don't get your hopes up, Judge," Max said as he filled the dishwasher.

"I know, but I want to see with my own eyes."

I understood. I wanted to see Sean too. We needed to tell him we knew, at least we thought we knew. Brody had specifically said that Sean had broken into his home and found his photos. What other secrets could he have had? "Max, I didn't mention this to the police because I didn't know if it was true, but Brody said Sean found photos in his home. Maybe there's something to that? Maybe that's why Sean wanted to speak to you the night he was shot?"

"Photos? Where would Sean have those?"

Dad answered before I could. "In his apartment. I've gone over there several times, but since the boy doesn't even have a plant to water, I didn't stay long, and I sure didn't pry into his computer or his desk. His lease is coming due soon. We may need to pack it all up—"

I grabbed Dad's arm. "Then we will." When I glanced over at Max I could tell he was thinking about the information Sean might have stored that could help us. I was thinking the same thing.

"We need to check out his apartment." Max pulled his car keys out of his pocket. "Gio," he called out. "We're going to Sean's place. You and Bobby lock up."

I scurried past Max and Dad on my way through the sitting room. I ran into the men as they were leaving the suite. "Gio, I need to speak with you right now." I pulled him over into the corner of Rose's room by my little desk. "Rose's husband pushed Brody down those stairs. I provoked him, and he came after me, but Max pulled me back. Brody wasn't so lucky."

"That man comes around when times are bad. He's scary. Charlotte, you need to tell Max that you're not safe here. That's the second time he's tried to hurt you, right?"

"Yes, I suppose. I've never run into a spirit so angry, so malevolent."

Gio looked up at Rose's portrait. "That man was the same way when he was alive. He's stuck in his own hell. I've often wondered why he would want to remain here."

"To never leave Rose in peace." The words fell quickly from my mouth as though they weren't my own. "Gio, we need to get rid of him."

"Are you thinking of an exorcism?"

I wasn't sure. "I don't know. I think eventually you and I should talk to him. Are you up for it?"

"Charlotte, to make you safe, I'll do anything."

I hugged the little mobster and kissed him twice to make him blush. Now, it was off to Sean's apartment.

When we arrived, Max noted that the lock had marks on it. "I bet Brody has been here."

He was right. The apartment had been completely ransacked. The television was on the floor as was any piece of paper or magazine that Sean kept. "Here's his stack of comic books." I showed Dad one of them.

Max headed to the bedroom. It looked like a war zone. "Where would Sean hide his computer?"

I left Dad alone in the small living room. "Have you tried in between the mattresses?"

Max pulled up the top mattress, and I looked under. "Nope. Hopefully, Brody didn't grab the thing."

"He would've been smug if he had. He wouldn't have attacked. He would have destroyed the thing and no one would have been the wiser, especially if Sean had ..."

Max couldn't say it. "If he had died. I'll say it for you. What about the bathroom?"

"Too much water for a laptop, honey."

"You two! I found it," Dad yelled. "It was hidden in the stove. Obviously, Sean never cooked."

"Of course," Max and I said together.

Dad handed the laptop to Max, and he turned it on. "Do either one of you know his password?"

Dad frowned. "Try one, two, three, four."

"Oh come on. Sean is crazy, but he's not dense. He's a cop for heaven's sake."

Dad and I shrugged. Max did as he was told and was immediately granted access. "Seriously?"

"That's my boy."

Max and I reviewed files and came across one marked with the number five. That was Conor's placement in the family. As it opened, we saw nothing. "Maybe Brody did find it and wiped it clean?" Max scanned for more files, but found nothing that was useful. "He has two cartoons on here and recipes. Recipes?"

Sean really didn't know the difference between a spatula and a rake, and Dad was right. Sean's oven was immaculate and seemed to never have been used. I hit on the file, and instead of recipes, there were numbers. "They're dates and numbers."

"They're dates and amounts of money, Charlotte. Judge, look at this."

We reviewed five pages of Sean's research. "Max, hit the cartoons."

At my suggestion, Max played what should've been two series of the famous moose and squirrel adventures. Instead, there were two videos and over one hundred photos. "He's stored them on the cloud too." I closed the laptop in front of Max's face. "I'm taking this with me, and I'm not going to let it out of my sight until we have time to look over every piece of evidence."

Max's disapproving scowl didn't phase me. "What? Don't look at me that way. You have no search warrant. You're not involved in a local shooting of a police officer. We need to distance you from whatever is on this computer. You need plausible deniability, Max."

"Damn, you're beginning to sound like me." Max looked toward my father to plead his case, but Dad waved him off.

"She's right, Max. You know it. I'm Sean's Dad, and Charlotte is his sister. We are supposed to be here, not the friendly federal prosecutor. Charlotte will look at it. She'll show it to me, and I promise we will bring you in when we can."

"Sean could have evidence in my corruption investigations."

"You can argue all you want. Could is not a good argument, counselor." I smiled, but it would've been more effective to stick my tongue out at him. I held the laptop close. "Let's go see Sean and stop arguing."

Max complained to Dad. My wonderful father pointed me at me and warned him. "Look, this is the real Charlotte. She's a bossy one. Do you think you can handle her, Mr. Shaw?"

Max was a bright man. Wisely, he didn't answer, but instead followed me as we left the apartment and headed to the facility. I sat in the back seat of the car remembering as much of Brody's ravings as I could. I tapped on the laptop wondering what Sean had found and why. In the apartment, I thought I saw a few photos of familiar faces. That's when I had stopped Max.

Conor and I figured out a long time ago Sean wasn't as idiotic as he pretended. With his photographic mind, Sean had never studied for one test in school. Tom suffered through hours of worrying while Sean just read his comics. Yes, he was a goofball, but there was the police side of him that was pragmatic and unrelenting. I was proud of the information Tom, Sean, and I had compiled on Conor's murder. All of our work had paid off, but now it was time to really help a brother out. My brother discovered more than just Conor's murderer. He'd possibly uncovered a crime that literally almost cost him his life.

I brushed away a tear. None of us really discussed that Sean might not ever be able to talk or walk. He might not ever have a goofy family that dressed in the same ugly Christmas sweaters. He might not be home for Thanksgiving in just a couple of weeks, or sleeping over on Christmas Eve. Alone, in the backseat of Max's car, I realized my brother could be gone forever even if his body still lived on this earth.

Max caught sight of me in his rearview mirror. We exchanged glances, and I could see his concern. Every time we were stopped at a traffic signal, he looked back. Luckily, Dad was oblivious, praying the rosary gripped in his hands as if it was his only lifeline. He was hopeful that Sean would yell a hello when he entered the room.

Sean's facilitator met us before we entered his private room. She updated us on his condition confirming that Sean's ability to focus was improving. No, he had not spoken, but he had attempted to pinch a therapist's butt. That's our Sean!

All three of us, and the laptop were allowed to visit. He was awake, but still remained on a feeding tube and needed oxygen occasionally. He attempted to smile and then saw the laptop in my hands. One finger pointed at it as he began to become agitated. "Mmmm ..."

"Max? Are you trying to say Max?"

Sean nodded slowly. He shut his eyes. I could only imagine how much effort it took to attempt to speak. I leaned in and kissed his forehead. "Sean, was Brody here? Do you remember?"

My brother nodded again. He pointed frantically at the laptop. "Sean, we know. Brody killed Conor."

Sean nodded once more, but kept pointing at the laptop. "Mmmmaaxx."

Max and Dad wanted to ask dozens of questions, but I warned them. "Let's take this one step at a time." I directed my attention back to Sean. "I'm going to look at the stuff on your computer. We found the numbers and the money amounts, and we figured out that the cartoon videos are where you hid the videos and the photos. You have everything in the cloud, don't you?"

He nodded affirmatively and grabbed my hand. "Bad."

Dad was delighted with his son's progress. I was worried we were pushing him too much. "Sean, just rest. Let me look at all of this."

He became upset, clutching at my hand desperately. He kept looking in Max's direction, pleading. Max came closer on the other side of the bed. "Sean, let us do this for you. You've done a great job."

Sean's eyes darted from me to the man I loved. "Max. Danger."

Again, I heard those bone chilling words. The threat was real, and it still remained. Dad pushed Max back and addressed Sean. "Son, calm down. We understand that Max is in danger. He has security. Brody is in custody. I know there's more. I can see it in your face. Let us review the information. We will find it because you did a great job of figuring it all out. I'm so proud of you. I love you, Seany."

One small tear passed from my brother's left eye as he took Dad's hand in his. Poor Sean was trapped in his own body. "And Sean, as soon as you can, you'll be able to type or write out what you're so upset about. Or, you'll be talking." He pursed his lips tightly in frustration and then relaxed in surrender. My sibling nodded affirmatively, but his eyes held his doubts.

Dad held my gaze. "Charlotte, why don't you and Max get some rest. I'm going to stay here today. Maybe someone could check in on us later?"

"Judge, we'll leave and grab you something to eat. Sean, we will see you in a bit, and I promise you, I'll be careful." Max's compassion showed me once more who he really was. Mom said I'd meet a man who left me breathless, who would carry me when I couldn't go another step. I had met a man who did that, but also loved my family as his.

I kissed Sean again, struggling not to cry. I blew a kiss to Dad and left with Max. He was quiet as we drove to one of Dad's favorite hamburger joints in the suburbs. He left me in the car as he ran in. In a few minutes he reentered the car with two greasy brown bags. "I got us food too. It's not the healthiest, but right now we need all the energy we can get."

Yawning, I nodded. "I need more coffee." I watched Max blow on his hands as he started the car. It was getting colder. We might have snow before Thanksgiving.

"I'll drive through. There's a coffee place down the block from the rehab center. Charlotte, we need to look at that information together."

"No, we don't. Sean thinks this is big, and this information may be dangerous for you. You will remain impartial and away from it."

Max hit the steering wheel with his left hand. "I'm not impartial. I'm involved. This, whatever it is, involves me. I'm involved with you. See how that works?"

"Don't patronize me, Max. You sound like your mother."

"Well, maybe you need to understand what I'm talking about."

"Oh, well then. Let's just stop talking before one of us says something they can't take back."

"Don't make me get a warrant."

Max had just thrown down the gauntlet. "Do it. Try it. No one will give it to you."

"Watch me."

I knew that a great crisis could create a toxic environment. Our family usually began fighting with each other so this behavior was nothing new for me. For Max, he probably had never run into a woman like me who wouldn't back or bow down to the great Mr. Shaw. "Try it."

Max pulled the car over and placed the car in park. His hand landed on the edge of my seat. "Why are you such a spoiled brat sometimes?"

"Why are you, *Poop Head*?"

I watched as he studied my face. I bit my lip so I wouldn't show any fear. Max looked over at the interstate. He was thinking. This was like a chess match with a master. My problem was I had never taken up the game. I was more of a checkers cheater.

"Charlotte."

"Max."

A smile crossed his lips. "Damn it." He reached over and grabbed my face softly. He pulled me to him and kissed me long and hard. When he finally broke his hold we both needed a cold shower. Preferably, not together. "You can't fool me. You're biting your lip. You are trouble. You always have been." He started the car and pulled back onto the street to drive to our destination.

"I prefer to think I am determined."

"You have your Irish up. That's what your father calls it."

"I suppose." The truce had been established for now. I still held custody of Sean's laptop. Chalk one up for the rook!

We ate with Dad in the dining room, said our goodbyes

to Sean, and assured my father one of us would pick him up when he was ready. Round two of the great game began as Max walked me into Dad's house. He removed his coat and followed me into the office.

"Aren't you going home?" I placed the laptop on the desk to charge.

"Not yet."

I pointed at the door. "I'm going to make this very clear. Max, you can't be involved in this. What if Sean received some of this information illegally? We already know he snuck into Brody's place. What if this danger is setting you up to go to jail? Have you ever thought of that? Someone wants to thwart you."

"Thwart?" Max began to laugh. "Baby, where did you get that word, the Middle Ages?"

"Why? Don't you understand it?"

Max turned around on his heel to face me. "What are we doing?"

"Protecting you, you jackass. Go home. You know I'm right. Go." I directed him out the door.

Max threw up his hands, almost surrendering. "You have a devious mind if you think the leader of our nation is setting me up. He's not the president of the PTA; he's the president of our country."

I pushed his back and continued to do so until he neared the front door. "Weirder things have happened, Max."

He finally balked. "You will lock this door. You will call me immediately if—"

"Yes, darling." I stretched to kiss him.

Max embraced me. "I'm going to have so much trouble with you, aren't I?"

"Probably on most days, but I'll make it worth your while. I won't shop like your mother. I won't spend money like water, and I promise to confront every demon you have. Oh, which reminds me, we have to have an exorcism."

Max rolled his eyes. "Don't throw holy water on me again."

"You should be good for a while. It's not you."

Max leaned against the hall wall. "I knew something was off. Now, what or who?"

"Your grandfather."

"He pushed Brody and you like he did that one day, didn't he? Do you know I felt this coldness rush over me? And I think I heard Rose tell me you were upstairs."

I patted his face. "That's wonderful, honey. Now, go home to your haunted house. If you can, maybe talk to them."

Max kept shaking his head, mumbling something about crazy ghosts and a nutty girlfriend, but he did leave. I locked the door behind him and set the alarm that Nate and Bobby Mack had installed. Once I showered and changed my clothes, I headed to Dad's office and began to tear apart every file on Sean's computer.

There were files labeled vacations. The man never went

anywhere except to his nearest bar. Another file boasted it held his bucket list. Sean yearned to be a police officer since the age of five. When he figured out he could arrest his siblings, or at the very least pull them over for a non-functioning turn signal, the career was for him. I went one by one. I soon discovered that our brother, the goofball, was one smart cookie. I called Tom around five and told him he needed to come over to help me with a graph. Not only was money involved, but real estate too. There appeared to be federal court case numbers in a file with a judge's name beside each one. Two judges were listed. Max's real estate criminals could actually be a part of this entire scheme, and his corrupt judge was at its center. I'd never hear the end of this if this actually ended up being his prosecution.

Tom was a wizard with numbers. His fastidiousness bridged on a disorder of some kind. He had to have his column straight and perhaps loved chronological order more than his wife. Then he alphabetized. "Charlie, I don't know what these codes are. They are some sort of routing numbers, but I haven't seen them before."

I looked over at his list we printed out from Sean's work. "I haven't either." The security system blared that someone was entering through the front door. "That can't be Dad, can it?" But it was. I heard Max's voice too.

"Where are you two? Tom, Charlotte?"

We piled our research in the middle of the desk and tidied

up. With one of the sheets I had printed in his hand, Tom and I met them in the living room. Dad looked exhausted as he almost fell into his chair. Max didn't look much better. He began to sit down on the couch as Tom handed him the paper.

"Brainiac, have you ever seen sequences like these?"

Max took the sheet, briefly looked at it, and handed it back to Tom. "They're Swiss bank account routing numbers." Max seemed unphased. Finally, a light went on in his head, and he tore the evidence away from Tom. "They're Swiss bank accounts. Now, whose are they?"

"There're two or three different ones. Maybe the judge you're looking into is one of them?"

His eyes were veiled as he barely looked at me. "You mean I could be right about the real estate debacle?"

I turned away. "I don't want to discuss that right now."

Tom, Dad, and Max fell into laughter. Max patted the seat cushion next to him. "Charlotte, sometimes you'll be right, and sometimes I'll be right. It has to work that way."

"I'm not sure about that," I answered flippantly, but I did take the seat, cuddling up against him as his arm fell over my shoulders. For the first time in well over twenty-four hours, I relaxed, pulled my legs up on the couch and stretched as I watched Max.

"What else does your brother have on that computer?"

Tom smiled. "A million things, and not one file is actually what it seems. He's compiled a ton of information. It looks like he began this little undercover project right after Conor was killed. Charlotte and I thought we were the super sleuths. No way. He has us beat. Paddy, the real detective, isn't going to like this one bit."

"He moved his entire right hand today," Dad muttered.

All of us looked in his direction. Finally, Dad looked up and smiled. "Sean moved his right hand, not just a finger. He was able to hold a red solo cup."

"Oh great, he'll still be able to drink." Tom's joke fell on deaf ears, but our father laughed out loud.

"He even reached for a pencil, but he's having an issue with holding it. Max, he is desperate to tell you something." I could tell my father just didn't understand how important Sean's message probably was. "Do you think someone is still after you?"

"I don't know, Judge." Max looked down at the accounts and tucked me closer under his arm. "There has to be something else that Sean needs to tell me. There's other forms of danger, aren't there?"

Tom took Mom's chair and began to list them off. "Your career, your money, your house, your friends, your family–"

"Right. It keeps coming back to the overarching heading of the family," Max admitted. "They've attempted to burn down the old house. Someone has broken in. Maybe they were after my birth certificate, my real one. They've shot at us, and they selected a deranged loyal friend to muck things up instead of them doing the dirty work. There's some mighty deep pockets pulling the strings."

I agreed, but I wasn't about to tell him all of the things Tom and I had already connected. Max did need plausible deniability. He was at the center of this storm, but swirling around him was a tornado of an epic nature. From what I was seeing on Sean's laptop, no one realized what they had set in motion when they assigned Max to take down a corruption and real estate fraud group. The problem was that the president of the United States and the attorney general might not do a thing to help. And what if powerful people were setting up Max? What had he done to receive this retribution? Was it because he was a senator's illegitimate son? If they took Max down, could they take down one of the most powerful statesmen in the country? Ironically, I decided I needed to bring in even bigger guns.

Chapter Twenty-One

Lucky for me, Max was embroiled in the final stages of another trial. His second chair was in charge, but Max was behind the scenes making sure his office was working like a well-oiled machine. And he was busy watching, constantly searching for any little piece of evidence to reveal the mole. We talked on the phone and met for lunch, but I stalled him off of my brother's treasure trove of information and evidence. It took me two weeks to put together a comprehensive timeline with dates, monies transferred, and presumed activities cross referenced with the payments. I shared my findings with my father and Gio with strict instructions that Max wasn't to know anything. I'd take the fall. If he hated me, then so be it. It was worth sacrificing his love to keep him safe and to honor all of Sean's hard work.

I'd made the call early on a Tuesday, but didn't expect quite a quick response. It was ten in the morning when my cell rang. The caller's identification was restricted.

"Charlotte O'Donohue."

"Edward Shaw. How are you Charlotte?"

"I'm good. I saw you had snow."

"Yes, just in time for Thanksgiving. Here, this city shuts down with just an inch. I remember the time I drove your father down to the courthouse because the streets were so bad, and that's when Kansas City had ten inches. In our nation's capital, that amount of snow would be forewarning of the end of the world. Before we go any further, do you know you're being blamed for the fact that Max isn't going to my wife's Thanksgiving dinner? She swears you've brainwashed him."

I sighed. I knew. He told her when we had visited, but apparently, she hadn't really thought it would happen. "Yes, and I'm absolutely fine with that. I wouldn't have it any other way. Do you have plans?"

"I have invitations, but I just might order Chinese, stay home, and watch football all day. I will go really wild and not put on a tie."

Edward Shaw was even more charming than his son. "Come here. I know Dad would love to see you, and we're taking pie down to Sean. He's talking in bits and pieces, but his memory of that night fades in and out."

"It's a terrible thing to remember. Sometimes the mind does the body a favor. You know, I'll see if I can get a flight out. I'd love to do that, besides it would make Olivia furious. I always enjoy doing that to her. We could text her photos of all of us. Enough fun, your message said it was important?"

I convinced myself I was doing the right thing for Max. "Sir, Mr. Shaw—"

"Edward."

"Edward, I've discovered a significant amount of evidence that could be quite damaging to some public officials. These people are very well connected. Max doesn't know anything about this, and I haven't told him I'm contacting you."

"Very well. Why is that, Charlotte?"

"Will it sound ridiculous if I say, to save him from himself?" I waited for the director of the FBI to yell at me.

Instead, I heard a chuckle, a real chuckle. "You know my son very well. Can you email me what you have?"

"I don't trust the internet, not with this information. It is very sensitive. Come for Thanksgiving, and maybe you and I could do a little Christmas shopping alone. My brother has been working on this too, but this is all from Sean's laptop. We have assembled timelines, graphs, spreadsheets, correlations–"

"Charlotte, how bad is this?"

"Devastating to the wrong people, the end of careers for others, and Max could pay the price. He's being set up by some very powerful people. I'm not sure, but one of them may be your boss."

"My boss," Edward Shaw murmured. "Charlotte, this is coming out of the blue, but what do you love about my son?"

Considering what we had been discussing, the straight-forward question threw me. "Um, well, I love that faucet over the stove. You can fill the pan for pasta right on the spot. I love the commercial faucet on the sink, and all the renovations he's made so far to the house have been amazing. But I do like those faucets. Then there's the waterfall edge on the island, the shower, and that amazing tub–"

I heard laughter, deep and full out on the other end of the phone. "I see you're really into the plumbing fixtures, and it's none of my business."

"I'm sorry, I didn't mean to joke about it, but there's so many things. I believe he is an honorable and very generous man. He is a good man."

"I agree, and you make him an even better one. Charlotte, tell your father to place another setting at the table. I'm coming. Let's just surprise Max all around."

"I'm good at secrets, and not so good at lying. You'll have to be the one to convince him we are shopping for him, and he can't come along."

"I'll take care of it. Luckily for my profession, I'm very good at deception. I do it every time I tell a congressman to have a good day."

"Then I'll see you on Thanksgiving."

Edward Shaw was a man of his word on that Thursday. Max was mashing the potatoes when the doorbell rang. I thought Paddy would hyperventilate when he opened the door to see his idol, the current head of the FBI standing on our porch. "Max, there's someone here for you," Paddy yelled very unceremoniously.

"What is he bellowing about now? Does he ever not yell at

me?" Max wiped his hands with a towel and headed out of the kitchen. "Paddy, what are you ... Dad?"

"Surprise!"

I stood behind Max, waving. "Welcome, Mr. Shaw."

The father and son embraced, and Max held on just a little longer. "What are you doing here?"

"I wanted to spend Thanksgiving with all of you. Charlotte invited me, and I came. Where's my old friend?"

"I'm here, Edward." Dad walked out from the dining room, adorned with his *Kiss Me I'm Irish* apron. They shook hands as the director removed his overcoat and handed me a large box.

"Charlotte, I brought my favorites from a bakery in Georgetown. If the adults don't want them, I know the grandkids will."

Max grabbed the box and opened it. "No way! You brought the chocolate chip cookies? These are the best. They add brown sugar and caramel. We are not giving them to the kids."

"Okay, simmer down little Maxie," I joked as I received the box. "I'll keep a couple just for you."

Screaming came from the den at the back of the house. Paddy and Linda's oldest son arrived in the hallway. "They're crazy in there. Is there any room at the adult table for me this year?"

Dad nodded. "This year there is. Come on, help me with the turkey."

We all recognized what Dad had just realized. None of us had thought that there would be another empty spot. Mr. Shaw would fill it, but usually Sean would bring a police friend who was alone for the holiday.

"And I'd like to help too. Let me get my jacket off." Mr. Shaw followed his old friend.

Max and I went back to work in the kitchen. Gio removed another pie from the oven. "Will the head of the FBI be okay with me around?"

"He has to be," Max answered calmly. "You're family, and so is he, right?"

Max looked around at the other ladies in the kitchen. Of course, they all agreed.

Max kept watching me. "You invited him?"

"I did."

"Is there a reason why?"

"Max, maybe I just did it because I thought it would be a nice thing to do." As soon as I'd answered him, I turned away, pretending to be busy with the gravy. I could feel his suspicious eyes on me. I knew that look. Those luscious caramel eyes were veiled by dark, long lashes. And they were boring a hole in my back.

"Charlotte?"

I kept stirring. "Yes, Max."

"Is that the only reason you invited my father?"

"We're going shopping for you. And I thought it would

really piss your mother off, how's that?" Olivia Shaw was furious, we were shopping, and technically Mr. Shaw was here for his son. Jane stepped in to save me, although she didn't know I needed to be thrown a lifeline.

"Oh, for heaven's sake, Max. We're all expecting you to give Charlotte a ring later tonight. How's that?'

I don't think I've ever seen a man turn red and choke on nothing at the same time, but Max was the first. I patted his arm. "She's kidding. No one's expecting that. You're off the hook." I kissed him on the cheek and shared a laugh with everyone else in the kitchen.

"Off the hook?"

"Nevermind, Max." But there was something in his question and the way he was looking at me. Surely, he really wasn't ... No, he wouldn't. I had to tamp down any anticipation. Max Shaw would never do something impulsive like that without planning and hours of deliberation with me. Besides, he would make me sign a prenup!

Dinner was lovely. Edward's personal detail enjoyed dinner in the kitchen at my father's insistence and then took hot coffee out to the agents in positions on the street. I felt very safe. During the meal even Paddy was half human and well mannered. Gio had nothing to fear. The three oldest men at the table huddled later in Dad's office sharing the best bourbon in the house. Eventually, they closed the door to Paddy and Tom's dismay. We watched football and waited to have room for all the pies and desserts still in the kitchen.

Max's head was in my lap as we laid on the floor. He looked up and tenderly wound his finger in a few strands of my hair. "This is much nicer than my mother's party."

"You're on the floor because there's not enough room for us on the couch, and you had to fight with a teenager for the drumstick. How is that nicer?"

"You're here, and I'm wearing jeans and a sweatshirt. I'm about to fall asleep. The food was way better, and the company is the best. I know Gio's cannolis are out there, and my favorite cookies in the world will be mine in a couple more hours. And did I mention that you're here?"

"Well, aren't you the charmer?" I leaned down and kissed him quickly. "And I'm glad you're here too."

Max smiled and his eyelids fell and opened slowly. By the fourth time, they shut, and he was sound asleep. Paddy looked down at me from Dad's chair.

"Is he okay?"

I nodded. "He's just tired."

Paddy leaned over, his hands almost in a prayer-like position. "Charlie, are you two, well, will you be–"

He was so cute when he was awkward and embarrassed to ask his baby sister anything having to do with her love life. "I don't know." I smoothed an errant strand of Max's hair. "This is nice, but we have a lot to work through."

"You're okay with taking time?"

"Yes, I am. Mom used to say that sometimes the good things take time to simmer before they're perfectly delicious."

"That she did." Paddy made himself more comfortable in the chair, turning his attention to the television screen. There was no private space in this group.

The grandchildren became unruly and invaded our adult area an hour later. Max suggested a game of football, making him the best guest in the house. There had been years in the past when I was out there with them, but my mind was somewhere else.

"Charlotte, you are quiet," Meg commented as all of us ladies of the family were still watching the game on tv. "What's up?"

"I was just thinking this has been a lovely day, but it's so quiet without Sean."

Jane chuckled. "Sean is loud."

Linda agreed. "Sean was loud." She looked at all of us as we stared in her direction. "I didn't mean it that way."

We knew. "It's okay. It's true. He may never be the way he was."

Jane smirked. "You mean he may grow up just a teeny bit?"

"I just hope he's still with us next year."

His prognosis was day-by-day. He had his good days, and then way too many bad ones. It was wearing on the entire family, but Dad took the brunt of the emotional roller coaster. I wasn't sure how much longer he could live like this.

Jane moved to the couch. I was below, leaning on it. Feeling her stares, I looked up. I yawned. "What? I'm exhausted."

"That's not all, is it?" Before I could answer, Jane's eyes lit up. "Are you pregnant? Oh my gosh, you are!"

"What? No, I'm not."

"But you could be?" Jane's eyes were riveted on me. I wasn't. Was I? No, I wasn't. Max and I hadn't even been together ... I couldn't remember. I began to count.

"I can't be pregnant, Jane. Stop it." I wasn't sure if I was telling the truth or forcing myself into believing what I was saying. Now all eyes were on my adamant reply and indignation. "All of you, just stop it. I am not pregnant."

Everyone went quiet again. Dad, Mr. Shaw, and Gio broke from their sanctuary. Dad looked around. "What have you girls done with all of them?"

I pointed through the window where Max was throwing the football to Tom. "The kids were bored so they all went out to let off a little steam."

Dad watched. "It looks like Max can still throw the ball, and Tom can still catch a pass. Edward, they look pretty good."

"I think they need a referee. That kid under the pile isn't doing very well."

The oldest members of our group headed outside as my sister and sisters-in-law continued to examine me. "Stop it. Stop looking at me."

"She's testy," Meg whispered to Linda.

"I think she's gained a little," Jane added.

I stood up quickly. "Look, I ate too much today. We all did. I am not pregnant. I haven't been to the gym in weeks."

Meg huffed. "You never go near a gym unless you have to pass by it to get a burger. But if you are pregnant, you might have to change your imaginary workout."

All three women were looking past me. I turned to see Max. His face was white. "Charlotte, do we need to talk about something?"

I stood up quickly. "We do not." I touched his arm as I fled to the kitchen. Why did he have to follow me?

"Honey, what's going on?"

"Nothing. I'm getting the pies together. Everyone will be hungry in a bit. We'll take his favorite down to Sean later. Everyone will go. Did your team win?"

He touched my arm and turned me around into his arms. "Charlotte, are you pregnant?"

I rolled my eyes. "They are being silly. No, I don't believe so."

"But you could be?"

"Max, things have been so crazy, and we've all been stressed. I'm pretty sure I'm not. Don't worry about it." I hurried around the kitchen as though it was a race to gather plates.

Max leaned against the counter watching me. "Don't you start examining me too. I already have three women analyzing my every move and if my waistline has increased. Of course it has. I had two helpings of potatoes, a roll, and every starch I could get my hands on today. Don't say one word."

"I haven't said anything. You've been distant the last couple of weeks. I've been busy, but it's like you've been avoiding me. Why? Is it a baby?"

I finally stomped my foot. "Stop it. I've been researching a family case." I wasn't exactly telling a lie so I figured he would buy it hook, line, and sinker.

"It wouldn't be the worst thing to happen if we did have a baby, would it?"

I moved all of the pies onto the kitchen table. "This really isn't the place to have a discussion. You've made it clear you aren't ready for, for–"

"Us? I never said that."

"You did, well you didn't, but you said weeks ago that you had things to work out."

"Maybe I've worked them out?" Max touched my arm. "Look at me for just a second." He took the knife out my hand and placed it on the table. "And without a weapon."

I tried to mask any emotion I was feeling. I even looked up at him through veiled eyes, shielding my heart from his direct eye contact.

"After the holidays, we need to spend time together and talk, Charlotte. So many things have happened this year. I've doubted over the years if I would have a wife or even children."

I shoved away from him. "We don't need to talk today," I insisted. Slowly, I extended my hand up to touch his cheek. "You've made it abundantly clear you aren't thrilled about kids, about a family, or even a wife. I'm not pregnant, and if I ever am, and it's your child, you will be the first to know, but you don't have to worry about being responsible."

"Good, wait, if I'm the father? Who else is in the running?"

"I've been meaning to tell you about the guy at the deli. He and I have been having a thing, and there's the mailman who delivers to my office."

Max smiled. "Enough." Leaning down to kiss me, Max stopped before he brushed my lips. "Seriously? What's so special about them?"

"One feeds me, and the other brings me ads for groceries and occasionally money."

He slowly touched my mouth, pulling my body to him. When we parted, he grinned. "They don't kiss you like that."

"No, but food and the occasional circular for my favorite dress shop does make my day."

Max's mouth neared my ear. "But none of them can make you feel like you do when you spend the night with me," he whispered. My entire body remembered his touch, and muscle memory quickened my heart. He stood back proudly and bowed, smiling at my blush pink face. "My job is done." He began to walk away knowing he had me in so many ways.

"Max, we've only been together for such a short time, but

these past few months are like years to me. You need to stop dangling the carrot in front of me every time we make love or want to get your way. You have it on a stick, and I'm the bunny running toward it. I'm not patient. I'm not pregnant. I'm a woman who knows what she wants now in so many ways, and I know one thing for sure. Eventually, I'll either catch that damn carrot or I'll hop away to find food somewhere else. Got it?"

Sometime during my speech, Max had turned to face me. I could always tell when he was thinking. He began to open his mouth to answer me but stopped. He smiled. "I understand, and I know that's who you are. It's very clear to me that this isn't a game between the two of us. Just give me a little more time to clear things up."

I nodded as I fought back tears. He leaned down and kissed my cheek before taking the pie plates out to the dining table.

I hadn't lied to him, but I hadn't told him the truth either. I could lose him if all of this went horribly wrong. I had to have faith and patience that I was doing the right thing. Those were two attributes I never had my fill of in my life.

Chapter Twenty-Two

"Max seems to have bought our explanation," Edward Shaw commented as we sat down at Tom's desk in the real estate office.

I nodded. I felt awful when his dad told Max we were shopping for his Christmas present. Then, we would lie when we told him we didn't find what we were looking for, but on the other hand, it wouldn't be a lie. If you actually didn't shop, you wouldn't find anything, would you?

Tom had all of our evidence placed on the conference table in the office. Luckily, Meg believed he was going into the office to catch up on a few things the day after Thanksgiving. The fewer members of our family that knew what was going on kept the secret intact.

"Tom, Sean seems to be improving," Mr. Shaw said before we began. "It was great for all of us to visit him last night."

Tom nodded. It was difficult for my brother to talk about Sean. They'd been close over the years, probably closer than any of us with another sibling. When Conor died, Tom stepped in. He knew that if Sean was left to his own devices, he might do something stupid like take a bullet so no one else would be hurt. "Here's what we have. We have bank accounts from the Caymans."

Director Shaw picked up a sheet. "And from Zurich. I know these codes very well. This is unusual." He pointed to another random code. "This is a New York City bank, and here's one from Washington."

"It's not that unusual when you see the photos I found on the internet connecting with a few of these deposits, if that's what they are." I removed the envelope from my bag and handed it to Mr. Shaw. "These confirm my worst suspicions."

Edward Shaw looked at me as though his best friend had died. He slowly opened the package and pulled out the photos I had printed out at a shipping company store in Kansas just a mile from Dad's house.

He reviewed photo after photo and saw the dates on each. He knew the man in some of the photos and knew the others as staffers of two of the most powerful men in the nation. Occasionally, his eyes found mine. "Charlotte."

He saw what Tom and I had seen. We all knew now. "This is why I wanted you here. I'm not sure you'll be able to trust anyone in Washington."

Calmly, he slid the photos into the envelope. He stood and placed them on the table. When he sat down he almost collapsed in the chair. First, he rubbed his chin. Then he closed his eyes and remained quiet. Tom and I thought he might be having a heart attack.

Finally, he opened his eyes and drummed his fingers on the envelope. "Max needs to know. If he knows, he can distance himself from that case. If he knows, he can prepare."

"He'll want to kill someone." Tom walked to the side cabinet and pulled out the bottle he kept hidden along with two glasses. "Director?" He held up the bottle, and Edward Shaw nodded affirmatively.

"Charlotte, what was that operative after when he broke into the house? Do we know?"

"I'm pretty sure he was looking for the birth certificate. Don't ask me how I know, but Rose, Max's grandmother, placed the original birth certificate in a hiding place. It remained there for all those years. She's the one who told the nurse the name of the biological father. But, another document was filled out and filed fraudulently with your name on it."

Tom passed the glass over, and Max's father slugged it down. "I knew Olivia was pregnant, and back then the husband was always listed. But I didn't know about another birth certificate. And I was none the wiser because the gentleman involved, and I say that loosely, had it all fixed, didn't he?"

I nodded. "I believe he did. At least someone did, maybe even Rose. Of course, I have no proof except for hearsay. Gio didn't even know until recently." I couldn't possibly tell the FBI director that a ghost admitted her subterfuge from decades ago.

"Now, we have this mess." Mr. Shaw offered his glass for a fillup.

"We would never have known of any of this if Max hadn't been tapped to investigate that real estate scheme. The AG and the president may have had no clue, I hope, of what they put in motion. Then, Max was having a problem with his sugar."

"He found out I wasn't his real father."

I couldn't believe my confidence, but I took his hand and held it. "You are his real dad. This man is nothing, and from what I've seen of his actions, he will remain a nonentity in Max's life."

"But that bastard has always been in my wife's life. He has some hold over her." Mr. Shaw's eyes softened. "If he could do all of this, he could be holding this over Olivia. Maybe he's blackmailing her?"

I nodded. "He could be, and he probably is. At the least, she doesn't want the embarrassment from the wounds it would open. He's a very powerful man who could make her a social pariah. She couldn't live like that."

"You're right, Charlotte. You have seen her in action. It's all about the smoke and mirrors, never about the intimacy of just having love and a wonderful family." He stared at the remnants of bourbon in the glass. "You all are so fortunate to have each other. I have done an injustice to both of my children. My daughter doesn't want to be around any of us, and my son has been alone most of his life."

I strengthened my hold on his hand. "Max adores you, and I'm sure that will never change. My biggest fear is that they're, and I have no idea who they are, setting up Max to take a fall or as retribution toward the senator. We need to protect Max at all costs."

"Charlotte, call him. He should see all of this."

"Max once said this was war." I was fearful he really meant it.

"My son doesn't take fondly to being cornered. He will embrace his fury and aggressively fight his way out. If we give him the ammunition he needs, he can plan. He'll take his time. When he finally fights back, it will be a missile attack, clean and deadly. Call him."

I understood completely as did Tom. My brother had considered Max days before. He said we needed to tell him as soon as we could. Now was the time.

Within twenty minutes, Max stormed into the office. At first, he thought his father was ill. Then he thought Tom was losing the real estate agency, and finally he really did think I was pregnant. Tom poured him a drink and sat him down at the table. We explained what we had been doing since we delved into Sean's laptop. He frantically read the deposits made. He looked over our spreadsheets and timelines. When we finally deposited the photos in front of him, Max's eyes darkened. He knew one of the staffers as a deputy for the attorney general. There were other staffers he suspected worked for the senator. And then there were those photos. The senator was here. The senator was there. The senator met with this person and that person. He knew the Martins. There were even photos of the senator at a party with Max's friend who had taken his own life when he'd lost everything. The Martins and Max's friend had done business with Hughes. The senator wanted the family house destroyed with all of its secrets lost forever. There were banks and elite locations involved such as Nantucket and Hilton Head.

Max's eyes concentrated on the material before him. I touched his arm. "Someone took these photos. We aren't sure whom, and then the rest were accumulated online. We matched the dates from them, correlating them with events and deposits."

Unexpectedly, as Max came to the last photo, he pushed all of them off of the table, sending several of our pieces of evidence flying throughout the room. "He's setting me up."

"It seems that the judge you've been investigating is involved up to his eyes," his father admitted. "When you compile all of this, you'll see the circle of corruption. Charlotte believes Brody was jammed up in all of this since he knew the O'Donohues. It was easy for him to catch up with the judge. Maybe at first they wanted Judge O to be part of the conspiracy, or they suspected the judge was forming a group of his own to counteract the deceivers. At the very least, during a casual conversation Brody could keep tabs on you, especially after you and Charlotte began spending so much time together. You also have another problem. The mole in your office has been relaying information to the senator since you arrived here in the city."

I watched the distress not just on Max's face, but in his entire body. His shoulders stiffened and his arms were extended out onto the table as though he was building his own barrier. My brother attempted to explain. "Max, your assignment on this investigation seems completely by accident. You were just very good at your job. I prefer to believe the president and AG didn't know that Hughes was involved. But the AG could be involved. It is unclear." Tom's comments went unheard. Max remained silent.

Max took a drink and looked at all of us. "They knew a senator was involved. That was my secret assignment. They didn't realize it was him or his association with me. Hughes has power." He eventually focused on me. "The AG's deputy is in one of these photos. He seems very tight with the senator. This is why you've been so distant."

"You needed to be far away from all of this until we knew. I told you it would be safer for you until we discovered what all of Sean's investigation meant."

"Sean had been doing all of this? Why?"

"I have no idea," I admitted quickly. "Tom and I have no explanation why our brother decided to go rogue and combine all of this evidence."

Something on the desk caught Max's eye. His right hand pushed through the papers and landed on the bank statements.

Tom and Edward were talking, but I was watching. Max was studying the bank routing and checking account numbers. What was he seeing that I wasn't? His body tensed; his jaw tightened. "Max?" What was he thinking?

Max stood up and grabbed his coat off of the back of the chair. He began to walk out.

"Max?"

He turned. He faced Tom and his dad, but stared at me. "You should've told me, Charlotte. You knew this for a few days, and you kept all of this secret. We said there couldn't be any secrets between us. I told you my family had enough for everyone. You even contacted my father. You didn't just have him come for Thanksgiving. You had him come for this." Max's hand extended toward all the papers remaining on the table and on the floor. "I can't believe you did this when I've been trying so hard to do everything you wanted me to do, to be who you wanted–" He turned his back on me.

"Don't you dare! Who are you protecting now? You need to stop running, and I don't mean that ritual you do every morning to supposedly clear your head." I was shocked when he glanced back at me.

"What exactly am I running from? You seem to know all the answers. Enlighten me, Charlotte."

I stood up so he couldn't look down on me. "Me. Us. You have this fear that you can't have better, do better with a real relationship. I don't want you to be anyone but yourself. And you need to learn to trust me."

Max shook his head and shrugged. "You ask too much. Now, I'll tell you. Back off. You can't be near me. You'll lose everything." He turned on his heel and stormed out.

"Max, come back here! You are my everything," I screamed, but he didn't return. We heard the door slam. I reached for my coat, but Mr. Shaw stopped me.

"Charlotte, let him go. He knows the truth. You did nothing wrong. You protected him until you knew for sure. He knows you did the right thing. You did what he would've done for you. Apparently, he had his own secrets."

"He saw something. He knows something. I kept telling him he couldn't be close to all of this when I realized what might be on Sean's computer. He's using this to end it. Damn him. A coward always finds an excuse." My eyes filled with tears, but I straightened my back and my resolve. Tom came over and held me in his arms. "Tommy, I think it's over."

Tom's arms enveloped me tighter, closer. "If it is Charlie, then Poop Head never had any intention of your relationship lasting. He was looking for a way out. You were right when you told him he is afraid. I had this feeling he'd do this to you. Honey, it will all be okay."

I nodded. It was one thing to say if we ended we'd still be friends, but when you ended after trying to protect the man you loved, the betrayal seemed to be the most hurtful feeling I had ever experienced. And what was that garbage about not being near him? Was he attempting to protect me from some threat?

"Charlotte, he'll be back. You're probably right. My son knows something, and obviously we haven't figured it out yet. Give him time. Give him a chance." Max's dad's words seemed meaningless to me. "I know my son. I also know him as a formidable attorney. I'm not so sure he's not playing one of his wiley games and pushing you away on purpose in an effort to protect you. Let him go for now."

What had Director Shaw said ... let him go? I knew what I needed to do. That evening, Dad, Max's dad, Gio, and I had a quiet meal of leftovers at the house. All of us left messages for Max. Finally, he called his father when we were drinking coffee in the living room.

"He'll meet me tomorrow before I leave," Edward Shaw said slowly. "Charlotte, I'm so sorry about all of this. I thought, nevermind. It's not important at this point."

I stood up, pasted a smile on my face and headed for the kitchen. "I knew this would and could happen. I'm good. I just want him to be happy and safe. If this is what he needs to do–" I walked away quickly. I wasn't sure why, but Gio was the one who had pulled the short straw.

When the elderly mobster touched my shoulder, I dissolved into his arms. He smoothed my hair and murmured everything would work itself out, but I didn't believe him. We all knew Max Shaw by now. He was at war, if not against the bad guys, then with himself. He had no room for love in his life. I'd asked too much of him. No, I had demanded too much from him. Didn't I deserve the love I needed?

Chapter Twenty-Three

When I used my key to enter Taylor House, I heard crying. It was Rose. I went upstairs and packed up the few things I had in Max's master suite and headed down to the sitting room. I looked over at the sweet desk near the window and thought of the nights of making love with Max and falling asleep in his arms.

"Charlotte, sorry."

"I know. Me too, Rose. Sometimes things don't work out, even if heaven is on your side. Right? Look at you and Gio."

"Max, yours. Trust."

"No. I'm okay. I've cried enough." I smiled for some weird reason. "Rose, at least I know what love is really like, and he's made me so much stronger in my life and career. I'm so happy I broke it off with that other jerk, and I'm delirious that I did throw a beer at him in that bar that night."

Now, I heard laughing, and I smelled her sweet perfume. "By the way, your nasty husband was very quiet upstairs. I hope you banned him from your house."

I heard the security system ping and the door opened. Grabbing my bags, I turned to see Max standing at the edge of the sitting room. He looked like hell.

"I should ask for your key back," he murmured.

I looked down at it in my hand. I slowly held it out. "Yes, I'm sorry. I wanted to grab my things and be gone before you came home. I was going to give Gio the key so you wouldn't have to worry about it."

"What's Rose saying?"

"Nothing. I hear nothing."

"Charlotte." Rose's sweet voice filled my head, but I didn't answer in any way.

"So, it's all over?"

"You mean the voices in my head?"

"That too," Max murmured. He looked down at the floor. "Charlotte, I cherish our friendship. I appreciate everything you've done for me."

My voice caught in my throat. He really was ending it. Edward really didn't know his son as well as he thought. Wanting to scream and pound my feet on the floor, I chose to nod, agreeing to his conclusion. Eventually, I found my voice, but it was low and shaky. "We will always be friends, *Poop Head.*" I quickly passed him and placed the key in his cold hand.

I thought he might pull me back and into his arms like in some romance movie, but I fled freely to the safety of the outside and to my car. I saw the lights turn on in the large master bedroom. Paddy would be upset that I wouldn't have millions. Tom wouldn't want to speak with his best friend for a while. Jane and the others would be crushed that there was no baby and no wedding to plan. Dad, well he would be Dad. He'd be friends with Max, take care of Sean, and he'd tell me something inane like Mom's old line ... what will be, will be, and if it doesn't happen then it was never meant to be.

As I drove away from the big house, I was leaving behind the best part of my heart.

I headed to see Sean, but my visit was short lived. My brother was having a bad day and had been sleeping for hours. The staff informed me Dad had gone home, and I just missed him.

By the time I entered the house and threw my bags down at the base of the stairs, I was ready for the biggest piece of pumpkin pie with a humongous amount of whipped cream that a dumped girlfriend had ever created. Dad had beat me to it. He sat at the kitchen table, his mouth full.

"You look like a chipmunk."

"That's not very nice. You look like roadkill."

I was shocked. "Dad, you're not supposed to say that about your daughter."

"Well, someone needs to. Edward filled me in on the latest festivities. You and Tom can not become investigators. We already have a detective. Have you figured out why Sean started all of this?"

"I have no idea. Our goofy brother got himself into

something, but why or how he even began compiling all of this information is beyond me. We'll have to ask him."

"He's not good."

"I know." I piled the whipped cream at least three inches high. "I just came from there. He looks tired."

"Charlotte, Max is still paying for Sean's extra care, and he sent me a text about providing private care here at the house. He'll also pay for the construction we'll need to do to the guest room and the first-floor bathroom."

"That's wonderful, Dad." I sat across from him and began to eat the pie. I wanted to send a photo to Olivia Shaw to show her exactly what I was digesting.

"And now what?"

My mouth was full. Dad's question was confusing. "Rut?"

"You and Max."

I swallowed. Yes, that was about one hundred calories. "There is no Max and me. I'm fine."

"Oh please, you are not fine."

"We'll remain friends."

"Cut the crap, Charlotte Rose O'Donohue. You can't remain friends."

I stared my father down. "We will be cordial."

"You two are ridiculous. I thought he was shielding you, making you mad so you wouldn't be around, but–"

"Maybe, but Dad, I hid something from him for his own protection. I made the decision without consulting him. I called his father instead of telling him as soon as I could. I told him he's scared of what we have, had. He's mad, and he has the right. I think he's being stupid and controlling. I gave him back my key, and I grabbed my things. You're stuck with me for a bit now."

"Charlotte, I'll be happy to be stuck with you until the end of my days."

I waved my fork in the air. "Now see, why can't men say stuff like that anymore? No, all they say is I should get your key."

"What did Rose have to say?"

I shut my eyes tightly. "She's sad. I'm sad, damn it. I hate feeling like this again. I need ice cream." I rose from the table and headed for the freezer. "Did the kids eat all of the strawberry? I need to ban them from the kitchen."

I felt Dad watching me. Shutting the freezer door, I cut myself another piece of pie. "Dad, do you want anything?"

"Yes, cut me another, bartender."

"I suppose it is better than drinking ourselves into a stupor."

"I wanted him so much as a son-in-law."

I landed each plate with a thud as I sat back down. "You too? Paddy wanted his money."

"I wanted the football tickets." Dad sighed comically. "Charlotte, what did you want?"

Where did that question come from? My father! "I just wanted him, Dad. He has the best heart when he reveals it."

"Ah, that's the best answer. Don't think it's over yet."

"I can't wait. I need to get my life back on track. I'm at work on Monday, and I'm going to be the best family attorney I can be. Max can do his thing."

"And when you see him again?"

"I'll say hello, smile, be cordial as hell, and wish him well."

"We'll see how long that lasts. Paddy is betting two weeks before you throw a beer on Max."

"And what's your bet?"

"I give you a month. Tom has two days–"

"You all are terrible."

"No, honey, we're your family. We know you. You haven't reached acceptance yet. You're still in the grieving stage, and it's very fresh. You'll peak at revenge soon, and that's the part where I'll have cash on hand for your bail."

I laughed so hard, whipped cream fell from my mouth. Cash. My thoughts turned to the bank statements. When Max had looked over a few of them, it almost appeared as though he knew the accounts. Thinking back on that moment, I realized as he swept the papers from the stack, he'd pocketed one sheet. Whose accounts had piqued his interest, and how did he know? Is that the reason why he ended it all? Maybe Max wasn't just protecting me? Maybe he was protecting someone else he loved?

Chapter Twenty-Four

There were murmurs in the courthouse on Tuesday morning. I heard the word recusal. As I walked out of the building to head to the office, I saw numerous television station vans set up at the federal courthouse. One of my father's friends, Judge Murphy, passed me on the sidewalk and said hello.

"Do you know what is going on?"

"The U.S. attorney is recusing himself from that big real estate case. I think you found the body of one of the perpetrators, didn't you, Charlotte?"

"Yes, you mean Max Shaw is stepping down from the prosecution?"

"Exactly. The entire office has been compromised in some way. On request from Shaw, the federal investigation and the scheduled trials are being transferred. I have to go. Tell your father I'll meet him next week for cards at the usual place."

Instead of heading back to the office, I walked briskly over to the courthouse. There was a crowd of reporters, each one shoving a microphone in Max's face. He was acknowledging he was stepping down, recusing himself for personal reasons. His office had been compromised. He looked tired and wan, very unlike the tanned attorney who had come to town at the beginning of the year.

I wish it had been like the old days when two people on the silver screen would catch each other's eyes. He would run to her, and they would embrace as they promised to never let each other go, but it wasn't that way. He saw me. I saw him. He hurried into the building, and I walked back to my car alone.

I entered my office to see Phoebe smiling. There was a vase of flowers on her desk. I saw the card had my name on it. "These came for you."

I took the card and walked into my office.

"Don't forget the flowers." Phoebe set the vase on my side credenza. "This way you don't have to look through them when you meet with Mrs. Sotter later today. I've pulled all her notes from the last visit, and she promises this time she won't change her mind on who her executor will be."

I removed my coat, readied my desk, and sat down, reading the card out loud. "Charlotte, you and I know how much you care. My biggest hope is that somehow the two of you find your way back to each other. Sincerely and thank you, Edward Shaw." When I looked up, Phoebe's smile had vanished, and it seemed her entire face had fallen.

"Max's dad?"

"Yes. He was in town for the holiday, and things didn't go as planned."

"Your father hasn't told me any of this. What is going on?"

"Phoebe, it's a long story better told over a cold beer on a hot summer night." I wanted to avoid the subject. I began to go over my notes on my desk.

"Charlotte, I've known you since you were a little bit. What happened?"

Was it possible to cry so much that you just couldn't anymore? "Phoebe, Max and I are finished. There is no more plotting to press the two of us together. There's no more, well, we are no more."

Phoebe fell into the chair, dramatically protesting. "What the bloody hell? Did he do this? I'll hurt him. I have some thoughts on how we can–"

"Stop. It's okay, really. I believe it is for the best." I hadn't figured that one out yet. For whom was it the best outcome? I suppose I could realistically believe it when I thought of the life Max led. There was no way I was adept with the social graces needed to run in his circles, or of his family's. I smiled slightly. His mother was probably throwing a party after hearing the news that the snot-nosed little sister of the large Irish Catholic family had been unceremoniously dropped on her ass.

"For whom? You know when you called him the devil? You were right. Only the devil would say all the right things, make you love him, and then crush your little heart over a freaking holiday. Your family must be livid."

"No, everyone is good. They understand. Paddy is a little upset."

Phoebe's face lightened. "Paddy will kill him?" She seemed gleeful, and it scared me. Who was this woman?

"No, Dad and he are just upset they won't get Max's football tickets."

"Right, there's a big game this Sunday."

I cleared my throat, held back the tears, and smiled. "Now, what else do we have?"

Phoebe not only gave me the rundown on the day, but for the entire week. I had work. My life would be full again, and on Friday night, I would snuggle with Mickey on the floor and watch Christmas movies where the girl and guy finally kissed at the end. My life sucked.

By Friday night, I was exhausted, not just from work, but from the inept attempt at feeling happy. It wasn't working. My family overcompensated. Dad took me to lunch; Paddy dropped by just to see his baby sister; Jane brought my favorite pumpkin bread; Tom and Meg called every stinking day; and Sean smiled when he saw me. His effort meant the most. I talked to him about the laptop, but his memory was still altered. I could've been speaking in tongues, and he would've understood just as much.

Saturday morning, Dad served me coffee, an omelet of sausage and mushrooms with my favorite cheese melted on top. He was humming. I was suspicious.

"What's up, Dad?"

"Um, I need to tell you something. I'm not proud of myself,

but Max is taking Paddy and me to the game. This is a make-or-break game, Charlotte. Please understand."

A bite of omelet put me in a better mood. "It's okay. That's how it should be. Enjoy."

"Are you sure?"

"Yes, leave me alone. I'm eating. This is good for all of us."

But when Max arrived Sunday morning to pick up two of the men in my family, I opened the door and just stared at the man. I had no words, not even the ones to ask him to come in. Paddy pushed me to the side.

"Come in Max. We're all ready." Paddy literally had hidden me behind the open door. "Dad, Max is here. Let's move it."

Max pulled the door closed as he entered and smiled. "Hi."

"Hi."

"How are you?"

"Good." I crept out of my dark place, standing uncomfortably in the hallway while Paddy threw coats into the air.

"Charlotte, maybe we could–"

"Let's go. The traffic is going to be crazy. Did I tell you my unit has a tailgate party? I'll have to text the captain to see which lot. I figured we could drop by. One of the sergeants smoked an entire pig." Paddy began to push Dad out the door while Max hung back listening. "Come on, Max, let's get going. No time for chitchat."

I noticed Max looking at me. He didn't move a muscle. Paddy yelled again. "Give me a second, tiger." He searched my eyes. "We should meet for lunch next week."

"I'll have to check my schedule. I suppose you have some free time now?"

"I told you I was going to take some time off, but I was going to spend it–"

"Max!" Paddy literally pulled at his jacket.

"Gee, Paddy, give him a break!" My scream filled the neighborhood.

"Charlie, you're screeching like you're five again." Paddy reprimanded me with a finger stuck in my face. I almost bit it like I used to do when I was that age too.

"And you are acting like a brute of a brother!"

"Charlotte, I'll call." Max turned. That was the last I heard from him.

As soon as they left, I grabbed some candy from Dad's private stash. Mickey jumped into Dad's chair and was barking as the car pulled away.

"Come on, you neurotic dog, let's get you fed." I made sure Mickey had his water filled and had made one trip around the backyard. Afterward, I pulled my keys from my purse and headed to Sean's. He and I would watch the game together. When I arrived, Tom and Meg were visiting.

"We're having our own tailgate party," Tom announced, holding up a hotdog.

"You didn't bring a grill in here, did you? You'll get us thrown out." I removed my coat and kissed Sean on the head.

"No, of course not. I wouldn't let him," Meg announced. "We pre-cooked and brought in the warmer. We have potato chips, mac and cheese, and brownies."

"That sounds like the meal of champions."

Tom smiled at me weirdly. My attention was on Sean. He looked good today with color in his cheeks and fewer wires and tubes.

Tom touched my arm. "Charlotte, I wanted to be here, and I just couldn't go to that game."

"I know, Tom. Thanks."

"But," Tom added, "we'll have a great time here, won't we?" Tom's weird smile worried me.

I turned my attention to my other brother, brushing his hair with my hand. His warm smile made everything better. "Hello, Seany."

"Hi, Charlie."

"What?"

Meg began to cry and Tom clapped. "He has been practicing just for you."

I brushed away tears of joy. "Oh my God, Sean. I'm so proud of you." He pointed at me.

"Proud of Charlie," he said slowly.

"I haven't done anything."

Sean moved his head from side to side. "For Max."

"What?"

Tom's wife stepped near me and placed a protective arm around my shoulders. "Apparently, Max told Sean what you and Tom were up to. He also thanked Sean for all the information on the laptop."

"Charlotte, I think Sean is beginning to remember," Tom added.

Sean nodded affirmatively. "Max, danger."

"I know, Sean. I get it. He was in danger from some very powerful people."

"And that's why he recused himself, Charlie," Tom added. "Also–"

"What?"

"Charlie, he did it for you."

I was completely confused. "Tom, I don't understand."

"Don't you? He distanced himself from you, and he probably won't be around all of us for a while. He backed off so he wouldn't affect your career, your life. Of course, Dad and Paddy are with him today, but they'll be sitting in a box with a group of the police hierarchy so it seemed safe and natural."

"Okay," I answered slowly. "I understand." But, the two of us only being friends now had nothing to do with distance. We still had a problem with trust. I was being trustworthy in my effort to protect him, but he couldn't trust me to make my own decisions. I kissed Sean's head. "I'm so proud of you."

Sean took my hand and looked at me. His eyes were clear. I could tell he wanted to say so much more. Soon, I hoped he would.

"Let's have a party," Meg cheered.

The game was enjoyable, but Sean's hand holding mine was more of a win than anything that happened today on the football field. My brother was coming back.

Chapter Twenty-Five

"Is herself in?"

I heard Paddy's deep voice bellowing from my outer office. He didn't wait for me, rather entering my space and shutting the door behind him.

"Why are you here today?"

Paddy frowned and sat down. "Is that anyway to greet your dear older brother?"

"It is when you are acting like a decent human being. What's up?" I saved the document I was working on and gave him my full attention. "Has my lovely sister-in-law finally figured out she can do much better than you, and you're here for divorce advice?"

"Ooh, you are harsh. You're sounding like a woman bitter about love."

I threw my pen at him. "Don't you dare. That isn't fair."

Paddy caught the pen in mid-air and placed it on my desk, away from my reach. "Have you heard from Max?"

"Well, no. You bum rushed him out of the house Sunday, remember?"

"I did. Dad and I had a great time."

I leaned back in my chair. I needed to show no fear. My brother always intimidated me from an early age, and even now it was difficult to go up against Paddy. "Yes, Dad said the game was great."

"Max is leaving for the holidays," Paddy announced.

"Good for him. He said something about calling me for lunch, but he's probably very busy."

Paddy seemed uneasy. He looked around my office and stared out my window before speaking. "He's going back to New York City. I think he's going to get some stuff straightened out."

"Do you know this for sure, or have you deduced this for yourself, being the great detective that you are?" I sounded sarcastic. I meant to be smug and condescending.

Paddy leaned forward, resting his arms on my desk. "Charlie, Charlotte, I want you to know I've been completely wrong about Max."

"Okay." Where was he going with this? Was he trying to convince me of something?

"I don't know all the details of what went down with you two, but you should know that this ... this separation is for you."

"Uh huh. That's sweet." Tom and even Max's dad had said something similar. In my mind, I had hoped that Max was only placing distance between us to protect me. "Well, you're making absolutely no sense. What I know for sure is Max and I will see each other in a hallway or at the house. We've proven we can be adults about this breakup. But you know what? When I think about it, we have always been friends. There was nothing more to it than that."

Paddy expected me to tear up, but instead I smiled sweetly and completely confused him. "Don't say that, Charlotte. You mean so much to him."

"Since when have you become Max Shaw's cheerleader?"

"Since, I know he loves you."

I stood up quickly and walked around my desk. I opened the door. "Paddy, I have a lot of work to do, and if Max Shaw needs to say something to me then he can do it himself. He doesn't need you to do what a man should do."

"But he is," Paddy pleaded. "You need to think about this. Why has he suddenly dropped you?"

I laughed nervously. "Seriously? Dropped me? He walked away. He ended it. He can't trust me, and I now know I can't rely on him. Paddy, I need you to leave, please."

I saw Phoebe watching intently. My brother got up slowly and stood in front of me. "Charlotte, don't give up on love." He leaned down and kissed my cheek. "Just think."

I never thought in my wildest dreams my oldest oaf of a brother would speak of love and defend Max so intensely.

"What was that?" Phoebe's question pretty much summed up the visit. "Is the world coming to an end?"

"I'm supposed to think. I think I'll do it over a copious

amount of egg nog." Merry freaking Christmas to me.

And I did. By Christmas night, I was drunk. My nieces and nephews enjoyed my rendition of a rather naughty Christmas parody, and my siblings just smiled and allowed me to wallow in self-pity. I stretched out on the couch and watched the fire Dad had roaring. Mickey sprawled below me on the rug.

Once the family left for the night, the house seemed so very empty. But I was ready to be alone. As soon as Dad sat in his big chair, Mickey moved his sleeping position in front of his feet. As Dad drank his brandy, he threw a card across the room that fell on my stomach.

"What is this?"

"For you."

"Dad, did you forget to give this to me earlier?"

"It's not from me."

I downed my latest eggnog and set the glass on the floor. The card had a fragrance to it. It was Rose's perfume. Slowly, I opened it. It was a *missing you at the holidays* card. I read the printed words and saw the signature. He had signed it love, Max. That was it. There was no explanation, nor as Paddy might expect, a gift of any kind.

"Dad, I'm going to bed."

"Honey, did it say anything?"

"It says he misses me during the holidays. It's the perfect sentiment from a card company."

"Charlotte, you're not going to throw a beer on him the

next time you see him, are you?"

I smiled widely. "Of course not, Father. Friends don't do that to each other." I kissed my Dad's head, wished him a goodnight, and headed to my bedroom.

I decided to wear my heavy pajamas tonight. Tom and Meg had gifted these beauties as a joke present last year, but I loved them on cold nights. Every inch of my body was covered in flannel. What did it matter? No one was going to attempt to disrobe me, or tell me how much they loved how the snowman design favored my curves.

"Damn you, Max!"

"Charlotte Rose!"

"Mom? What do I need to do?"

"Charlotte, trust him."

"I'm giving up on men. Really, I'm done. He has so much baggage, and I don't think he'll ever get his act together. He'd probably be a lousy husband and a cranky dad."

"Teach him."

"Nope. I'm not taking him on. He's too high maintenance."

"Charlotte, trust him."

I fell back on the bed and hit the mattress with my fists. "Fine, I'll trust. Could you please give me a clue? Something? Anything? These cryptic messages really get old, Mom."

There was nothing. "Merry Christmas Mom and Conor. Keep looking over Sean. And protect Max wherever he may be."

I fell asleep soon after my tantrum. My dreams were of my family, each of us happy. Sean was walking and yapping about how I had eaten all of the chocolate covered cherries. Dad fixed the best ham ever, and Linda had miraculously managed to get every ingredient into the jello salad. Every year, she always forgot something, but not in my dreams. Paddy was happy with his new golf clubs and Tom and Meg announced they were finally having a baby after trying for so many years with no luck. All of the grandchildren were smiling, and I opened the door to greet Gio and Rose. Mom and Conor walked in next followed by Max. He kissed me and said he was home.

When I woke up, I realized I'd been crying into my pillow. My dream had been better than my reality. I dried my tears, looked out to see it had snowed overnight, and decided I was done with lost loves. I needed to take care of myself.

Chapter Twenty-Six

New Year's Eve, Beautiful Hotel, Downtown, Kansas City, Missouri

"Paddy took me to lunch. I think it's the end of the world." Max Shaw threw back his drink and laughed with his companions.

Tom and Meg O'Donohue were enjoying themselves at Max's expense, serving as their friend's plus one and two. They never wanted to pay the hefty price tag for this exclusive party, but when Max suggested they go as his guests, they jumped at the chance to have New Year's Eve out. Tom decided Max was his favorite brother or non-brother-in-law when he saw the two-room suite the boy wonder reserved for them. Max booked his room across the hall.

"It's frightening how you and Paddy have bonded." Meg was enjoying the live band. She couldn't remember their last night out as a couple that didn't require bringing a wedding gift. With Max along it was like the good old days. But, someone was missing. She even noticed Max surveying the room. Was he looking for Charlotte?

"I'm happy everything has worked out, and I'm overjoyed

that this awful year will be gone in thirty minutes," Tom said while looking at his watch.

Meg noticed Max's smile vanish. He sucked down the remainder of his drink. Looking back on the past year was bittersweet, part of it had been wonderful, even magical. He hadn't expected that Charlotte would become such an integral part of his life. He missed her. He didn't miss how he'd stumble over her shoes she cast aside in the most bizarre locations. He almost face-planted in the middle of the night from the ill positioned sneaker at the top of the stairs.

He missed Charlotte sleeping next to him. She would reach over and pat his leg to make sure he was still there in the darkness. And he missed the way she shyly touched him in the shower after they'd made love in the morning. Her touch ignited such a fire in him he couldn't control his need for her. But when Max had realized the bank statements were well known to him, he knew what he had to do. He couldn't turn Charlotte's world upside down. Besides, he couldn't really trust her, and she wouldn't trust him.

Tom noticed the change in his friend, and he knew the reason. He saw the same look on his sister's face. Charlotte was at home with the dog. Dad was even out with friends. He offered to cancel the plans, but she insisted they go. Charlotte should be here with the three of them. "Max, please dance with my wife. She had a pedicure, and doesn't want me anywhere near her pretty little toes."

"Honey, I love your effort."

Tom laughed. "Face it. I'm not good at dancing."

Acting like the perfect gentleman, Max took Meg by the hand and led her out onto the floor for the slow dance. "Tom shouldn't allow someone like me to dance with his beautiful wife."

Meg was always charmed by her dancing partner and understood how a woman could succumb to the man's smoldering good looks. How he moved, his words, his low voice, and especially his touch was nearly perfect. But when he was with Charlotte, Max Shaw was adorable. He'd laugh at her jokes and smile at her lack of patience. As a couple, they shouldn't work, yet they did. "Tom trusts you."

Max seemed to be in pain. "Trust. That's a word that will get you into a lot of trouble."

"Or, it will bring you a lifetime friendship."

Max turned his head. "I miss her tonight."

"It was your decision."

Max sighed. "I know. You, Tom, Paddy, and even your Dad know why I did it. She's just beginning her practice. All of my problems were going to blow up if I didn't take a step back in every way. I needed to protect her until I could figure out my next move. My family–"

Meg thought she understood. "I think you could've talked it over with her, and allowed her to make her own decision. You have to admit that my sister-in-law understands familial insanity. Charlotte may balk at taking the spotlight or stepping in one direction or another, but she's tough, and she's not stupid, Max. She knows why you recused yourself from that trial. She understands your situation, but she also thinks you're a coward. You acted like one when you dumped her. I don't even understand that."

"There's days I don't either," he admitted truthfully. "She said I was afraid."

"You are. You are just making up excuses to escape a commitment. Tom said she told you off."

Max chuckled. "Even then she did it nicely. Besides, I knew I needed to straighten out some family things. My biological father is a piece of work. My mother is a social snob and could be looking at a very uncertain future."

"But your dad and Gio are wonderful."

Eventually, a thin smile formed on Max's face. "They both absolutely adore Charlotte."

The old friend patted him on the back. "And you?"

"I adore her too. She's my best friend."

Meg created a face. "Stop lying to yourself. If I hear that word one more time, I swear I'm going to scream. You two were lovers, not just friends. All of us girls even thought she was pregnant in November, remember?"

"I do. I thought maybe–"

It was time to ask the hard questions. "Would you have been happy if she had been?"

Max wondered to himself why it felt like an oven in this ballroom. "It would have been an adjustment."

"Would you have been happy?"

Before he could think, he answered. "Very, but I'm damaged goods. I told her from the very beginning I wasn't ready for a commitment. She wants so much so quickly."

Meg felt so sorry for her friend. "Max, Charlotte isn't looking for perfection. She knows who you really are, and yet she accepts you. She's willing to wait if she knows how you truly feel. She's looking for a good man who is generous, thoughtful, and willing to risk it all for love. Maybe even risking everything for her? She's quiet now. She doesn't say a word about you. We interrogate her, and we get nothing. She's back to being perfectly content in a corner. She's meant for bigger things. She's reconnected with a couple of friends, and she had a date the other night."

Max stopped dancing. "Do I know him? She didn't spend the night with the–"

Meg laughed. "Ah, you can be jealous."

"Well of course. I worry about her. Was the guy nice?"

"I have no idea. She didn't say anything. Tomorrow, she's attending a New Year's Day luncheon for an old high school friend who is getting married this spring. I'm proud of her for getting out there, unlike you, my sorry friend."

"Let's take a break." Max hadn't even noticed the band had stopped playing a minute ago. He pasted a smile on his face as they joined Tom at the table. In just a few minutes it would be a new year. He had no wishes, no hopes, not even one resolution. He had uncertainty and a future that could hold a career collapse and a fight with people so powerful that they could pound him into the ground as though he never existed. This was war, and he'd welcome the fight, but he felt very much alone. He'd been alone before, but now he knew what it was like to be part of a real family, and to have a partner who had been willing to sacrifice her love to save him.

Tom nudged his friend's arm. "Max? What are you thinking?"

He flashed his signature smile. "You don't want to know, Tommy."

Tom slowly took a drink from his glass and turned to stare into his friend's eyes. "I already know. You're an idiot."

"Your wife said much the same thing."

"She's right, and so am I. You know, right now my little sister is probably opening up the front door and letting this crappy year out."

Max figured Tom was drunk. "What on earth are you talking about?"

"It's an old Irish thing. Mom used to do it every New Year's Eve, well except for the year she was so sick. She made Charlotte do it. You open the door to let the old year out and to welcome in a new one, a better one. Charlotte deserves a better one, and you do too."

Max laughed nervously. "I'm not so sure I deserve anything."

Tom used his finger as an instrument of poignancy. "You can do something about all of this," he said over the noise, poking his friend until Max winced.

At midnight, the throng toasted, cheered, and kissed their significant others. Max gladly received the kisses and hugs from his friends and even perfect strangers. But at a minute after midnight, while the room was filled with balloons and the champagne flowed freely, Max texted Charlotte and wished her the best this year.

"Damn you, Charlotte," Max said out loud while the entire room celebrated. How had she managed to make him want so many things he never thought would be possible? He knew exactly how. Even her obnoxious habit of biting her lip seemed endearing to him. She made him laugh; she smiled way too much. Charlotte would yell at him and debate every little thing, but in the darkness she sighed his name sweetly when she was beneath him. Most of all, Charlotte had no clue how damn sexy she was, how desirable she was to him. He missed every inch of her. Most of all he missed her capacity to love him no matter what.

Chapter Twenty-Seven

The luncheon was lovely and expensive, and I was totally bored hearing about the wedding plans. Other stories were about former classmates' children and spouses. I smiled, and I even laughed occasionally as I ate my plate of stuffed chicken breast, spring carrots even though it was the dead of winter, and a potato that looked more like a small cube of tofu. I would've preferred a beer and a hot beef sandwich. I waited patiently for the dessert. There was no need to when the small scoop of lavender ice cream was placed in front of me. Someone mentioned it was divine. That wasn't exactly my adjective for it.

The women sighed, marveling at its beauty. Shaped in a design of a blooming flower, the ice cream seemed an unusual option for New Year's Day. I lifted the first bite to my mouth and tasted the lavender. It was okay. You know you're eating after a breakup when you go ahead and do something you normally wouldn't. I ate the damn dessert. It was better than the other night's date.

Jon was a very nice attorney who I talked to several times at the courthouse. He moved here from Nashville and didn't know many people, and so I agreed to go out with him. He selected a sushi bar, and I had to look over the menu to find an item that was appetizing enough to eat. I just couldn't eat sushi. Give me some cooked fish, and I was good. Fry it, and I'm thrilled. After dinner he treated me to a fine arts movie about a woman who lost her entire family. I was in tears by the end of the film, until the audience realized she dreamt the entire story. Well, crap, I can do that! The best part of the night was talking over coffee. I think we both came to the realization that we were really good at just talking. Jon and I agreed on every subject we discussed. We didn't bicker, and there was no playful or seductive banter. He agreed with every opinion I had and enthusiastically insisted I was the nicest person he'd met in the city. He was sweet, but he wasn't Max. If I was being honest, no one was Max.

When I went to bed that night, I pounded my pillow until it was flat beneath my head. I turned on my side and patted the open space. Max wasn't there. When I stayed the night at Taylor House, I always used to fall asleep with one hand on his bare chest. When I felt his heart beating, I became so relaxed that slumber came within minutes. And truth be told, I missed his low murmurs and his lips nuzzling my neck. I missed his lovemaking, making me feel like the only woman in the world, in his world. But we were always attempting to conquer each other. I thought when I came to him that first night, my surrender would bring him into my reality, my needs for existence. Obviously, I was wrong. Miserably, I couldn't survive in his orbit.

"Charlotte, I saw you at your cousin's wedding last year, and you were with the most gorgeous man."

I looked up from my melted lavender treat and blinked my deep thoughts away. "Yes."

"Details, honey."

Celeste always wanted details since I met her the first day of high school. "There's not much to tell. He's an old family friend."

"You two looked very cozy. If that's what you call a friend, I'd like his number."

"You're married," I remembered.

"Yes, but a man like that on the side would really make my life complete."

He would've done the same for me, minus the husband. I looked around the room. Celeste began to tell the table all about my date that night. The tux fit him like a glove; he was tall, dark, and handsome; his smile was dazzling.

"He looked at Charlotte like she was his everything."

"What did you just say?"

Celeste looked like a deer in the headlights of a pickup truck. "Honey, he looked at you like you were everything to him."

"Wow."

"Wow, indeed. He left me breathless, and I wasn't in those arms. It was just the way he looked at you. Oh, and girls, the way he held her was so sexy. It was too intimate for just a family friend. His hand on her back—"

And that had been before we slept together. I cried last night when he wished me a happy new year through a text message. I couldn't do this anymore. I stood slowly, pushing my chair back. "I need to go. I have to see my brother in the rehab center."

When I mentioned Sean, they all nodded understandingly. They cooed their sympathy. I apologized to my friend and her mother before fleeing the club. Our family was meeting at two in Sean's room for a celebration with him. Being a little earlier to visit one on one would be a blessing.

Sean was doing so well with the extra help he was receiving. Max was true to his word, and my brother had everything and more he needed for his recovery. Dad could never repay his generosity.

Gio and Dad were busy renovating the room and bathroom for Sean, and next week Tom and Paddy had committed to moving Gio into his suite at Max's house. I hadn't been in the Taylor House, but Dad said that the entire first floor was finished including the expansion of the new living area off of the kitchen. Bobby Mack would stay in the guest room until his own apartment over the garage was finished. Max hadn't told me about those details, but he didn't need to anymore, did he? He never needed my approval from the very beginning, but he had always asked my opinion.

I greeted several patients as I walked into Sean's wing of the center. I was stopped by one of the therapists telling me Sean walked on his own this very morning. She also said that my boyfriend was already visiting with my brother. Really?

I stepped softly, not choosing to announce my entrance. I could hear Max's voice. He was telling Sean that last night was fine. He had to go to the event and took Tom and Meg with him. He would've preferred to have been with all of us watching an old movie or a football game.

"Sean, do you need water?"

"No, Max. Talk."

"About what, buddy?"

"Charlotte."

What was my brother up to? His speech was so much clearer today than it had been last week.

"You can't tell anyone."

"Okay," Sean said slowly.

"I love your sister. I had told her, but when I did, it was more of a response to her telling me how she felt, but now–"

"She loves you."

"Well, I messed up. She won't trust me now."

"Fix."

I barely moved into the doorframe to see with one eye what was happening. Sean sat in his wheelchair with Max sitting across from him.

"I don't know what to do." Max looked tired, even a bit distressed. He ran his hand through his abnormally longer hair.

"Tell truth."

"Sean, I had to do what I did to protect her. She shouldn't have to sacrifice her career for me. It could still get rough if I can't get all of this settled."

Sean reached over and pulled on Max's sweater. "Scared, Max."

"Yes, I'm scared. Charlotte thinks I'm a coward. Sean, she'll grow to hate me, and if she doesn't then I'll sabotage this relationship. I've never committed to one person which makes it infinitely easy to date several women. It's easy not to have a family or responsibilities."

Sean began pulling at Max's arm. "Scaredy cat."

"You're not being very nice, but I was afraid. It was all too fast."

"Stupid, Max."

Sean looked away and caught me watching. "Charlotte," he yelled out. "Come fix."

I held my head down as I walked in. "What's going on?" Finally, I looked up at Max. "Sean, are you okay?"

"We were just talking," Max answered calmly.

"He seems very agitated." Sean raised his right arm with his left and pointed at me.

"Charlotte, fix Max. You do. You. Enough."

Max and I stared at each for the longest time while Sean looked back and forth. He wanted one of us to make a first move. Sean's eyes focused on me.

"Charlotte, please. You do. Max scared." With all of the pain and frustration Sean had been through since September, he was pleading with me. I couldn't let my brother down. My heart was breaking.

"Stop looking at me like that, Seany. Fine, I'll try one more time, but this is it."

Sean smiled and clapped. "Do it."

And I heard my mother. *"Charlotte, he leaves you breathless; he holds you as if you are his everything."*

I removed my coat as though I was going to battle. Max and Sean were surprised by my ensemble. I could dress up if I had to, and this gray dress hugged every curve I had. If one looked closely, one could see the pizza from last night's feeding frenzy now taking up occupation on my left thigh. Featuring a v-neck and a deep back, this dress left me more exposed than I would normally be for any court hearing. I had added my tall black suede boots and was wearing a small silver cuff bracelet and drop earrings. I flipped my hair back comically and attempted to stand as tall as I could.

I began to speak but was shut down by Max who stood in front of me. "Look, hear me out. It's a long story why I did what I did. Frankly, what is going on, the information you, Sean, and Tom discovered may just be the beginning of the storm headed my way."

I took a step closer. "It seems like we're always in a storm, you and me."

Max nodded. "That first night was a flood."

"Of many things." He and I shared a very intimate, all-knowing look. I smiled as I noticed Sean trying to unsuccessfully push Max with his wheelchair.

"I'm not hurt," I admitted. "I'm very disappointed. I began to hope you and I, well, it was a real shock. I expected, well, I knew why you were backing off."

"I didn't want you hurt or your practice taken down because of some things that have come to light. It's my family."

I nodded. "I figured something was up."

Max focused on my eyes. "I'm sorry for what I did."

I smiled. "The great Max Shaw just apologized?"

"When I need to, I do."

I took another step. "Max, are you drunk?"

His cocked head as if he was a confused puppy, led me to believe I was confusing him more than helping him in any way.

"No, why?"

"Well, I'm not drunk either." I took another step until I could feel his all-consuming body heat. Sean was watching with wide eyes, but I didn't care. "I tried this last March and it was a serious fail. I'm trying just this once–"

As I closed in, just like I had on the St. Patrick's Day's float, he kissed me instead.

"Charlotte, I want you in my life because you are my life. Do just one thing for me please?"

"There's always conditions with you as though you're negotiating a plea bargain." I stepped back and crossed my arms across my chest. "What?"

Max cleared his throat before speaking. I steadied myself for his summation. "Charlotte, I don't understand how all of this works. I also need you to have faith."

"I do, Max. I believe in God, my family, my country, my career choice–"

Max reached out for my hand. I extended it with uncertainty. "Charlotte, you have faith in so many things, except for yourself. I just want you to have faith in you, and in us. My life has changed in so many ways this past year, and I have no idea what the future will bring us. My world isn't one you're comfortable in, and I understand that. You are the only woman I've ever met who can shut my mother down, and if you just have confidence in yourself, you can do amazing things in my world. I want to let the bad year go, and welcome this new one. You're going to carry a load with me, but I promise I will try my damndest to be the man of your dreams."

Before I could answer him, he pulled me into his arms. Despite my brother in the room, Max's mouth was on mine. His hands were planted firmly across my back, holding me securely against him. Sean clapped slowly but enthusiastically. I didn't notice my entire family entering the room much happier than when they'd arrived to visit. A few seconds later, Max pointed in the direction of the doorway.

"Can we all fit in this room?" His question was appropriate. Everyone did seem to be here.

Sean pointed at Dad. "Dad. Look. Charlotte and Max."

My dad wiped tears from his eyes. "Yes, I see, Sean. It's going to be a good year."

With my father's proclamation, all seemed right in our world. Sean would continue to heal, eventually we'd know all the secrets he'd compiled, and Max and I would be happy. But, as I looked into those amazing caramel eyes that seemed to burn me alive, I didn't need a spirit's insight or a voice in my head to know that the barometer could change at any minute. We were headed into a storm, one that could destroy all we possessed and a future that seemed just beyond my grasp. Perhaps Max was right? I needed to have faith in myself to survive. But would faith be enough?

Chapter Twenty-Eight

The O'Donohues' Home, January 2nd

"Here you go." Judge O'Donohue handed a glass with a healthy measure of Irish whiskey to Max. He took his place in his favorite chair, Mickey sleeping at his feet. "To what do I owe this visit?"

Max took a slow drink and then sat back on the couch. He loosened his tie and took a breath. "Now that I believe Charlotte and I are back together–"

"And I'm happy about that. I knew you'd finally come to your senses. Smooth, isn't it?" He pointed at the drink in his visitor's hand.

"Yes, yes it is. I've told you before, if I'm going to marry, it will be to your daughter."

Judge O'Donohue smiled and saluted his visitor with his glass. "That's good to hear, but you better do it fast. Charlotte doesn't like waiting, remember?"

"I know." Max cleared his throat as if he were about to offer his closing statements in a murder trial. "Judge, I'm not here to talk about Charlotte. We need to talk. Then, I need to speak with Charlotte."

"Good. So, you're finally going to ask her?"

Max smiled and shook his head. "No, not yet. We need to discuss Conor."

"Conor." The judge looked down into his glass. "Go on."

Max placed his glass on the table in front of him and edged up on the couch. He held his hands firmly together in front of him. "Charlotte and her damn voices–"

"They can be helpful," the judge interjected.

"Possibly, well, Conor told her I would know about him. Nate and I have been investigating, searching everywhere for something. Finally, I was talking about Conor to a friend of mine in the NSA. We were at Annapolis together, and I trust the man. Well, he told me about a rumor a few years ago, and that sent me into a direction dealing with corruption in the justice department."

"You know that happens. Look what's going on in your office. You were sent in to investigate."

Max bowed his head. It was way past time to get this out in the air, but before he began, the judge chimed in.

"I'm happy you and Paddy have mended your fences. I wasn't surprised to hear he was your inside man."

"Paddy has been very helpful. He's a good man. He's just a little overly protective of his sister. I'm not sure he realizes Charlotte is every bit as tough as he is, just in her own way. Judge, I've talked to Tom. I gather Conor was missing for a couple of years?"

"He wasn't missing. He was away." Judge O'Donohue heard the tone change in Max's voice. So, he was to be interrogated by the U.S. attorney? He had wondered how long it would take Max to stumble on some fragment of the truth.

"He was in Washington, D.C. That's quite a leap from his high school days of drugs and performing in every play and musical in the city," Max said plainly, void of any emotion. He looked straight into Judge O's eyes. His judicial idol didn't flinch. A bell rang in the kitchen.

"That's my casserole. It's a new recipe." The judge stood up quickly and left Max alone in the living room.

"Damn." Max stood up and looked outside the large window where the Christmas tree probably stood just a few days ago. The judge must have just taken it down because there was a piece of tinsel left behind on the carpet. Max removed his tie completely and stuck it inside his pocket. Moving over to the mantle, he surveyed the family photos. Conor looked so young. They all had been so young, so uncorrupted. "I've got to do this." He turned and walked quickly into the kitchen before he lost his nerve.

The judge wasn't surprised to see Max. "This is an enchilada casserole. Everything is in it. Why don't you sit down and eat? It's hot." He motioned toward the table.

Max removed his coat and threw it over the chair where Charlotte usually sat. "Judge, we need to talk. This is serious."

But the judicial giant made himself busy with cutlery and

plates. He placed them on the table and quickly began to remove items from the refrigerator. "Lettuce, tomatoes, and onions are amazing on top of this supposedly. Then, you top it with sour cream. I'll pull extra salsa in case you want it. Will you get us a couple of glasses of water?"

"Sure." Max did as he was told, finally placing them on the table. The two men sat across from each other, the casserole and all of the extras in the middle.

When the judge bowed his head, Max did the same. They said grace and the judge began to serve. "I've never known you to beat around the bush, Max. Spit out whatever you have to say. It probably has something to do with what Edward told my daughter and you in New York City a few months ago?"

"Of course Charlotte told you. You knew Conor was undercover. Why didn't you tell the others?"

The judge handed a full plate to his guest. "It wasn't something that needed to be said. Supposedly, his death had nothing to do with his job."

"But I think it did." Max watched as the judge stopped moving.

"What? How? Why do you think that?"

"I put it together when I combined Dad's information with a file my friend forwarded. Conor was investigating corruption within the entire justice system, specifically judges at the federal level who were suspected of forming their own little club."

The judge spooned on a dollop of sour cream. "And why does that have anything to do with Conor's death?"

"Because he was sent in to investigate his own father."

Judge O'Donohue dropped his fork. "Max, are you making some accusation?"

"You knew." Max took a drink of water.

"That doesn't mean that Conor was killed because of his job."

Max shook his head. "I'm sure you didn't think it at the time, but now, I know more than you did. Did you even tell your wife?"

The judge pushed back from the table. "Max, you are on thin ice. Be very careful."

"What were you thinking? What were you doing with your little judge club?"

Judge O'Donohue slammed his fist on the kitchen table. Mickey came running out of his hiding place, his wide eyes looking from one man to the other. "Max, I wasn't thinking. I thought it was just a terrible tragedy. Are you telling me Conor is dead because of me?"

Max shook his head. "No, God no. But he stopped the investigation, and I have a feeling his handler didn't take that very well. Did he tell you who it was?"

"No, he didn't." The judge looked down at his plate. "I'm not very hungry."

Max stood up and gathered their plates. "I'll clean up. Go

sit down, and I'll bring in fresh glasses."

As the judge began to leave the kitchen, he turned. "You know, you're just like Charlotte. Both of you are bossy."

Max chuckled. "She says I can be demanding, domineering, pushy, commanding, unrelenting–"

"My, she has your number, doesn't she?"

"She does." Max put away the containers, sour cream, and salsa in the refrigerator. He returned the lid to the casserole and let it set on the counter to cool. Grabbing the glasses, he joined the judge.

When Max joined his friend, he managed a smile. "Judge, Charlotte thought I weaseled my way into the family to spy on you."

"I never thought that, but I wondered how long it would take you to discover our little judge club as you call it." There were a few minutes of silence between them until the judge began to talk. "Conor had me meet him at the park. There's this bench–"

"I know the one. Charlotte goes there, and Conor did too."

The judge nodded. "Yes, that bench. He told me what he had been doing. I suspected he was investigating, but I wasn't sure until that day which department he was working for. He told me his search led him to me and a group of my friends. Our opinions differed with the department's policies at the time, and there seemed to be a push to have all of us retire en masse. We thought it was strange, and we began to look into the AG."

Max got up from his seat and grabbed the bottle, pouring another measure. He did the same for the judge. "Why did the AG want you all out?"

"To this day, I really don't know, Max. I suspect it had to do with upcoming cases that would soon be in our hands. Our group of judges had a few members from all over the nation. We had been friends for some time, but when we noticed something wasn't quite right in the way trials were assigned and sentencing requirements were altered several more joined our group. It all began at a judicial conference two years before Conor returned home."

Max took his seat again. "Whoever was Conor's handler realized the connection and used him to get to you."

Ironically, the judge smiled. "But that's wrong. Nothing ever came of it."

"With Conor dead they couldn't just have someone else come snooping around. You all would've figured it out. When he told you–"

The judge slammed his glass on the side table. "He sealed his death warrant. Jesus, Mary, and Joseph. My son is dead because of me."

Max's hand flew up reactively. "No. We don't know that. The police were certain it was a random shooting outside of a very popular bar. They were certain, Judge."

"And you and I both know how **they** can make something look absolutely ordinary, even a shooting."

Max was stumped. Of course, the man was correct. Powerful people could get away with almost anything, even abandoning their own son. "Judge, Brody admits to killing Conor, at least he does today. We have the old statements, the evidence that he did do it. Hell, Sean's investigation and Charlotte's notes seem to confirm it."

Judge O nodded. "But does that mean Brody was Conor's handler?"

Max shook his head. "I have my doubts about the entire situation. Brody kept telling Charlotte about his boss. I think it was an office insider or the judge I was looking at. Brody doesn't have the gravitas to pull anything off by himself, or even to make a substantial decision."

"I feel sorry for him. Is that wrong of me?"

Max searched the eyes of the man across from him. "Brody was in a desperate situation. I feel sorry for him until I think about the fact that Charlotte could've been killed that night."

Now the judge nodded. "She seems to have put it out of her head."

Max took a drink. It did seem like that, but when Brody went on trial, Charlotte would have to think about that night for days. "Judge, at least now I know what Conor's warning to Charlotte meant. He told her I would know about him. I do now. He was an investigator just like I am." Max's thoughts turned in a different direction. "And maybe I'm being used in the same way?"

"By the AG?"

"Maybe, or even by the president. Who the hell knows anymore? Now, I need to know a couple more pieces of information. Did your merry little group ever form any kind of conspiracy, make plans, etc? I need the truth before I stumble right in the middle of something all of us hang for."

The judge shook his head. "Of course not. After my son's shooting, our family was too devastated to do anything except eat, maybe sleep, and go to our jobs. Our merry band of judges had no reason to make any plans. A few of us retired. The legal system seemed to be as it should be. Trials were put into a hat, and we pulled out our next assignment. There were no unusual verdicts, appeals, or orders from on high."

"Okay, so it all just stopped and everything went back to normal. Next, I need a timeline from you with dates, just years are fine when your suspicions began, and when everything was normal again. This might span over administrations, and if it does that might limit our list. Also, you'll need to trust me on this. I need the list of your group, and I suspect you're not the only name on it whom I know and respect. I have an idea that I'll be able to cross reference dates with cases, maybe even litigants that might offer a clue."

"Max, this is dangerous to unearth if you really think there was a puppet master in the DOJ." The judge's concern was etched on his face. His usually soft blue eyes penetrated Max's and heightened his fear.

Max chuckled. "Judge, isn't there always a puppet master? There's always a handler and a fixer too. We need to search for all of them. One of them put Conor in danger, and the other could be his real murderer."

The judge held up his hand to stop Max from continuing. "His real murderer?"

Max sighed. "I'm not so sure it was just Brody. His attorneys are contesting his admission that night at my house, and he is still undergoing competency tests. The judge assigned has been taking his time because of the holidays. Besides, could Brody really shoot his friend?"

"Brody pulled the trigger and killed Conor, and he almost did the same to Sean."

Max took a sip from his glass. "We know that's what he admitted. Yes, perhaps physically he did, but someone else ordered that trigger pulled. That person could also have been the one who put Sean in peril. The puppet master is who I want."

The judge grimaced. "And that means if Brody didn't really want to shoot two of my sons, then there's someone else out there who did and is still running the show?"

The two men looked toward the hallway. The front door had opened. "Dad? Max? The snow is beginning to really come down."

Charlotte entered the house and stood at the entrance to the living room. She began to remove her coat but stopped. Her eyes focused on her father. He smiled widely.

"It's good that you got home before it gets bad out there, honey."

Charlotte turned her attention to Max who quickly came to her side to remove her coat and hang it on the hallway hook. He smiled sweetly as he gave her a kiss on the cheek. "Hi baby. I thought I'd drop by to see you."

Charlotte squinted. Something was very wrong. "Your car has been here for a while. It's completely covered in snow, and there's no tracks in the driveway."

"Can't I just visit your dad?"

"On the day after a long holiday? No. You should be at work."

Max smiled again. This time she noticed he held his hands tightly together forming one ball. "I have a light schedule right now."

"I see." Charlotte then removed her suit jacket, hanging it on the hook in the hall. She flipped off her shoes and placed her bags on the floor. As she walked into the living room, she suspiciously eyed Max, but kissed her father's cheek. Max returned to his seat. "I would love a hot cup of coffee."

The loving father immediately rose. "I'll put some on right now. In fact, I could go for a hot cup myself. We are eating a great casserole tonight."

Max shook his head as he watched the doting dad leave the room. "Don't expect that sort of behavior from me all the time."

Charlotte's finger shot out in his direction. "You. You are going to tell me what is going on. We just got back together, and there's secrets, right?"

Max wasn't expecting the accusation. He leaned back on the couch and feigned ignorance. "I have no idea what you're talking about. I came to visit your father."

"And you've been discussing Conor. You know. When are you telling me? Why did you come to Dad first?"

"Where are you getting these ideas?"

Charlotte stood in front of him, her toes up against his shoes. "Where do you think, Max? My brother has been frantic ever since I put my hand on the doorknob."

"Damn voices. Damn ghosts."

"Max?" Charlotte stared at him. She held her breath to steel herself against those caramel eyes of passion. Yesterday, they had finally been in each other's arms. The great holiday war between the two of them had ended. Here she was ready to fight again. As she stomped her right foot, Charlotte yelled his name again.

"Fine. Sit down." Max straightened up as Charlotte's body landed up against his. She offered a peck on his cheek as she snuggled to share his body heat. "I came to talk to your dad about my theories. You should hear this from him, but I'll tell you I know about Conor because Conor was doing a job much like mine."

Charlotte pulled back from his side. "I know. Your dad told us about all of that."

"Yes, right, well he specifically worked for the DOJ. He was investigating a conspiracy of sorts just like Dad said. Before you ask, we have no idea who else was involved."

"I don't understand how he got involved. Conor never thought about law or justice, maybe some illegal stuff now and then." Charlotte clenched her teeth on her bottom lip. "I shouldn't have said that out loud."

Max chuckled. "His drug use was mild, and we all knew he was a pothead. He had no record. Your brother got his act together. None of us may ever know why he did. Apparently, your dad knew. I suspect your mom did too."

Charlotte thought back. She had been away in her first year of college when she came home to register her car. She stayed overnight and remembered her parents had received a phone call from Conor. She was only told he was fine, but she hadn't even bothered to ask where the heck her brother was. "Okay, so what are you not telling me?"

The judge appeared in the doorway. "I think I can eat now. Are you two ready for dinner?"

Charlotte nearly toppled over on the couch as Max shot up. "I can eat now too."

"And during dinner, you two are telling me the big secret?" Charlotte saw the nods as both men turned away from her. "Dad? Max?" Charlotte uttered several words of profanity as she shuffled toward the kitchen. "What didn't Edward tell us last year?"

Max glanced back as he quickly made his way to the kitchen. "Edward, is it?"

"Yes, your father is a lovely man, unlike his son. I want to know the big secret before I begin eating, like now."

As the judge was placing fresh plates on the table, he turned to his daughter. "Charlotte, Max has found out that a group of judges were plotting the overthrow of the justice system of the United States."

Max watched Charlotte as she passively sat down in her place. "So it's just another Tuesday then?"

Max burst with laughter. The judge filled a glass with water and placed it in front of his daughter. "I'm not kidding, Charlotte. It's a long story, but there was and is corruption. You know, you kids aren't the only ones who can investigate. I'm pretty good at it, and I don't tell anyone I'm doing it."

Charlotte glanced in Max's direction. "He's not kidding, is he?"

"Nope." Max leaned back against the kitchen counter and crossed his arms. "Please remember we aren't together because of my job. I do love you, but apparently, I really will be investigating your dad."

"Dad?"

"Daughter dear, it will be fine." The judge tasted the casserole. "It's still warm. Max, do you think they'll allow me to bring Mickey with me to the big house?"

"I think we can arrange it, Judge."

Charlotte looked from one man to the other. "You two think you're funny. Well, I don't know what to think. Oh no."

"What, honey?" The judge served dinner onto Charlotte's plate. "Max, get the sour cream, lettuce, tomatoes, all the stuff."

As Max became a server, Charlotte shook her head. "I just realized you two are just alike. I'm dating my father."

Max and the judge shared a smile. Max kissed her on the cheek as he handed her the salsa. "Honey, you should know by now you are not dating your father." He added a wicked wink after the declaration.

Chapter Twenty-Nine

"Max? Are you asleep?" I whispered then shoved him just to make sure he heard me.

"I was until now." As he opened one eye, I patted his bare chest. "What is wrong? You told me there's nothing better than sleeping in on a Saturday morning when there's a storm outside."

I nudged my body closer for warmth. "When it's a rainstorm, but it's a blizzard out there. Look." I pointed to the large bedroom window. "It's nothing but white."

"And you woke me up for this, why?"

I turned over onto my back and stared up at the ceiling. "I have no idea. Sorry."

"Ha. That's a first. Charlotte O'Donohue has no idea. I need to call all of your family and alert them of your uncertainty."

I shoved his body hard. "No, you do not."

"Ow." Max rolled over quickly and hovered over me. "I'm awake now. It's–" He looked over at the clock and glared down at me. "It's six in the morning, Charlotte. You owe me." When he arched that left brow and his lips formed that slight smile, I knew I was about to be preyed upon, but it was always in a good way. "I've missed you."

"I noticed. I wish you hadn't pushed me away during the holidays, *Poop Head*. It was terrible. Not unexpected, but awful."

Max began by kissing my forehead, then my nose, and finally bringing his soft lips to lay on mine. "I promise it was for a good reason, and I will make it up to you."

"What did you do in New York?"

Max's trail of kisses continued down my neck to the top of the sheet. "Digging, setting up an army. Being very certain–"

"Tell me."

Max began to laugh. "Now?"

"Yes, now. We can do the other later. It is only six in the morning." I stretched up and kissed him on the cheek.

"Fine." He threw himself back onto his side of the bed like a petulant child and took my hand in his. "I'm walking a fine line. Someone out there is pulling all the strings and targeting me, maybe you, and your entire family."

I released his hand and slid my body closer, placing my arm around his waist. "Then we need a big pair of scissors."

"That's a good one, honey."

Usually, Max was decisive. I didn't like this unsure model. It worried me. "Max, now that we know what Conor was doing, what exactly was Dad and his cronies looking at when they formed their little club?"

"Well, the justice system doesn't always appear so just. Your dad said he was seeing a trend in the dumbing down of charges, guidelines, and sentences on some very big cases.

Usually, it involved political and business biggies. Someone on high was manipulating the system for their friends."

I moved back into my original place on his chest and leaned my chin on my hand. "Do you think the president did it?"

"It was the prior administration if that was the case. No, I think there's a group of government elites who might be involved. They may be coming for me."

"The senator?"

"He may be part of the club."

"Then, if he comes for you, we go after him." My voice was monotone but cold. Max glanced down at me suspiciously.

"No, **we** don't."

"Yes, **we** do. We are in this together, and this time buddy, you won't argue your way out." I stabbed my finger into his chest. "Decide right now if you and I are together. You have thirty seconds. If not, it's been fun and very pleasurable, but we're over."

"Geez, Charlotte, that's cold."

"I won't tolerate this hot and cold thing you've got working for you. I was miserable when you walked away, and I promise, if you do that again, I won't be waiting. Got it? Have you decided?"

I saw Max's thin smile forming. "I understand. I'm deciding."

"And your verdict is?" I looked up hopefully, but I was prepared for his response to shape the end of our relationship.

"Let me think."

I leaned over his broad chest to glance at the clock. "Time is ticking. You had thirty seconds, and I believe an answer is due. You shouldn't even need that much time for you to decide if you–"

Out of the blue, Max maneuvered me onto my back and looked down. "Charlotte, do not test me."

"Don't give me a reason to do it ever again."

"Fine."

"Good."

Max's eyes were darker than usual. His lips were within a whisper of mine. "Charlotte, I love you. I'm not sure you know what you're getting into, but you are here, and from now on, you are with me. I'm not walking away, God help you."

Before I could answer, his mouth took mine in a ferocious onslaught of emotion. When he finally released my lips, I smiled.

"Do you want to play out in the snow?"

"What? I was being romantic there."

I patted his shoulder. "We can do that anytime, but the snow won't always be there."

"It's a darn blizzard out there," Max slowly answered. He fell back onto his pillow and pulled me closer to his body. "I like it right here."

"It isn't a blizzard. It's just a little snow."

"You only want to dump the stuff on me."

I couldn't help but laugh. "You do know me, don't you?"

"I do. Besides, you would be the one who ended up encased in snow."

I snuggled up closer to him. "You are very confident."

"Always," Max growled. "You can't play with the big boys."

I quickly rose up and hovered over him this time. "Excuse me? Where on earth did you get that idea?"

I saw the twinkle in his eyes. He was pushing my buttons. "I thought you weren't that confident, counselor, but it seems you are, or you can be when you need to be."

"I can, and I am. Do you enjoy making me angry?"

Max smiled. "No, I enjoy you when you have this fire in your eyes. You can be with the big boys. You can run in my world. You just choose not to, don't you, Charlotte? Why?"

"Your world can be very nasty. Just look at the place you're in right now with all of those special people." My murmured statement created a silence in the bedroom. I pushed off of Max and returned to my own pillow. "Max, your world frightens me."

"I know. It frightens me too, but Charlotte, I'm glad you're on my side." Max tenderly reached for my hand and took it in his.

I could hear Max's breathing, slow and steady. He was still grasping my hand when he fell asleep. Within a few minutes I did the same.

Chapter Thirty

The snow was still falling as Max stoked the logs in the fireplace. We slept in late, and Gio created a magnificent brunch around eleven in the morning. I was nursing a hot cup of coffee as I watched Max from the couch.

"So, what shall we do?" Max glanced back. He winked. "I have several ideas."

"I bet you do. We won't be able to begin working on the float today."

Gio entered the living room with his own coffee in hand. He sat down in the largest chair and placed his feet up on the ottoman. "You all really work hard on that thing."

"We do, in fact, the only Sunday we take off is for the Super Bowl. Not even Valentine's Day is exempt from work on the O'Donohue Irish Parade float!" I raised my hand up in the air for effect. "We are dedicated, and we are Irish."

"Among other nationalities," Max added. "But you don't speak of that."

Gio laughed. "The boy is catching on, isn't he, Charlotte?"

"He's coming along. There's a playoff game later today."

"Yes. I'm making pizza." Gio stared into the fire.

Max joined me on the couch. He draped one arm over my

shoulders and pushed me closer to his body. "I like this. The three of us are just watching the fire and doing absolutely nothing. We can watch football later."

"We should be organizing our attack," I murmured. Gio gave me a side glance.

"Who are we attacking?" Gio asked. "Just let me know. I still have a few tricks up my sleeve. I know a couple of guys."

"No," Max said sternly. "By the way, where is Bobby Mack? I thought he was moving in last week."

Gio nodded. "He's in Vegas visiting friends."

Max shook his head. "I don't want to know. I'm constantly afraid that you are setting up a gambling establishment in the cellar."

Gio smiled. "Charlotte, did you tell him?"

I pretended to lock up my lips, throwing the imaginary key into the air.

"I never know if you two are kidding or being absolutely serious." Max's lament was received with laughter.

I kissed his cheek. "Seriously, what are we going to do about this mess around us?"

"I told you we aren't doing anything."

"I have some theories," I added. "I've been making notes, and I think–"

"Charlotte, it's in my wheelhouse now. Let it go. By the way, I need to get my hands on Sean's laptop."

I ignored his request.

"Charlotte."

"Max."

"Charlotte, I need that laptop, and the information on it."

I patted Max's sweatshirt covered chest. "Get a warrant."

"Are you kidding?"

"Nope. Remember the term plausible deniability? And there's the fact that you took a couple of the printed pages from our investigation?"

Max began to say something brilliant but closed his mouth quickly. "We will talk about this later." His eyes were tiny slits of displeasure. I loved it when he didn't get his way instantly.

I pulled away. "Crud, I left my phone upstairs. I need to call Dad and make sure he's okay. He won't be able to get to the rehab center today to see Sean." Before Max could stop me, I was on my way to the second floor.

I felt the cold breeze as I climbed the stairs. Once I was on the landing–safely closer to the wall than the steps–I whispered. "What do you want?"

"You are out of your league."

"I'm not sure what you're talking about."

"You have so many doubts. This will never last."

Damn this ghost. "What do you know?"

"I know you aren't looking in the right place. You, of all people, should figure this one out. You'll never be able to live in his world."

Every muscle in my body was shaking. Just under the

surface, my confidence was always fragile. It had been that way since I was little, and Tommy Brewster called me ugly and fat in kindergarten. I'd believed him. I couldn't allow myself to believe an irritating, mean spirited ghost.

"Just shut up." I quickly headed into Max's bedroom and found my phone. There were two messages from Dad. I called him immediately.

"Hi honey. Is everything okay?"

I bit my lip before responding. "Um, I'm not sure you can help me."

"What's he done this time?" Dad's question made me smile.

"He hasn't done anything bad. It's cranky old man Taylor, well it's his ghost. He is nasty."

"What did he say? I'm not sure I can help, but I can listen."

I loved my father. "I really appreciate that. He said I could never live in Max's world. Dad, I'm not good enough."

"Charlotte Rose O'Donohue, that's enough. That nasty ghost is just hitting you at your weakest point. You are the strongest woman I know. Just stop it."

My father's reprimand began to buoy my confidence, but my doubt was just too strong. "Dad, he said I above all people should be able to figure out Max's mystery, at least that's what I thought Mr. Taylor was saying."

I heard my father take a deep breath. "Charlotte, you've always been the one who took so many things to heart. That made you caring, but it also made you open to so much hurt.

Yes, you want things done now and you take off without thinking, but when it concerns your wants and needs you hold back. You over analyze. The doubt sets in. You went to work for your brother and didn't follow the dream of your own law practice until now. You were afraid to fall in love so you picked an easy going guy, someone who didn't challenge you. He hurt you so you assumed every man would do that to you. Do you want me to go on?"

"Wow, you've really thought this out."

"I suppose I've watched you the most out of all of my children. Just go for it. Max believes in you, and he loves you."

"I know," I answered softly.

"Then act like it. Be the bossy Charlotte. Do what you do best, take control of your family, the family you are making."

Family. Was it really that easy? Is that what cranky old Mr. Taylor was talking about? "Dad, I think that's it. It's all about family, not saving an election or a legacy. Well, it is about a legacy, but not the senator's."

"Are you talking about the judicial conspiracy?"

"No. Nevermind. I have some research to do. Mickey and you take care. We'll be over tomorrow to shovel. I love you! I have to go."

I did wait for Dad to say goodbye, but as soon as the call ended, I began to search through my purse for the card. Frantically, I threw the contents onto the bed and began to separate credit from business cards.

"Ah hah," I said out loud as I held the small piece of information in my hand. "Mr. Taylor, you won't stop me with your nasty taunts. Why am I even talking to you?"

I read the card ... *Mrs. Beatrice A. Hughes, wife of Finley Patrick Hughes*, Financier. I really should fill Max in before I make this call. If I did, he'd probably stop me. Max should be told, but I would wait until the early morning hours when he was barely awake. He would mutter his okay and not be the wiser of what he had just agreed to. Was this activity under the heading of secrets, lies, or investigating? It was definitely investigating. "Well, here goes nothing."

The call was answered quickly. "Charlotte, my husband told me you'd be calling today. How are you, dear?"

"It's snowing, and the roads are terrible. It's a typical January day in Kansas City."

"We're expecting snow tonight. But how are you? Are you and Max doing well?"

"We are now. The holidays were rough." Idle conversation pained me.

"Charlotte, we have a mess on our hands, don't we?"

Thank the heavens for an adult! "Yes, Mrs. Hughes, we do."

"Oh Charlotte, call me Bea. What can I do to help?"

"Your son, the senator–"

"Has always been a handful. We kept telling him how amazing he was, and he took it completely to heart. By the time my dear husband and I realized we should have used the stick more than the carrot, it was too late. But he is the perfect politician."

I giggled softly. "That he is. Mrs. Hughes, Beatrice, who knows about Max, I mean, about who he really is to the senator?"

"Let me think. Of course, he does and I do. I'm not sure if his wife does or his children."

"His children wouldn't be too happy about an older brother, would they?"

"Charlotte, what are you saying?"

How would I say this? "Would they be welcoming to another sibling?"

"Oh my. I never thought of that, but dear, I'm sure they are not aware of Max's existence, nor would it really matter to them. They have good lives and are very happy."

"I suppose it wouldn't matter." I sighed heavily in sheer exasperation. I wanted to have all of these mysteries behind us, and I suppose I still wanted to blame everything on the senator in some way.

"Dear, what made you think of my grandchildren?"

"I'm a family lawyer, and sometimes families can be–"

Mrs. Hughes' sweet giggle humored me. "A handful? Mine certainly is. We have a large family and everyone is a fan of the mine theory."

"Mine theory? I don't think I've heard that one."

"I'm sure you understand, Charlotte. They all think everything is theirs. Mine, mine, mine!"

We both laughed out loud. Who knew that this living, breathing piece of American history could be so normal? "I do understand. My oldest brother thinks everything is his."

"And my oldest son does too."

I stopped laughing. Could it be about money? Wasn't everything always about money? "Mrs. Hughes, Beatrice, the Taylors and Shaws have trusts and a foundation for their charities. I thought I saw that your family had the same."

"Of course, dear. My husband amassed a fortune. He worked hard and was very shrewd. My children and their children are well taken care of, as am I. We help many with charities that are dear to us."

"Then, your husband probably had a will, trust, all the usual documents so the family would be cared for years into the future."

"Of course."

"I don't mean to be rude, but I'd be interested in seeing his original will. Would that be possible? I'm currently working with a client that will need to set up something similar. Of course, the fortune isn't as vast as yours, but it's substantial." I was perfecting my fibbing.

"Charlotte, I'd be happy to have that sent to you. I'll call my attorney on Monday, but I believe it may be available online. It's a public document now. Just in case you were wondering, everything was fairly forthright. There are no secrets in that will. However, I'll have a copy of the original sent directly to you."

I gave her my information, and we discussed the weather again as I noticed the snow had finally stopped. I turned away from the window as I was saying my goodbye. "I'll talk to you soon, Beatrice. Thank you so much."

I was still smiling when I completed my turn to see Max glaring at me, his arms crossed in front of his chest. His stance of authoritarianism reminded me of Paddy. My smile vanished.

"Do you want to explain why the hell you are talking to Beatrice Hughes?"

Chapter Thirty-One

"You mean your biological grandmother?"

"Charlotte?"

"Max?" His one brow arched suspiciously. "Fine. I just wanted to check in with her. I thought maybe one of the senator's children might not like having an older brother. We talked about the weather–"

"And a will? What was that stuff about having a client?"

I stayed put near the window, keeping at least fifteen feet between us. "I will have a client like that one day, and I'd like to see an example of–"

Max threw his hands up. "I give up on you! You can't stop yourself, can you?"

There was a crack in his facade of irritation. I closed the gap between us and wrapped my arms around his waist. "Maxie, she's a sweet woman. You might want to meet her someday."

Max growled.

"Max, you aren't really mad." I kissed his cheek. "Are you?"

"Yes. I don't understand why you need to do this detective stuff. You have a brother for that. I have Nate for my investigations, but all of you amateurs just can't help yourselves."

I kissed him quickly on the lips and pulled away. "No, because we love you, and we want you safe and happy."

"Were you going to tell me what you were up to?"

"Yes, I was." Max laughed out loud. "I was." I stamped my foot for emphasis. "I was."

Max grasped my hand and pulled me into a hug. "If you say it three times, does it make it the truth?"

"Yep. I love you, I love you, I love you."

Max kissed my forehead and pulled me closer. His chin landed softly on top of my head. "Charlotte, you're asking for a love that I'm not sure I'll ever be able to give you."

I shoved off of his body to look up into his eyes. "Max, now you're the one who doesn't understand. You're wrong. You're already giving me the love I want, and the love I need. Again, for someone so smart, you are certainly stupid when it comes to me. Just you is enough."

Max nodded acceptance. He looked more like a lost little boy than a confident boy wonder. "I came up here to tell you Gio has the dough ready for the pizza and wondered what toppings you want on it. I didn't know I was going to walk into the middle of your sleuthing."

"Whatever Gio makes is great with me, but I do love it when he puts mushrooms and that special Italian sausage on it."

Max agreed. "Are you coming down with me?"

"Um, give me a second up here. I need those fuzzy socks I brought over."

"Well, pre-game is on so I'll head down. Charlotte, please don't go headlong into thinking that all of this chaos is personal. I believe it is business, my business."

I knew what I wanted to say, but I should agree with him and enjoy the game. "Max, everything is personal, even business. You should realize that."

Max didn't argue, and he didn't voice his agreement. "By the way, you're getting pretty good at lying. Keep practicing. You might have a future in politics." He turned and waved goodbye as he headed toward the stairs. I found my fuzzy socks quickly and walked into the hallway. Slowly, I softly crept into the room where I usually found the cranky old Mr. Taylor.

"This is all about family, isn't it? Are you going to be mute now that I think I've figured out a route to discover the truth?"

There was complete silence. Nothing. I suppose challenging a terroristic ghost wasn't the brightest move on my part. I still needed to walk down the stairs.

"Fine. Don't talk. I really am happier that way." I began to shut the door of the room, and I heard my name. I entered again. "What?"

"I have underestimated you."

"That must've hurt to say."

Mr. Taylor appeared by the window. He stood stoically, straight as a rail, dressed in his full suit. *"Are you really ready to fight for that boy?"*

"You mean fend off the women? Sure." I smiled at the thought. "I had brothers. I'll take them on."

"No, the senator and the others, even my daughter."

I leaned against the wall. "That's a lot of people. My dad was just afraid I'd lose myself in Max and in his world."

Miraculously, Mr. Taylor smiled. *"I'll help in any way I can. Get that will. The answer may be contained in the codicil. Hughes knew his son had begotten a child. The man was as shrewd as they come. He may have mentioned any illegitimate children, or perhaps even made provisions. Someone knows something, and they certainly don't want Max around to discover it. The senator may not even know the extent of how the world would change if the wrong person knew Max is his son."*

"Okay. I appreciate your help. You may not like this, but to bring light onto despicable people, sometimes you need a despicable person to do it."

Again, the cantankerous ghost smiled. *"Happy to be of assistance. Old man Hughes was a lot like me, especially in business. I know that kind of a man."*

From what Beatrice Hughes had said briefly, her husband was nothing like old man Taylor, but that discussion would be for another day. "Thank you. I better get downstairs."

My hand was on the knob when he stopped me.

"Charlotte, don't you worry about his world. You'll do just fine, and when you take on that mantle, you'll make it your own. You'll have the power, the prestige, and the money to help people like you've always wanted to. Damn do gooders. The boy is like that too."

"Yes, he is, and that's just one of the reasons why I love him."

Max and Gio were in the kitchen arguing about red onions when I arrived. Max looked up at me, his caramel eyes actually twinkling. His smile comforted me in every way. I came to his side, and his arm immediately wound around my waist.

"Charlotte, are we okay?"

I stretched and kissed his cheek. "We are more than okay."

"Gio, *Melon Head* is getting a copy of old man Hughes' last will and testament. She thinks she'll find something." Max leaned down and whispered in my ear. "You owe me tonight. I'm thinking of a nice bubble bath." I nodded my agreement.

Gio looked up from the almost perfect pizza and winked. "Charlotte, you may be onto something. Those people like their paperwork. Maybe the old coot put a secret piece of evidence in the darn thing. My Rose kept that real birth certificate."

Max feigned shock. "Do you agree with her?"

"Sure." Gio placed the last red onion and pushed the pizza into the oven. "Charlotte has good instincts. She has intuition, common sense, and her knowledge is just not from the voices from beyond. Max, you would do well to listen to her more."

I stole a slice of green pepper that was sitting on the cutting board. "Max, listen to your grandfather."

"I'll listen to you when you listen to me," Max argued as he grabbed me from behind and began to kiss my neck.

"Stop it."

"Never."

"Okay, you two. We have food on the counter. Don't get any ideas." Gio waved his finger in our direction.

Max released me immediately. "The game is starting." Max seemed to be under the spell of the playoff football game as he headed toward the large television.

Gio put a skillet and a cutting board into the sink. "What do you expect to find in that will, Charlotte?"

"I'm not sure." I munched on my pepper and began to think. "What would be worth killing Max and becoming a murderer?"

Gio's eyes widened. "Are you done with him already?"

"Heaven's no. I'm wondering what could be so bad that someone else would need to kill him or to scare him off so badly–"

"Back to Senator Hughes."

I shook my head. "I'm not sure, Gio."

"Maybe the boy inherits everything. Wouldn't that be something? Just what he needs, more money."

I leaned on the kitchen counter and wondered. "I do think

it's about money. Could it be that he would inherit all of Hughes' fortune? Wouldn't Mrs. Hughes know that?"

"Husbands didn't always tell their wives back then, remember?"

"Right." I picked up a piece of celery and waved it in the air. "If Mr. Hughes knew about Max, and he would've, then he would make an allowance for his grandson, wouldn't he? That grandson would be the eldest. That was a big deal back then too."

"You bet your life. The oldest son, the male heirs were everything to hoity toity families like that. They acted like royalty."

"Or this could be all about Max's job, his assignment. Either way, they want him stopped."

Gio grimaced. "Whoever **they** are."

"Exactly.

We heard Max's shouting from the living area. "You two just missed a touchdown!"

"We better get in there before he thinks we're conspiring against him," Gio muttered.

"That's for sure." I hugged the mobster and headed him into the direction of the flat screen. "Coming, honey."

Chapter Thirty-Two

"Mrs. Rubin, please tell your daughter hello. She was the best babysitter I ever had." The lovely woman I was escorting out of my office used to be our neighbor. Her daughter Rachel usually acted out my favorite childhood books to entertain me on evenings when Mom and Dad went to a charity dinner and didn't trust my siblings to supervise me. Apparently, the one time Paddy was allowed to supervise my well-being, he dressed me up as a pony and gave me grass to eat.

"I'll talk to her tonight. She's on Broadway in a great show. You should see her, Charlotte."

"I'd love that. My friend's mother lives in New York City."

"There you go. You could stay with her."

"Right. Sure." No, never again. "I'll have the final papers ready by next week."

"Thank you, dear. Just give me a call." Mrs. Rubin said goodbye to Phoebe.

My assistant handed me a huge padded envelope. "This came for you. I had to sign for it."

I looked at the return address and saw it was from a law firm in New York City. "This is Mr. Hughes' will."

"That'll be some heavy reading. Maybe you and Max could read it together?"

"No," I answered emphatically. "I mean, I want to look it over first just in case. Besides, Max is in St. Louis for regional meetings. I'm having a quiet night with my father."

"That's one weighty will."

I opened up the envelope and saw almost three inches of paper. "I bet this is all the trust, foundation, and charity documentation too." As I looked at the table of contents it was as I suspected. "They were certainly thorough."

Phoebe turned off her computer, grabbed her coat, and began to gather her things to go home. "I know what you're really going to do tonight. You'll be reading that thing, won't you?"

"Yes," I answered slowly. "Why not? It can't hurt anything, right?"

Phoebe chuckled. "Really? I can't believe you just said that. Depending on what you find out in that document, you may set the world on fire, especially Max's. Think about it."

"I'll see you tomorrow."

Phoebe had a point. I had thought about the ramifications, but it could be all for nothing. If Mr. Hughes didn't have any allowance for Max or any other progeny then nothing was gained or lost. I would just need to mark off any family suspects I had on my list. It would come back to Senator Hughes just being a jerk.

I was almost out the door when I felt the presence. "You're here, aren't you?"

"Apparently so."

"Could you tell me your name?"

"No."

"Fine. I'm leaving. Enjoy your solitude."

"How can you hear me?"

I dropped my bags down in Phoebe's chair. I sighed loudly. If I had a dollar for every time some spirit wondered that I might be as rich as Max. "I honestly have no idea. I've been able to hear people since I was little. Is there something I can do for you? I'm tired and have a lot of work ahead of me once I get home."

"I'm not sure. I knew Olivia Shaw."

That statement widened my eyes. "How?"

"I was her friend."

"Okay. When?"

"In high school. I never graduated."

That answer had a solemn tone to it. "Did you pass on before graduation?"

"In a car."

"An accident?"

"Olivia was driving."

I swore I could hear an anvil drop. "You died in a car accident that Olivia had?"

"Yes, right out there."

This spirit wasn't visible. "On the street out there?"

"Yes. I came in here because it was so cold. It was Thanksgiving."

And the plot thickened. "Will I find it in an old newspaper?"

"Yes, but not the truth. They covered it up to save her. We were arguing."

"What is your name? I want to help you."

"I can't say. You need to take care. You need to watch yourself or I'll lock you in your office again."

I shook my head. "Oh no. We need to get one thing straight. You won't do anything to me, or I won't do anything for you. I won't even respond to you. Do you understand?" I wasn't going to be afraid every day at work. I had enough fear in spades. "Do you understand?" I repeated as I received silence in response.

"I understand. I won't anymore. You may call me Ginger. It was my nickname."

"Ginger. Fine. I need to get home. You don't happen to know anything about Hughes' last will and testament, do you?"

"I don't know who that is."

I picked up my things and shut off the last light. "Goodnight, Ginger."

"Goodnight, Charlotte."

In just the short drive home, my thoughts reeled. Ginger had really thrown me for a loop with her story. Cover ups seemed to be the history of Max's family. Now, I had another mystery, and I was beginning to believe that the investigation into the corruption, my brother's murder, Sean's shooting, and the targeting of Max was going nowhere. Maybe it really had been Brody and the corruption at the federal level? But Brody wouldn't have done all of this just to hurt Max, would he? My doubts filled my head as I kicked my shoes off in the front hallway. Then, would the will hold any secrets? And where would that get me?

"Dad, I'm home. What smells so good tonight?"

"A new recipe Gio gave me," Dad yelled from the kitchen. "It's ready."

"I'll be there in a second." I removed my coat and dropped my bags. Removing the envelope, I walked toward the kitchen. "I received the Hughes estate information and the final will today." I held it up for Dad to see.

"It's a big one. I really am surprised she had it sent to you. Of course, you could've found parts of it online. I wouldn't trust that family as far as I could throw each and every one of them. Do you want wine with dinner?"

I looked at the dish that apparently had just been removed from the oven. "Italian? Yes, please."

"You may have already tried this when Gio made it."

I retrieved the cutlery and Dad's bowl of salad. Taking my seat, Dad joined me. We said our thanks for our food and dug in. "I have had this. This is the casserole that Jane loves. Dad, this is so good."

"I suppose our entertainment tonight is reading your gift." Dad's words seemed to be spit out.

"If you don't mind, but you don't have to. I always appreciate your help and feedback."

"My feedback? Do you want my opinion?"

He was not pleased. Into the fire I walked. "Sure, of course."

"I think this will be a dead end, as it should be. Max has a father, Edward. He doesn't need a man who walked away as though his son was an abandoned puppy he brought to the pound."

I took another bite and chewed. Those doubts in my head were mingling with the fact that I was somehow making my father angry.

"Charlotte, your father spoke with Max earlier today."

"Oh, I get it." Dad looked up at me, his brow furrowed in confusion. "Dad, you talked to Max today, didn't you?"

"What? How?" Dad dropped his fork onto his plate. "Is your mother telling you that, or do you actually know me that well?"

"Well, Mom told me, but I would've figured it out. You and Max tag team up on me. So, what's the discussion you had with him, and what do you really think?"

My father pointed at the voluminous envelope. "That, or something in that could break this wide open. We need to tread very carefully, daughter dear."

"Yes, sir. After dinner, after I finish my glass of wine,

and when we eat the last of the chocolate cream pie in the refrigerator, I'll make us some hot tea."

"And then we begin reading," my father added. His smile said everything. All the misgivings faded.

We were almost finished with our dessert, and Dad had just completed the update on each grandchild when I decided I'd tell him about Ginger. "Dad, do you remember a wreck that killed a young woman on the corner of my office building?"

"When?" Dad collected our empty plates and began to fill the dishwasher.

"Well, Olivia Shaw would have been in high school so well over forty years ago."

"I'll have to think. Your mother was better at remembering stuff like that." Dad turned away from the counter and faced me. "Why? Wait, do I really want to know?"

"Maybe." I bit my lip and wondered. "I don't know if this is related, but I have a spirit in my office."

My dad's eyes lifted to the heavens. "Of course you do. What does this one say?"

"She says Oliva was driving the car when she was killed in the accident, and that the entire incident was covered up."

"Holy Mother of God." My father made the sign of the cross. "You can't believe it, can you?"

"I can, and I do. I've never been lied to by anyone beyond. I'm not sure they can misrepresent themselves. Not even old cranky Mr. Taylor can tell a fib or pretend to be something or someone he is not."

"What's the woman's name?"

"Ginger."

My father's face fell. "Mary Margaret Hennessey. She was a redhead, and they called her Ginger. She was driving Olivia's car, speeding on Wornall around the Thanksgiving holiday. She lost control and wrapped the car around the light pole."

"That's not what she says. Olivia was the one driving, and they were arguing. I don't know any more than that."

"Oh no. You aren't going to do that super sleuthing on this too, are you?"

I smiled as I brought my glass to the sink. "Well, not right now. Ginger can wait, but I'll keep it at the back of my mind when dealing with Olivia."

Dad shook his finger at me. "Don't mess with Olivia. If they covered up that accident then that could be a mess. Just leave this alone ... for now."

I was hopeful. "For now? You mean in the future we can look into it? O'Donohue and O'Donohue on the trail again?"

Dad kissed me on the cheek. "Yes, daughter. But tonight, we have a will to read."

Chapter Thirty-Three

I yawned. Looking up at the clock on the mantle, I realized it was nearly midnight. "Dad, we both need to quit for tonight."

"No."

"Dad, it's late. Even the dog gave up on us. Mickey is snoring."

"Charlotte, no."

I stood up and tried to take the paper from his hands. "Dad. Stop. We can read tomorrow night."

"Charlotte, I found something." Dad's hopeful eyes looked up at me. "It's in here."

"What?"

"The reason why someone might want Max dead. He gets it all, if he wants it."

I gulped. That one statement almost made me lose my long-digested dinner. "All? Gio was joking about that. Mr. Hughes really did provide for him?"

"He did. Here, read this page. It is in a codicil that was added almost five years before the man died. It may not be public knowledge since it technically isn't part of the original document. I'll look online tomorrow. His wife is mentioned as agreeing to the stipulation if Max is of good standing. She would make the final decision, but it doesn't state that she knew of the agreement. Maybe she has read it by now. These older wills, like this one, had unique features within them. The oldest son would inherit, **and his oldest son**. That's Max, not the other kid."

"So does that mean that Max's half-brother is trying to kill him?"

Dad shook his head dismissively. "No, he would lose everything. That son probably knows nothing of this unless he was attempting to break the will, but he'd have to get rid of his own father too. That seems unlikely, besides what does that kid do?"

"I think he's an intern in Boston or New York. I'm not sure. I'll look it up later. He has two sisters too. One is in New York City. She works in the family's foundation, and the other is still in college."

"Well, Charlotte this may be the smoking gun, no pun intended."

I swiped at my eyes. "We haven't even looked at the trust pages yet. Let's stop for tonight. I'm done reading legal crud."

Dad's laughter woke the dog. "Legal crud, huh? Fine, honey. Let's call it a night. Do you want to keep it?"

"No. Would you lock it in your safe?"

Dad nodded. I kissed his cheek and headed up to my room. My voices didn't even wait until I had closed the bedroom door.

"Charlotte, Max doesn't need any more money."

"I know, Mom. I'm not looking at this for the money. I'm trying to find whomever is messing with him and with our family."

"Max needs your love and direction."

I pulled back the covers and began to undress. "He has done just fine without me. Wow, maybe that's the problem, why we argue?"

"You two will always argue. It's what he does for a living. Charlotte, he has never had the love you can give him, and he certainly has not had your directness. Your father is right. There are many paths to get to the same location, to home."

"He is my home."

"Exactly, that's what Rose has been telling you."

"I guess that little Kansas girl and her dog had it right all along." I laughed at my own joke. There was silence from the great beyond. "Oh come on, that was funny."

"No, it wasn't. Go to bed."

Suddenly, I was five again. "Yes, Mom." I paused as I slid under the covers. "Mom, do you know anything about Ginger Hennessey?"

"It was in the newspaper and on the television."

"She says Olivia was driving."

"I can see that. The Hennessey family was devastated. She was their only child. I suspected something was not right. The girl didn't like driving. She took the bus."

"I don't have time right now, but who could I talk to about the accident?"

"Phoebe and her friends."

"Wow, great."

"Be careful what you may uncover. Concentrate on you and Max."

"Yes, Mom."

"Go to sleep, Charlotte."

I had already closed my eyes and was dreaming before I could answer.

Chapter Thirty-Four

I was waiting within the door frame of Taylor House when Max pulled into the parking lot. His head was down as he walked slowly up to me. When he saw me shivering, he smiled.

"This is a surprise."

"I hoped it would be. Gio let me in. Welcome home." I took his one bag and quickly gave him a kiss on the cheek. "The meetings were good?"

"As good as can be expected. You know, that wasn't a proper welcome home kiss, don't you?"

"Then close the door and get in here. I'm freezing."

Max dropped his briefcase and backpack, pulling me into an embrace before I knew what hit me. Now, this was a welcome home kiss. When he finally released me and began to remove his coat, I piled his items at the base of the stairs. "You really missed me."

"You have no idea how much." Max clapped his hands. "What are we doing tonight? Are we going upstairs for a nice long bath first, or a shower, or are we eating?"

"You really have simple needs, don't you?" I shook my head as I walked into the kitchen. "Gio, is making meatloaf."

I directed Max's attention to the small man who was mashing potatoes.

"Oh."

Gio winked at me. "The boy doesn't want to eat first. I can't imagine what else he might have in mind."

"Yes, you can, but we are having dinner together. Just the three of us."

Max almost threw himself onto the kitchen counter. "What no family? No ghosties joining us?"

I glared at him playfully. "Just us three. I hope. We need to discuss a few things."

Max laid his head down. "Mom, I don't want to talk."

"Geez, you are such a brat."

Max's smile was sweet. I could tell he was thinking. "Charlotte, I have something for you."

I clapped like a child. "A gift for moi? I love gifts. Did you get me a magnet with a photo of the Arch on it?"

"I didn't get you anything. I already had something of yours." Max opened one of the drawers in the kitchen island. He pulled out a key and placed it in my hands. "This is not to be given back. Never again. This house is yours."

I remained speechless. Glancing at Gio, I noticed his wide smile. "But, Max–"

"No, never." He softly folded my fingers around it. "I was a fool."

"Am I supposed to respond to that acclamation?" I gave him a quick kiss on the cheek.

"Just take the damn key, Charlotte. Now, what are we eating?"

Max and Gio began small talk about the St. Louis trip while I pulled the salad from the refrigerator. I stirred the sauce that was bubbling on the stove. Gio had made everything from scratch tonight, and my small contribution of mixing salad ingredients didn't count for much. It took less than ten minutes and we were eating at the small table in the kitchen.

"The Italian food in St. Louis is amazing. Gio, yours is better."

Gio smiled as Max dug into the mashed potatoes and gravy. "I used to know some people there."

"Of course you did," I murmured. "This meatloaf rivals my father's."

"That's a high compliment, Charlotte. Your dad is a great cook." Gio reached for another helping of our entree. "Your entire family really puts out a spread."

"Mom began that tradition years ago. Every child had to learn to fix something. Paddy's specialty is macaroni and cheese. Jane can make a Denver omelet to die for, and Sean's pancakes are amazing. With Sean, that's absolutely the only food he can make. He's never baked anything in his life."

Max's gaze lingered on me. "Thus, why he hid his computer in the oven. And what about your other brothers and you?"

"Tom perfected baked beans and Conor was the Caesar salad guy. I haven't really hit my stride yet. All of the men in my life seem to cook for me."

"Sounds like you're a very lucky woman, Charlotte."

Gio's smile always warmed my heart. It was hard to imagine he had ever been anything but an angel, a good guy, but I knew better. Maybe it was because I could hear those voices on the other side of life that made me a little more forgiving. I searched for the better angel in everyone. There was a good and a bad. In his later years, Gio was making amends for his prior indiscretions.

I looked toward Max and then at Gio. I stopped eating, placing my fork onto my plate. "Indiscretions. Atonement. Correcting a mistake. Unfulfilled promises."

"Charlotte, honey, are you okay?" Max reached over and took my hand in his.

"I think so. Max, I looked over Mr. Hughes' will. Dad helped me. We saw something."

"Honey, I have seen it."

I withdrew my hand. "What? You didn't tell me?"

Max shrugged. "That was one of the first items I looked into. I wanted to know who would inherit and if I was a target because of some inclusion as a recipient. I saw the public record filing, but I had a hunch. An attorney buddy of mine did a deep dive for me and found the codicil hiding in some records."

Gio shook his head. "He's doing that lawyer speech stuff again." He turned his attention to Max. "Charlotte wasted a couple of days reading that damn thing. So did the judge."

"I'm sorry."

"But I told you I was looking into it. Why didn't you stop me?"

Max stood up. "Anyone want coffee? I want coffee."

"Max, why didn't you stop me?"

He turned around slowly. "Because I know you need to see it out for yourself. Coffee?"

"No. I want wine."

Gio pulled away from the table and scampered to the wine refrigerator. "I'll get your favorite, Charlotte. What about dessert? Are we ready for dessert?"

Max and I both answered with a firm "no".

I picked up Max and Gio's empty plates and headed to the sink. "You should've told me. I don't like to be played a fool."

"I didn't do that. There was no harm. Maybe you would've found something I missed. But what were you saying at the table? You sounded weird."

"Maybe you've already figured that out too," I answered with as much sarcasm as possible. "I love you, but you make me so mad sometimes. I'm taking my wine in the living room. You two can do the dishes."

I poured my glass full, stomped away, and didn't hear a peep from the kitchen. With the channel selector in hand, I scrolled through show after show.

"Charlotte, Max is Max."

"I know, and he won't stop being that way, and I won't stop

being me," I whispered. I heard a noise outside. I placed my half-full wine glass on the coffee table and plodded over to the large window at the front of the house. If silver tinsel had a sound, this was it.

The precipitation was sticking to the glass. It was ice falling from the darkness. We were having an ice storm.

"Well, crud. Now I have to stay with *Poop Head*, don't I?"

"I suppose you do." Max's low voice startled me when I was expecting to hear Rose's. "Is that a bad thing?"

"I suppose not." I didn't turn to look at him, but I felt those caramel eyes of his warming my back. His arms slowly encircled me, his hands clutching in front to capture me.

"I would hope you'd want to stay, but I've goofed up again, right?"

"No, not really, but you could've told me before I went chasing after an elusive unicorn. You gave me such crap for calling Beatrice Hughes."

Max nuzzled my neck. "Sorry. Would you have believed me? You would want to see it for yourself, besides, I really did think you and your dad might find something, to figure this all out."

"Oh, I've figured part of this out."

"You have? How does atonement, unfulfilled promises, and the rest make sense in your head?"

I touched Max's hands and he opened his embrace. Turning, I looked up and saw the man I loved. "I've told you before I'm not sure about the rules the spirits have, but I do know that there is a restlessness of some kind. That's the energy they convey; how they communicate with me and others like me."

"Wait, when and if we have children will they be able—"

I smiled as my one hand tenderly patted his chest. "I have no idea. Maybe. My mom said her mother had the ability, so did her sister, but unless Jane or one of my brothers has kept a very long-held secret, I'm the only one in our family."

"Charlotte, tell me your suspicions."

I took a deep breath. "I think old man Hughes is attempting to make amends. I think he regrets whatever agreement was struck with your great grandfather. I also think your biological father needs you out of the way. He has other plans, larger plans for his life, and that's been the problem from the very beginning. His own mother alluded that he was hard to control. He was the fair-haired son. Lineage was and may be very important with those people. Father to son to grandson, first born always."

"So you really think that all of this insanity is to get me out of the way?"

"But who wants you out of the way? Is it Senator Hughes? It's not Mrs. Hughes. It's not her attorneys. They sent those papers quickly and efficiently."

Max swept his hand over my cheek. "Unless, we still don't know everything."

"Yes. And then this could all be out of revenge or jealousy."

"Geez, Charlotte. I thought we were narrowing the circle of culprits. You've just made the list as big as three rings under a circus tent!"

"And then there's your judicial investigation with enough suspects to—"

"Kill me, or us."

Max's silence was unnerving. "Max, there is something more, isn't there?"

Max nodded slowly. "My mother is involved."

I clapped. "I knew it. I knew it. It's the bank records. They are her accounts! You took the evidence that day. You know, we still have it on the laptop, right?"

Max rolled his eyes and shook his head. "You are way too gleeful. Yes, they were her bank accounts, but I'm not sure why or how. Maybe Hughes used her?"

"Or she was a willing participant?" The ice was pummeling against the window. I reached around him, placing my head on his chest. "We don't need to talk about her tonight."

"Thank you. I'm still digging."

I kissed Max's neck. "I'm definitely staying the night now."

"Good. You know, I ordered the ice storm just so you'd stay?" Max's impish smile made me laugh. His distraction was welcome. We would talk about Olivia another time.

"I knew you were powerful, but an ice storm?"

"Fallen angels do have special skills." He cupped my face in his large hands and tipped my chin up. "We do well together in bad storms."

"Of every kind," I whispered against his soft lips.

The kiss vanquished my doubts. Yes, this was the man I loved.

Gio shouted from the kitchen. "Do you two want dessert or not?"

"He's made a chocolate cobbler."

Max smiled. "I suppose you want that, right?"

I nodded enthusiastically. "I'll take the coffee now."

"Yes, Charlotte. I'm your obedient servant." He bowed as he retreated to give Gio assistance.

"Rose, what is all of this about?"

"Family, Charlotte. Always family ... the love and the hate."

I gulped. I was so accustomed to the love of a wonderful family, I never even remotely wondered about hatred between blood relatives. Hate could move mountains, or at the very least could incite murder.

Chapter Thirty-Five

Max's even breathing was soothing. I concentrated on his low murmurs instead of the raging storm outside. We were always in the eye of swirling insanity, weren't we? His arm was possessively thrown over my body.

"Get down here, young lady!"

No, I wouldn't go. I shut my eyes tightly. Old man Taylor gave me a headache. There were times over the years when I trudged on despite head splitting pain of what doctors had determined were migraines, but not really. Really? I knew exactly why my head hurt. It was those damn voices!

Carefully, I lifted Max's arm. He stirred quickly. "Where are you going?"

"Bathroom. Go back to sleep."

"Okay." Max turned onto his back and was asleep once more before I even threw back the heavy bedspread.

First, I did go to the bathroom. I shoved my feet into a pair of Max's large slippers I saw in his closet, and I began to shuffle to old man Taylor's room.

"What do you want? I was perfectly fine, and then you yelled."

"You do realize you are a trollop, don't you?"

"We've been talking about getting married."

"But not yet. Talking and doing are entirely two opposing actions. This is intolerable."

"I won't be lectured on morality by you, sir."

"Ah, that was a good one."

I wrapped my arms around my body. It was so cold in this room. "Besides, you don't know your grandson. When he's talking, he always means what he says."

"Nevermind. We need to address how you used me when that lunatic was in my home."

"That's what you want to talk about in the middle of the night? Why didn't you yell about it right after it happened?"

The apparition turned to seemingly look out of the window. *"I will not be used or played."*

I shook my head. Unbelievable. Was I truly going mad? These voices, these ghosts could have hurt feelings? "I really need to get a few more hours of sleep, so if you don't mind, could you get to the point? You're a hardened man. You can take a little abuse."

He turned swiftly, glaring at me as though he could take my own life single-handedly. *"What has she told you?"*

I smiled. "Ah, you don't like me mentioning abuse? I can only imagine what you did to poor Rose."

"Poor Rose! That's a laugh. Can you really be that innocent?"

"Now who is attempting to play whom?"

"Learn that there are always two in a marriage, if not three or four. I'll forgive you for what you did to me."

I shook my finger in his direction. "You were trying to kill me again! That needs to stop now. I will get a priest in here and have you exorcized. It will hurt, at least I think it will. I bet it will burn, your skin will ... well you don't have any skin, so maybe your soul–"

"Please stop babbling. Does the boy tolerate that? It's very annoying."

I surprised myself with a low chuckle. "He usually stops me." I yawned. "Could we get over your hurt feelings and get to the point of this visit, this calling?"

Old man Taylor nodded. *"Indeed. I've been reviewing the situation. We need a plan of attack."*

I leaned against the door. "We? We do not."

"You realize by now I had nothing to do with that sham of an agreement, don't you? It was drawn by Rose's greedy father and that awful Finley Hughes."

"Wow, that's the pot calling the kettle black."

The apparition came into clearer, full view. I blinked and rubbed my eyes. The nasty man was actually smiling.

"Dear girl, is that phrase still used?"

"It is. Now tell me about the agreement."

"I was not involved. I was gone by then. Olivia had herself in a situation again. She wanted to marry that silver-tongued

manchild. He did not want her. She was a dalliance to him."

Again? What else had Olivia done in her life that was an uncovered secret? Was it the accident with Ginger? That was for another time. "But she still loves him," I said. His hands flew up in irritation.

"She has no idea what love is. She is like me in that respect. Although, love only makes your heart ache."

His stunning admission left me speechless. I yawned again, bringing my hand up to my face to stifle it. "Love can be wonderful. I'm sorry if you were hurt, but you hurt others too."

"And that is my sin. We need to focus on the subject at hand. Olivia's grandfather suggested a deal, and I know Hughes paid him off to get rid of the baby."

My sleepy eyes opened wide. "What? Is that why Rose–"

"Rose did what Rose always did. She took control. It was all a sham. It was all about money and inconvenience."

"From what I've heard, it was the same for you, wasn't it? Is that why you're still here?"

"You are the one who thinks she must atone for an ability that some might think is quite odd. You think your family is cursed. I know mine is. We all have our mistakes, don't we?"

His smile faded, and I thought I saw some form of humanity, of sorrow in his eyes. "Aren't we the pair?"

"It seems so. Tread lightly. The boy is formidable, but he has never gone up against powers like these. They are foes

who enjoy toying with their victim much like a cat with a small mouse. The clouds are circling around you both, and you'll be battered like no other storm has raged before. If you can survive this, perhaps you have a chance. Do you understand?"

I nodded. I gulped in fear. "Mr. Taylor, will you be with us or against us?"

His spirit began to fade. *"I will be here, dear girl. Do not tremble. I detest being taken for a fool. The Hughes' family thought they were better than me. Those Washington bureaucrats think they can ruin anyone at the drop of a hat. Even though I do not understand your lack of morals, I respect your strength and your pluckiness. No one ever used me like you did with that mad man. Hit them where they will hurt, Charlotte. They have hurt Olivia, and I will not tolerate it. Do it before they destroy everyone you love."*

The spirit vanished, and I gasped. I ran from the room, stopping as I entered Max's bedroom. I returned to the bathroom to finish crying and to calm down.

Slowly, I slid under the covers. Max's body immediately touched mine. "What is going on?"

"Max, you won't believe–"

"I will," Max murmured.

"Old man Taylor says you will be going up against your biggest challenge. He says we, I need to hit them where they hurt or they'll destroy everyone I love."

Max's hand softly rubbed my arm. "You're scared to death. I've never seen you like this."

"You said you were going to war, well I hope to God you still have some of those fallen angel skills because I think we're going to need them. Hold me tighter."

"Come here," Max directed. He pulled me over onto his chest and held me as if I was his life preserver. "Charlotte, honey, you have saved me, do you know that?"

I held onto him for dear life. All I needed to do now was to save us before the tempest swept all of us away. "That's my job now, Max. I'll always save you no matter how bad the storm is."

C.L. BAUER

"I always wanted to write romances. I read them, and our mom loved her soap operas. But at night, our family watched mystery and detective television shows. I was influenced to go in a different direction when I began my adventure in writing. I love a who done it that adds in a little humor, romance, and keeps you guessing."

C.L. Bauer's first cozy mysteries, A Lily List Mystery Series, debuted with The Poppy Drop featuring Kansas City florist Lily Schmidt. A spin off, A Lily List Mystery Exclusive introduced readers to the popular character, Gretchen Malloy. The premier event planner never met a pair of stilettos she didn't love!

Kansas City, Missouri native C.L. Bauer comes from a background in journalism and has received numerous awards as the owner of her family's wedding and event flower business, Clara's Flowers. (Many stories in A Lily List Mystery Series are based on true events.)

With Charlotte's Voices Of Mystery Series, C.L. Bauer has incorporated her love of mystery and romance with a bit of the paranormal. It's a little naughtier than your usual cozy, and with the introduction of the spirit world you'll never know what or who is just around the corner.

To contact the author or schedule special events/book club appearances, email clbauerkc@gmail.com. Visit her website at www.clbauer.com to join the newsletter for news about publications, contests, and upcoming events.

Other Books by C.L. Bauer

The Lily List Mystery Series
The Poppy Drop
The Hibiscus Heist
The Tulip Terror
The Sweet Pea Secret
The Magnolia Dilemma

A Lily List Mystery Exclusive
Stilettos Can Be Murder
Stilettos On The Run

Charlotte's Voices of Mystery Series
The Haunted Lost Rose
Haunted Decisions of the Heart
The Haunted Plot